NIKKI
ON THE
LINE

NIKKI
ON THE
LINE

BARBARA CARROLL ROBERTS

LITTLE, BROWN AND COMPANY

New York   Boston

Copyright © 2019 by Barbara Carroll Roberts
Interior illustrations © Shutterstock.com

Cover art copyright © 2019 by Sammy Moore. Cover design by Marcie Lawrence. Cover copyright © 2019 by Hachette Book Group, Inc.

Little, Brown and Company
Hachette Book Group
1290 Avenue of the Americas, New York, NY 10104
Visit us at LBYR.com

Originally published in hardcover and ebook by Little, Brown and Company in March 2019
First Trade Paperback Edition: March 2020

Little, Brown and Company is a division of Hachette Book Group, Inc. The Little, Brown name and logo are trademarks of Hachette Book Group, Inc.

The Library of Congress has cataloged the hardcover edition as follows:
Names: Roberts, Barbara Carroll, author.
Title: Nikki on the Line / Barbara Carroll Roberts.
Description: First edition. | New York ; Boston : Little, Brown and Company, 2019. | Summary: Nikki, thirteen, dreams of being a great basketball player but struggles on her new, elite team while also juggling school stress, her non-traditional family, and revelations about her biological father.
Identifiers: LCCN 2018017611| ISBN 9780316521901 (hardcover) | ISBN 9780316521833 (ebook) | ISBN 780316523615 (library edition ebook)
Subjects: | CYAC: Basketball—Fiction. | Single-parent families—Fiction. | Best friends—Fiction. | Friendship—Fiction. | Middle schools—Fiction. | Schools—Fiction.
Classification: LCC PZ7.1.R588 Out 2019 | DDC [Fic]—dc23
LC record available at https://lccn.loc.gov/2018017611

ISBNs: 978-0-316-52189-5 (pbk.), 978-0-316-52183-3 (ebook)

Printed in the United States of America

LSC-C

Printing 3, 2021

FOR MY FAMILY
Gary, Wesley, and Helen

Trouble

You know how you can tell you're in trouble?

You can tell you're in trouble when you're standing in a long line of girls in a basketball gym, getting ready to try out for an eighth-grade club team—an elite-level team, the kind of team you haven't played on before, the kind of team you really want to play on—and you all of a sudden realize you're staring straight-on, eye-level at the shoulder blades of the girl in front of you. Which means, as far as you can tell, the girl attached to those shoulder blades is a good nine or ten inches taller than you.

And that's right where I was.

And since I knew I was somewhere around five foot four, that meant the girl in front of me had to be over six feet.

In eighth grade.

I turned to Adria behind me and nodded toward the shoulder-blade girl.

"Maybe she's in the wrong gym," Adria said, her voice barely a whisper.

"Let's hope."

We moved forward with the line.

Girls who'd already gotten their tryout numbers shuffled over to the side of the gym to drop their bags, lace up their shoes, and stretch. Parents were over there, too, setting up folding chairs or camp stools because the bleachers had all been pushed back flat against the walls. With the bleachers pushed in like that, the big gym seemed even bigger than it was, and it felt cold and hollow, every sound bouncing off the walls. Nothing like the cozy little middle school gyms where Adria and I had played county-league games. It still smelled like a regular gym, though, kind of musty, with the leathery scent of the balls and the bite of floor cleaner all mixed together.

A few girls trotted onto the court to put up shots. Not particularly good-looking shots, I was happy to see. One girl snapped her hand sideways instead of holding her follow-through with her fingers pointing at the basket. Another flipped her hand backward, launching the ball toward the hoop with no arc and no spin.

Maybe I wasn't in such deep trouble after all.

"I wonder who taught them to shoot," Adria said.

"Not your dad."

Adria grinned. "Lucky for us."

A few more girls joined the shooters on the floor. One of them stood behind the three-point line and shot with plenty of arc and plenty of spin, and her first two shots dropped straight through the net.

Okay, I was still in trouble.

The registration line kept moving, and the shoulder-blade girl in front of me stepped up to the man handing out tryout numbers—squares of paper with big numbers printed on them.

"Name?" the man said.

"Kate Nyquist."

"Oh, Kate!" the man said. "Coach Duval told me he invited you to try out, but we didn't expect to see you. Your father said you always play with older girls."

The girl shifted her weight. "He's letting me play with girls my age this spring."

"Fantastic," the man said. "Love to have you play for the Action."

The girl took her number, mumbled "Thank you," and walked away.

I stepped to the front of the line, looked up at the tryout-number man, and waited for him to ask my name.

His gaze stayed pinned on Kate-the-giant.

I waited, waited, then finally stretched up on my tiptoes. "I'm Nikki Doyle."

"Hmm? Oh, right." The man still didn't look at me. He shoved a number at me, found my name on his clipboard, and wrote my number down, then looked over my head at Adria. "Name?"

"Adria Lawson." She took her number.

We joined the big clump of girls and parents by the side of the gym and dropped our gym bags.

"Am I wearing an invisibility cloak?" I said.

"We're all invisible next to that girl." Adria handed me her number and turned so I could pin it to the back of her shirt. "You think a lot of these girls have played on club teams before?"

"You think a lot of them were invited to try out?"

Adria held up her hands, fingers crossed. "Please don't let that be true."

Parents were talking to one another now, saying stuff like, "Played on a Nike-sponsored team last year" or "Duke coach watching her," and saying stuff to their daughters like, "Good luck" or "Try hard" or "Do your best," except one mom, who, honestly, looked kind of like a bulldog. She was bending down, her face about three inches from the face of her bulldog-looking daughter, growling, "Don't let anybody get in your way."

My mom wasn't there to say "Good luck" or anything

else. She worked some Saturday mornings, so I'd come with
Adria and her dad. And since he'd coached our county-league
teams ever since we were in second grade, he hadn't said
something dumb like, "Try hard" (*Really?*); he'd said, "Be
aggressive. Attack the hoop. Move your feet and keep your
backsides down and your hands up on defense." And to Adria
he'd said, "And stand up straight. Don't slouch."

I turned so Adria could pin my number to the back of
my shirt, then scanned the gym, doing a quick count of the
girls. Thirty or so. All different skin colors—brown and tan
and white. Skinny and stocky. Loud and quiet. But all with
one thing in common, it seemed—tall. Making me feel like
an ant in a field of giraffes.

I rubbed my hands along the sides of my shorts,
scrunching up the shiny fabric with my fingertips. I'd never
felt short before. Not in county league. And anyway, I was
a point guard, and point guards don't need to be tall. They
need to be good ball-handlers and make accurate passes and
call the right plays, and I was good at all that stuff. They also
need to get the ball to the girl who can score, which on our
county-league teams was usually Adria. And I was great at
getting the ball to Adria when she was open.

But some of these tall girls had to be point guards, and
all other things being equal, taller is better in basketball. I
knew that. Everybody knew that.

I took a long, slow breath, blowing it back out long and slow, the way you're supposed to before you shoot a free throw, then stood up extra straight and squared my shoulders. So what if these girls were all big? So what if I'd never played on a team like this before? I'd been the best point guard in all of county league. Adria's dad always said so. A lot of people said so.

I could be better than these girls, too.

I could be one of the best.

I had to be.

A whistle blew.

The tallest man I'd ever seen stood in the middle of the floor, waving us over.

I sprinted onto the court, beating out the giraffes to plant myself directly in front of the man, which was maybe not the best idea, since looking up at him from that angle was pretty much like looking straight up a tree.

"Ladies," the man said, "I'm Coach Duval, and this is the Northern Virginia Action. I'll take ten girls on this team. We'll play fast, up-tempo ball, but it'll be team ball." He paused and looked around at us. "Let me say that again. Basketball is a team sport and the Action plays team ball. If you want to be the only star of the show, this isn't the team for you." He paused again, as if giving girls a chance to leave, but no one did. "Okay, how many of you want to play varsity ball in high school?"

I raised my hand. So did all the other girls.

Coach Duval nodded. "So let me tell you something. I've coached eighth-grade club teams for twenty years. Some girls who play on my teams decide it's too much work. Decide they'd rather be shopping or hanging out doing nothing. But the girls who stick with it, every single one has made her high school varsity team. Quite a few played in college. What do you think got them there?"

"Talent," a girl said.

"Yup. What else?"

"Size and speed," another girl said.

"Well, yeah. What else?"

There was a long pause, then Kate-the-giant said, "Hard work."

"Bingo." Coach Duval pointed at her. "You want to play at the next level, you have to work hard. Doesn't matter how much talent you have, how big you are, how high you can jump. So hear me now. On the Action, we work hard. We have a lot of fun, but we work hard. Every practice. Every game. You don't like to work, you need to find another team. You got me?"

He picked up a basketball from the rack beside him, palming it in one hand, his fingers, dark brown against the orange ball, reaching way around—about like me holding a softball. Then he looked straight down at me. "You ready to show me what you got?"

I stood frozen for a moment, until I realized he expected me to answer, and managed to squeak out, "Yes."

"Then let's warm up." He handed the ball to me and tossed a few more to other girls. "Line up single file, dribble the length of the court, make a layup. Right hand first. Go."

Balls boomed off the floor, sneakers screeched, the basket rims rattled and clanked, all the noise multiplying, echoing off the walls.

When my turn came, I sprinted down the court, my dribble low and crisp, my eyes up, the way Adria's dad had taught me. I jumped to make a layup, and the ball rolled around the rim once, twice before dropping through. I got back in line just as Kate-the-giant started up the court. She didn't look like she was running very fast, but her long legs gobbled up the floor in a few strides and she had to slow down to keep from plowing into the girl in front of her. She barely had to jump to get her hand up near the rim, and her ball rolled across the lip of the basket and fell straight through.

I was having a hard time not hating her.

Our layup line kept going. Most of the girls looked okay

but nothing special, which wasn't surprising since there aren't a lot of ways to look special doing layups.

Unless you were Kate, of course.

Or Adria. She stood out on the basketball court no matter what she was doing. Her long, long arms and legs made her look like she was flying over the court instead of running. Like maybe gravity didn't apply to her. Even my mom, who was clueless about sports, said Adria made basketball beautiful.

I was glad she was my best friend. Otherwise I'd have to hate her, too.

"Kate," a man's voice said, sharp and loud, cutting through the noise in the gym.

She stepped out of line and walked over to a man who had to be her father—same thick blond hair, same stilts for legs. They had a short conversation, during which Kate shook her head several times. The only thing I heard was her dad say, "Reverse."

The girl behind me tapped my shoulder. "Go."

"Sorry." I sprinted down the court for another layup, caught my ball after it dropped through the net, and turned to watch Kate.

Her big strides ate up the court again, but when she got near the basket, she jumped sideways beneath it and swung the ball up backward over her shoulder. It tapped the backboard and fell through the hoop.

"Whoa!" the girl behind me said.

Coach Duval blew his whistle. "Okay, move your line to the other side of the hoop. Left-handed dribble. Left-handed layups. And we don't need anything fancy. Just regular layups."

Kate stared down at the court, her face suddenly splotchy red. She brushed past me as we moved our line, and even though I was still hating her, I couldn't help saying, "That was sweet."

She looked up. "Thanks," she said, so quietly I barely heard her.

Her dad leaned against the side of the gym now, frowning, arms crossed. Not very happy his daughter wasn't allowed to do reverse layups, I guess.

A lot of the other parents didn't look super happy right then, either, especially the bulldog mom, who stomped back and forth along the sideline, looking like she wanted to bite Kate on the leg. "JJ can do a reverse layup," she barked to the woman next to her. Then she whipped around and shouted, *"Intense, JJ. Get intense."*

I turned back to the court. A couple of the girls out on the floor fumbled with their left-handed dribbles. One completely lost her ball, and another jumped off the wrong foot to shoot her supposed-to-be-left-handed layup with her right hand.

And, okay, I know it was mean, but that made me happy.

Because I'm left-handed.

And just like every other lefty in the world, I'd spent my entire life learning to do things right-handed, because, duh, that's how the world works. So when it came to handling a basketball with my right hand, it was no big deal.

But, double-duh, right-handers never have to do anything left-handed.

Unless they play basketball.

And that's why some of the girls on the court were looking as clumsy as actual giraffes trying to dribble and shoot with their left hands.

We finished the layups, then dribbled around cones and ran catch-and-shoot drills and stuff like that. Then finally, it was time to scrimmage, to actually play basketball. The best part of any tryout.

Or practice.

Or anything.

Coach Duval put me on a team with Kate and three other girls I didn't know. One of them kept dropping the ball or throwing it out of bounds, but the other two were good, and Kate was fantastic. Also unselfish, which I hadn't expected from a girl as good as her. On the first play of our first game, I had the ball at the top of the key, and Kate set a pick, motioning me around. I dribbled in close, crashed my defender into Kate, and popped out on her other side. No one stepped between me and the hoop, so I drove straight in for a layup. Left-handed, of course.

"Sweet, Nikki!" Adria called. "Keep—"

"For crying out loud, Kate," her dad's voice boomed, drowning out Adria. "Call for the ball and take the shot."

But Kate just smiled a shy smile and slapped my hand. And I had a hard time hating her after that.

We ran down the court to play defense, but as soon as a girl put up a shot, Kate blocked it and swatted the ball out to me. I drove up the court, spotted one of our teammates sprinting ahead, and fired the ball up to her. The girl jumped for a layup, which she missed, but Kate came blasting up behind her, caught the rebound, and tipped it back in.

Everything else fell away—my worries about the giraffes, the parents yelling, every thought about anything other than what was happening out on that golden wood floor, with the ball in my hands, directing my teammates to cut across the court, then Kate setting another hard pick, motioning me around, then rolling to the hoop with her hand in the air, and my high lob over all the other outstretched hands to find Kate's, and her pretty pivot around her defender to put the ball up and in.

I was in the zone. Flowing with the game, feeling where my teammates were moving like there were strings between us, seeing the whole floor, all the girls, like a pattern, like a dance. The ball falling from my hand, booming off the floor, rising back up to skim my fingertips, *boom, shh, boom, shh, boom*, sure and steady as a pulse. The swish and rattle of the hoop. The shouts, the hands raised high for a pass. The grins, the fist-bumps. The joy.

I could have played like that forever.

And as it turned out, our team got to play a long time, because the first team to three baskets stayed on the floor, and another team came on to replace the losers. We won three games before we all got tired and Adria's team beat us.

The next time we got on the floor, things didn't go quite so well. All the other teams had seen us play, for one thing, so they didn't bother to guard our girl-who-couldn't-catch and instead double-teamed Kate. Plus, in one game JJ-the-bulldog-girl guarded me, and her mom kept yelling, "*Intense, JJ. Get intense,*" and JJ must have been listening to her, because she plowed into me, whacked at my arms, and even grabbed my T-shirt to pull me off balance. And then, just as I was about to throw the ball in from the sideline, she picked that exact second to lean up in my face and say, "What's wrong with your eyes?"

I jerked and threw the ball straight to one of JJ's teammates.

Great.

My team still won that game, because we had Kate. But in the next game, a girl on the other team with tight cornrow braids hit two quick midrange jumpers before we even took a shot.

Kate grabbed the ball and took it out under the basket.

"Let's press," the girl with the cornrows said, and her team closed in.

I took the ball from Kate. "Go long," I whispered. "I'll hit you."

Kate looked at me kind of sideways. "Really?"

"Yeah. Start at half-court, cut back toward me, then run for the other end."

Coach Duval blew his whistle. "Let's go, ladies."

Kate sprinted to half-court, took a stutter-step, and kept running. I faked a pass to our girl-who-couldn't-catch, then zinged a long pass up the court. Kate caught the ball on the run, turned, and jumped for an easy layup. She jogged back downcourt, pointing at me, and if I had even one teeny, tiny, little scrap of still-hating-her left inside me, it disappeared right then.

Kate's layup wasn't enough to win that game, though. In the next play, the girl with the cornrows slid around her defender and pulled up for another short jumper, and that made three, and we were done.

I walked off the court, breathing hard, looking for my water bottle.

"Hey, Lefty."

I looked up, expecting to see Adria's dad calling me, because he always called me Lefty. But it wasn't him. It was Coach Duval. He waved me over.

"You set up that play?" he said. "That long pass?"

It was hard to tell from his expression if he liked the pass, or if he was about to tell me it was dumb because it was the kind of pass that was easy to intercept if you didn't throw it hard and fast enough.

But I nodded because, well, because I'd set it up.

"Okay," he said. Then he looked back at the court.

I stood there for a minute, not sure if the conversation was over, but finally it felt weirder standing there than it did walking away without saying anything else, so I went and stood next to Kate and watched the other girls play.

And started to count.

Ten girls would make the team. Kate was one. So was Adria. And probably a girl I recognized from county league, Kim-Ly Tran, who flew up and down the court, darting between players, stealing the ball, streaking ahead of every-one else. What coach wouldn't want a girl as fast as her? That made three. There were two other really good guards who also happened to be tall. Taller than me, anyway. One was the girl with the cornrows who was such a good shooter, and the other was this goofy girl with wild red hair who called everybody "Dude" and jumped around slapping hands with her teammates. But goofy or not, she could whip the ball around behind her back and between her legs and spin away from defenders, moves I could barely do at half speed in my driveway, let alone on the run with a defender on me. That made five. Then, besides Adria and Kate, there were two more really tall girls who were good rebounders and pretty good shooters. That made seven.

Which left three spots.

And twenty girls to fill them.

In any tryout for any sport I'd ever played—basketball, softball, soccer, even lacrosse—I'd always known I'd be one of those three girls. But this time... this time I didn't know.

Sure, I'd made good passes, I'd been fine in the drills, I hadn't made terrible mistakes.

But had I stood out? Apart from being left-handed, apart from being a left-handed point guard, had I looked special?

Was I one of the best?

For the first time ever, I didn't know.

Some Kind of Heterozygote Advantage

It was only a fifteen-minute car ride from the gym to my house, but my muscles had already stiffened up by the time I got out of Mr. Lawson's car and thanked him for the ride.

"Come over later. We can shoot around," Adria said, pulling the elastic band from her hair and fluffing out her dark curls. She waved as they drove away.

I hitched my gym bag up higher on my shoulder and started up the steps to our side porch—three little steps that suddenly looked like Mount Everest. I grabbed the handrail, hauled myself up, and after about ten hours, made it onto the porch.

The door crashed open.

I jumped sideways, but not quick enough, because my

brother exploded out of the house like an eight-year-old rocket, hurtling straight into me. We went down in a heap.

"Sam! Can't you watch where you're going?" I untangled my legs from his.

"Sorry, Nikki." He jumped up. "Sorry. Sorry. You okay?"

"Yeah." I rubbed at my legs, which were now even sorer than they'd been a minute ago.

"Did you make the team?" Sam was already off the porch, sprinting into the garage. Two seconds later he sprang onto the driveway on his pogo stick, his hair flapping around his head. He looked like a giant bouncing mushroom.

"No," I hollered back.

"Nikki?" Mom stood in the doorway, still wearing what she called her librarian uniform—dark dress slacks, bright-colored blouse, dark jacket. And a hideous pair of clogs. Weird, shiny, plasticky-looking clogs. Weird, swirly green plastic. They hurt your eyes to look at, which I'd told her a hundred times but she just shrugged and said she was happy to look professional from the knees up, but had to be comfortable from the ankles down.

Like that made it okay to walk around looking so embarrassing.

"What are you doing down there?" Mom said.

I pushed myself up. "Run-in with Sam."

"She didn't make the team!" Sam bellowed, bouncing in a big circle.

"Oh no. I'm so sorry." Mom reached toward me, but I was already bending down to retrieve my gym bag from where it had landed, underneath the old rocking chair.

"It's okay, Mom," I said. "Nobody made it yet. There's another tryout next Saturday."

"Oh. Did I know that already?"

I sighed. "Remember, when I signed up, I told you there'd be two days of tryouts?"

"Well, I don't remember, but I suspect you told me." She put her arm around my shoulders, even though I was pretty sure my T-shirt was totally sweaty and gross. "Come and get something to drink."

"Look!" Sam let go of his pogo stick and held his arms straight out, still bouncing. "No hands!" He bounced two more times, then the bottom of the pogo stick hit the edge of the driveway, and he flew off onto the lawn.

I guess a lot of moms would have run over to pick him up and coo and stuff, but our mom was so used to Sam bashing into things she just folded her arms. "Any blood?"

Sam looked at his knees and twisted his arms around to look at his elbows. "No."

"Put your bike helmet on, please."

"Do I have to?"

Mom just looked at him.

"Okay, okay." He ran into the garage.

"And stay on the driveway." Mom went back inside.

I followed her, hung my gym bag on a hook in the laundry room, kicked off my shoes, and washed my hands at the kitchen sink. I tugged gently at the middle finger of my left hand, which I'd jammed a little in one of the scrimmages. I always seemed to jam that finger—probably because I reached for the ball first with my left hand.

"Mom," I said. "Why am I left-handed?"

"It's genetic." Mom took a pitcher of lemonade out of the refrigerator, poured some into a glass, and handed it to me. "As a matter of fact, I read something the other day about left-handedness. Researchers think it might be linked to some kind of heterozygote advantage."

You know, sometimes having a mom who's a university research librarian is a good thing, like when she helps you figure out how to find information for school projects and stuff. Sometimes it's beyond annoying.

"Thanks for clearing that up," I said.

"You're welcome. And what that means, in case you're wondering, is that they think left-handedness, or some trait it's linked to, might have provided an evolutionary advantage."

I wiped lemonade off my chin with the back of my hand.

"I hope it's linked to a trait that'll make me tall. I could use that advantage."

Mom smiled. "Don't worry, Nikki. You'll grow more." She leaned against the counter. "So how did the tryout go? Did you have fun?"

I gulped down more lemonade. "Tryouts are never really fun."

"No, I guess not. More like a job interview, I suppose. Stressful."

"Definitely stressful."

Mom smoothed some stray hairs away from my face. "I'm sure you played well. You always do."

"I hope so." I leaned against her, letting my head drop onto her shoulder. "You wouldn't believe how good some of the girls were."

She looped her arm around me and we stood like that for a minute or two. "Tired?" she said.

I nodded into her shoulder.

Mom turned her arm and looked at her watch. "Oh dear, I have to go."

"Where?"

"I have a haircut appointment and I need to go to the grocery store. Please make sure Sam keeps his helmet on when he's on his pogo stick."

"Wait, what? I have to watch Sam?"

"Just for a few hours."

"But I told Adria I'd come over to shoot with her."

"I'm afraid that'll have to wait."

"Can't you just do the haircut and not the grocery store?"

Mom picked up her purse and keys. "If I don't go to the grocery store, you and Sam won't have anything to pack for lunches this week."

"We could buy lunch in our cafeterias."

Mom raised an eyebrow. "Nikki, you know we run on a tight budget. If you buy lunch all week, we'll have to give up something else. Like a movie. Or dinner at a restaurant. It won't kill you to watch Sam for a little while."

I slumped into a chair. "It might."

Mom gave my shoulder a quick squeeze and headed out the door.

"Wait!"

She stuck her head back inside. "What?"

"You cannot wear those clogs to the hair salon."

Mom laughed. She stepped out of her clogs, set them on the shoe rack by the door, and slipped into black flats. "Better?"

"Better."

I made a sandwich and looked out the window to make sure Sam was still in the driveway, even though I could hear the *sproing, sproing* of the pogo stick. Then I sat at the kitchen counter, chewing my PB&J a lot harder than I needed to.

Why couldn't I have a family like Adria's? With older sisters instead of an annoying little brother. And why couldn't I have a dad like her dad, who loved basketball and would spend millions of hours out in the driveway with me, teaching me to dribble and shoot and playing one-on-one? Or even, just, why couldn't I have a family with a dad? A dad who liked to hang out with Sam so I didn't have to. Because, let's face it, taking care of Sam was about the last thing I wanted to do right then.

Or ever.

When I started seventh grade last year and couldn't go to after-school-care anymore because they didn't have it in middle school, Mom thought it would be a great idea if Sam came home after school, too. I'd be there to take care of him and the two of us could get our homework done and spend time "bonding." It took me two weeks to convince her that it would be a horrible idea, and that I'd be insane and Sam would be tied up and locked in his room every day when she got home. I think it was the tied-up part that finally convinced her.

That didn't get me out of weekend babysitting, though.

I finished eating, cleaned up, then texted Adria that I couldn't come over.

Poop, she texted back.

Double-poop.

I shrugged into a sweatshirt, pulled on sneakers, and went outside.

"Want to ride bikes?" Sam hollered.

"Maybe later. I need to practice shooting." I grabbed my basketball—my "Official WNBA" ball I'd gotten last Christmas—and dribbled it back and forth between my legs, jogging over to our hoop.

It was an old hoop and, honestly, it was pretty ratty-looking, scratched up and rusty in places. Mom said it had already been there, planted in the ground beside the driveway, when she bought the house before I was born. But it was the right height and straight and level, and Mom had helped me hang a new net on it, so it worked fine.

I stood in front of the basket to warm up with form-shooting, which is shooting with only one hand. It's the way Adria's dad started teaching us to shoot when we were little (on a lowered hoop, of course). *You learn good shooting form now*, he'd said, *you won't have bad habits to break later.* Which is probably one of the reasons why Adria and I were better than the other girls when we showed up for our first team in second grade. It's probably also one of the reasons why I always loved basketball—I was always good at it. And, you know, it's fun to do stuff you're good at.

Was I good enough to make the Action, though?

Oh man, I *had* to make this team. I'd been *dreaming* about making this team all winter long. Ever since Mr. Lawson took us to some games at the high school where Adria and I would go. Amazing games. The bleachers full of high school kids cheering and jumping around, a big scoreboard that lit up with the girls' jersey numbers when they scored, even an announcer. But the actual games were the best part, because the girls were so, so, *so* good. The way they played together, zinging the ball around, knowing where another girl would be before she got there, running their plays like they were connected to one another, like they didn't even have to think. Like they *lived* in the zone.

And from the first time I saw them play, I wanted to be part of that team more than I'd ever wanted anything in my life. Because how amazingly fun would it be to play on a team that good?

After one of the games, Mr. Lawson introduced Adria and me to the coach, and she told us we should play on a club team this spring if we wanted to be ready for high school ball and that the Action was the best club because they had great coaches.

So, yeah, I *had* to make this Action team. Which meant I had to get to work.

I squared my shoulders to the basket and started shooting, the ball balanced on my left hand at eye level, my right hand behind my back, bending my knees, then powering up, sending the ball toward the basket, holding my follow-through, and *swish*.

I had a regular warm-up routine, shooting from right in front of the hoop, then from both sides, swishing three shots from each spot before I could move on. Then I'd take a step back from the basket and do the whole routine again. After that, I'd work on the fun stuff—layups, set shots, jumpers—but I always did form-shooting first.

"Hey, Nikki, guess what!" Sam bounced up the driveway. "Mom says I get to play on a soccer team."

"That's cool. You run around a lot in soccer." My next shot clanged off the front of the rim.

"That's what Mom said." Sam bounced up next to me, still talking, his voice going *boing, boing, boing* every time the pogo stick hit the driveway. "Jeffrey's going to play, too. So's Omar. We all want to be on the same team."

"Cool," I said again, staying focused on the hoop, trying to screen out Sam's chattering, balancing the ball on my left hand, bending my knees, sending up another shot…*clang*. "Sam, could you back off? Your pogoing's distracting me."

"Sorry!" Sam bounced away. "I bounced a hundred in a row without falling off while you were inside. Wanna see me do it again?"

"Sure, whatever." Balancing the ball on my left hand, and

sending up another shot, and *swish*. Two. And balancing the ball on my left hand, and—*sproing, sproing, sproing* behind me, and Sam's voice, "eight, nine, ten"—and sending up another shot, and *clang*. Grabbing the rebound, and—*sproing, sproing, sproing* closer, "fifteen, sixteen, seventeen"—and balancing the ball on my left hand, and—*sproing, sproing, sproing*—and sending up another shot, and—

Bam! Sam bounced up, directly into the ball as it left my fingers. He flew into the little hedge that separated our yard from our neighbor's, and the pogo stick banged off my shin and landed on my foot.

"Yow!" I grabbed my shin, stumbled sideways, and dropped down on the driveway. "Oh my god, Sam, you practically broke my leg."

"Sorry," Sam said. "Sorry, sorry."

"You're a walking disaster area, you know that?" I pulled up the leg of my sweatpants. "Look at that! There's already a lump."

"I'm sorry, Nikki," he said again. "I didn't mean to."

I opened my mouth to yell at him some more, but stopped. Tears leaked from the corners of his eyes.

"You okay?" I said.

He nodded. "Are you?"

"Yeah." I pulled my sweatpants leg back down, being careful not to touch the lump on my shin. "You want to ride bikes?"

The Most Embarrassing Thing in the Entire World

At least I got to hang out at Adria's on Sunday.

I parked my bike in her garage, gave a quick little tap on the kitchen door, let myself in, and called out, "Hi, it's me." I don't think anyone heard me, though, because Adria's sisters were in the kitchen with what looked to be about half their high school dance team. Some of the girls were making cookies and the rest of them were dancing around to the music that blared from a speaker, shouting and laughing and pretty much making more noise than Sam could ever hope to make.

"Hey, Nik," one of Adria's sisters called. "Want a cookie? Adria's out back with Mom."

I waved at her and hurried out through their family

room to the backyard. Adria was sprawled in a lounge chair, one leg draped over the chair arm, with a plate of cookies in her lap. Her mom sat on a high stool, her big sketch pad propped on an easel in front of her.

"Well, there you are," Mrs. Lawson said. "I haven't seen you in forever."

I laughed. "I was here Friday after school."

"No, really?" Mrs. Lawson laughed, too, and pulled me into a quick hug. "It's so nice to hug you girls when you're not dripping sweat."

"Cookie?" Adria said, which sounded like "ookie?" because she was chewing.

I held out my hand and Adria tossed one to me, holding her follow-through like she was shooting a basketball. I caught the cookie near my knee. "I think that would've been an air ball."

Adria shrugged and bit into another cookie.

I looked over Mrs. Lawson's shoulder at her sketch pad. It was covered with drawings of birds. Birds hanging on the bird feeder, birds pecking at the ground, birds perched on branches. "What are you working on?" I asked. "No, wait, let me guess. A picture book about birds?"

She laughed. "Lots and lots of little birds. And a flamingo. Looks like I need a trip to the zoo."

Adria sat up. "Can we go with you?"

"You'll be in school," Mrs. Lawson said.

"We could miss a day," Adria said. "Remember how we used to go with you when we were little?"

"Yes, and I also remember never getting much work done when you were with me." She held binoculars up to her eyes, pointing them at the forest behind their fence. "Oh, look at that cardinal puffing out his feathers. Doesn't he look full of himself?" She set down the binoculars, pulled a pencil from over her ear, and with just a few quick lines, dashed out a sketch of a cardinal looking totally stuck-up.

I hung behind her, watching her sketch more birds. Ever since Adria and I started playing at each other's houses when we were in kindergarten, I'd loved watching Mrs. Lawson draw and paint. I always thought it was so cool that drawing and painting was her job. And that she didn't have to get dressed up like my mom did when she went to work. She could wear whatever she wanted, which was usually something like what she had on right then—black leggings, a big paint-spattered shirt, and a bright purple scarf wrapped around her head to keep her hair back from her face. Without the scarf, her hair was a fantastic riot of dark curls that danced and swayed whenever she moved.

Mrs. Lawson was from Brazil. No, actually her family was from Brazil. She'd only lived there as a baby, and whenever anyone asked her where she was from, she'd say, "Rhode

Island," because both her parents were professors at a fancy art school there, so that's where she grew up. I also thought it was cool that there were so many artists in Mrs. Lawson's family.

Adria and both her sisters were good at art, too, but only her oldest sister wanted to be an artist. Her middle sister was into science, and Adria was like me—the only thing she wanted to do was play basketball.

Adria stood up from her lounge chair and stretched, the empty cookie plate in one hand. "So are we going to spend all day watching Mom draw birds, or do you want to go shoot some hoops?"

Mrs. Lawson picked up her binoculars and waggled her fingers at us. "You girls go do what you need to do."

I snagged another cookie when we walked back through the kitchen, and Adria grabbed a box of little Goldfish crackers.

Out in the driveway we tossed the crackers to each other, trying to catch them in our mouths, and ended up laughing so hard we spit Goldfish crumbs all over the place. Then we got out our phones and a basketball and filmed each other taking goofy shots, tossing the ball up underhand, or kneeling on the ground and heaving the ball up at the hoop, or bouncing it off our heads like a soccer ball. When we couldn't think of any more dumb shots, we played H-O-R-S-E, and I won the first game and Adria won the second.

Then Mr. Lawson came out and said, "All right, let's get you two ready for the final tryout." He ran us through some drills, then played defense on us so I could work on ball-handling and Adria could work on shooting over a taller defender.

And we talked. Talked and talked and talked about the tryout—the size of Coach Duval (Mr. Lawson thought he had to be six eight or six nine) and how it seemed like he'd be a good teaching coach. And Kate-the-giant-girl ("Six one or six two," Mr. Lawson said) and how fun it was to play with her—"You were so lucky to be on her team," Adria said. And JJ-the-bulldog-girl and how rough she played—"Do you believe she asked what was wrong with my eyes?" I said, and Mr. Lawson said, "Oh, for god's sake, is that why you made that bad pass?" And the girl who was such a good three-point shooter—"She was a total lazy-butt on defense, though," Adria said. And the goofy "Dude" girl, and superfast Kim-Ly, and a tall, skinny girl named Taj who could get way up in the air and block just about anybody's shot.

"For once I wasn't the tallest girl on the court," Adria said. "I didn't have to feel like such a freak."

I swatted the ball at her. "I'd give anything to be a freak like you."

We all laughed, and Mr. Lawson patted my shoulder. "The point guard's the most important player on the court."

Adria rolled her eyes. "Yeah, Dad, we know, the floor general."

Now Mr. Lawson patted Adria's shoulder. "Sorry, honey, but it's true. No point guard, no team." He picked up the ball and tossed it to me. "Plus you've got that lefty thing going, Nikki. People don't expect it. Always gave our team a secret weapon." He dropped down into a defensive crouch. "Come on, let's get back to work. You girls did great yesterday, but you can do better."

Boy, I hoped he was right.

Adria and I were still talking about the Action tryout on the school bus Monday morning, and I was still thinking about it all through English, when I was supposed to be discussing *Under a War-Torn Sky*, and all through history, when I was supposed to be watching a movie about Pearl Harbor.

Third period was science with Mr. Bukowski, my favorite subject and favorite teacher, but I was still having trouble paying attention, only half listening to the lecture.

"Genotype," Mr. Bukowski said, writing the word on the whiteboard, his raspy voice filling the classroom. "Who can tell me what a genotype is?"

Several hands shot up.

"Sunil." Mr. Bukowski pointed at the boy who sat across from me at our lab table.

"It's the genes you have, isn't it?" Sunil said.

"Are you asking me or telling me?"

"Uh, I'm telling you," Sunil said, then more quietly, "I think."

"Well, you're right. Genotype refers to the specific genes an individual has." Mr. Bukowski turned back to the white-board. "Phenotype," he said, writing that word, too. "Who can tell me what a phenotype is?"

No hands went up.

"Nobody? Not one of you has read ahead in your text-book?" Mr. Bukowski scanned the classroom. "Now, why doesn't that surprise me?" He laughed like he'd told a really funny joke, making his hair—which looked like an exact copy of Albert Einstein's—vibrate around his head. "All right, phenotype refers to an individual's appearance or behavior."

He turned and wrote the definitions on the whiteboard, and everybody opened their science notebooks to write them down.

I opened mine, too, but I didn't write anything down, because now I was thinking about what I needed to do to stand out at the next tryout. I was a good ball-handler, I knew that, and I had a sneaky crossover dribble. I wasn't as quick with it as the "Dude" girl, but I could work on that after school this week. I was a pretty good shooter, too, especially if I was ten or twelve feet from the hoop, just left of the free throw line. I'd worked on that shot a lot because Adria's dad said that if I got good at it, defenders wouldn't be able to sag off me to double-team Adria. I had to make sure I showed Coach Duval that shot on Saturday.

And then, all of a sudden, Mr. Bukowski's voice said, "Nikki, do you have a suggestion?"

I blinked at him, glanced at Adria, who sat at the next lab table, then blinked again.

"Are you with us, Nikki?"

"Um."

"Would you like me to repeat the question?"

I nodded.

"Can you name a common, inherited trait with a dominant and a recessive form that we can all easily observe when we look at someone?"

Oh boy.

"Do you remember we talked about this last week?"

"Um." I glanced at Sunil, who seemed to be pulling at his ear, then at Adria, who, weirdly, was really pulling at her ear, then at this new kid, Booker, who sat beside me. He'd pushed back his shaggy, sandy-colored hair and was rubbing at the side of his face, right next to his ear.

My brain clicked. "Earlobes!"

Mr. Bukowski smiled. "What about earlobes?"

"Some people's earlobes hang down a little bit and some people's earlobes are attached to their heads right at the bottom of their ears."

"Excellent." Mr. Bukowski turned back to the whiteboard and drew a series of little boxes with lines connecting groups of boxes together, explaining how you inherit half your genes from your mom and half from your dad and showed how your earlobe phenotype depends on your parents' earlobe genotypes.

I was still having trouble thinking about anything other than the Northern Virginia Action, but I at least copied down what was on the board. I also leaned toward Booker and whispered, "Thanks."

I think it was the only word I'd said to him, other than *Hi* when he first walked into our class the week before and Mr. Bukowski told him to sit next to me, since it was the only open stool in the classroom. Not that I didn't want to talk to him or anything—it's just that, well, I wasn't that good at talking to boys, especially a boy who all the other girls in the class thought was cute. I mean, unless we were playing H-O-R-S-E in PE or something.

Booker glanced at me and smiled—a kind of crooked smile with just one side of his mouth turning up. "Glad to help," he said.

Mr. Bukowski turned away from the whiteboard, dropping his marker on the tray. "And now we're ready to talk about our genetics projects."

Everyone groaned.

"Yes, yes, I know you can't wait to get started." Mr. Bukowski picked up a stack of papers and handed them out. "This project will be half your quarterly grade, so you'll want to put in some time and effort, but I think you're going to enjoy it. You're each going to pick one of your easily identifiable inherited traits, such as dangling or attached earlobes, hitchhiker's thumb, dimples, or one of the others listed on the assignment sheet. Then you're going to make a phenotypic family tree, showing which form of this trait each of your relatives has. I want you to include as many family members as you can. Parents, brothers and sisters, aunts and uncles, cousins, grandparents, great-grandparents. You'll give a classroom presentation, and we'll hang your family trees in the science hallway."

Mr. Bukowski talked on, but I didn't hear him. And it wasn't because of the Northern Virginia Action or Coach Duval or giraffes or crossover dribbles.

It was because now I saw an enormous family tree growing in front of me, with dangling and attached earlobes for Mom and Sam, Mom's parents, her two brothers, and their children. And on my father's side . . . on my father's side, I saw a big, fat blank.

No, worse than a blank.

Two words.

Sperm Donor.

Oh.

My.

God.

Of all the embarrassing things Mom had ever done to Sam and me—or ever would do to us—nothing could be more embarrassing than giving us dads who were sperm donors.

What was I going to do?

How could I bring a family tree to school with…with those words on it? And stand up in front of the class and say those words? And hang my family tree in the science hallway so everybody in the entire school could walk by and read about my Sperm Donor dad?

I wanted to bury my head in my hands and scream.

For a minute, I thought about making up a dad and his family, but in the same minute I realized I couldn't do that. Half the kids in my class had known me since kindergarten, and they all knew I didn't have a dad. They didn't know *why* I didn't have one—I'd always let everybody think my parents were divorced and my dad had moved far away or maybe died or something.

Adria knew the truth, only because our moms were friends, and my mom didn't see anything embarrassing about talking about the most embarrassing thing in the world. But I'd sworn Adria to secrecy....

Wait. That was it. I'd get Mom to call Mr. Bukowski and tell him I couldn't do this assignment.

Perfect solution.

I hoped.

Special

"I have this assignment," I said the minute Mom got home from work that evening, with Sam blasting into the kitchen behind her.

But Mom threw a hand out in front of her, like a cop signaling *Stop!* and said, "Is it due tomorrow?"

"No. But—"

"Then I'm sorry, Nikki. I don't have time to talk about it tonight. I have to give a presentation in the morning and I haven't made a single slide yet. I brought home dinner." She set a supermarket bag on the counter, and I looked inside— a still-warm rotisserie chicken, and mashed potatoes and green beans that just needed to be heated in the microwave.

"Okay?" Mom said.

"Okay."

She gave me a quick hug.

"Nikki, guess what!" Sam bellowed. "Kritika got a puppy."

"Sam, please modulate yourself," Mom said, and disappeared into her office.

Great.

After dinner and cleaning up the kitchen and doing my homework, I sat down on my bed to do what I usually do when I don't know what to do, namely, have a little talk with Mia McCall.

Well, not actually *with* Mia McCall. With my poster of Mia McCall.

The poster showed Mia in her Minnesota Lynx uniform—just after she got drafted, first overall, to play in the WNBA—soaring up toward the basket with the ball in her hand, so far above the court her knees almost touched the shoulder of the LA Sparks player guarding her. At first I thought the picture was Photoshopped—like how could anybody jump that high? But it wasn't Photoshopped. Mia McCall has a twenty-six-inch vertical leap, which is only two inches less than the average vertical leap of the men who play in the NBA.

I know this because last summer Adria and I started watching WNBA games on TV, and her dad told us we should pick a favorite player to follow. Adria couldn't decide between Candace Parker and Elena Delle Donne because they're both tall, like her, but they're also so athletic they can play just about any position, which is what Adria wanted to be able to do. So she followed both of them. Mr. Lawson said I should pick a really good point guard, but once I saw Mia play, I had to pick her.

Mia's a forward, like Candace Parker and Elena Delle Donne, and it would have made more sense if I'd listened to Mr. Lawson and picked a point guard. But watching Mia play is like... it's like...

Okay, this probably sounds stupid, but my mom listens to classical music, which, honestly, I think is pretty boring most of the time, but there's this one Beethoven symphony that has singing at the end of it. First one guy, then a couple of people, then this whole huge choir of people. They sing bigger and bigger, and the orchestra swells way up behind them, and the music pulls you straight up from the middle of your chest, and makes you want to fling your arms out from your sides and throw your head back and spin around and around and around in the absolute gloriousness of those voices.

I asked Mom once what they were singing about—because they're singing in German—and she said, *Joy*.

And, yeah, that's exactly what it's like watching Mia McCall play basketball. Like listening to a huge choir of people singing out Beethoven's version of joy.

So anyway, there I sat, looking up at Mia, wondering what she would've done if she'd gotten a family-tree-of-earlobes assignment when she was in school, because I knew she'd grown up without a dad in her family, too. And as I looked at her, at the determination in her face, at the strain showing in her muscles, I could almost hear her say, *Just deal with it.*

I slumped back against my pillows. Mia was right. I had to talk to Mr. Bukowski—that's all there was to it. If I waited to talk to Mom the next night, she might be too busy again, and the longer I put off talking to Mr. Bukowski, the worse it would get. And I couldn't just ignore the assignment. I'd never not done an assignment in my life.

I'd have to talk to him.

"I wish you could go with me," I said to Mia. "But at least Adria will be there."

Except she wasn't. She had a dentist appointment, which I remembered when she didn't get on the bus at her stop the next morning.

I thought about waiting till later. Maybe talking to Mr. Bukowski after class. But then there'd be a bunch of kids around. It was better to get it over with. So as soon as I got off the bus, I hurried to Mr. Bukowski's room, hoping to get there before any of his homeroom kids came in.

No luck. There were already kids in his room. But at

least they were talking to one another, not reading or studying. Maybe they wouldn't hear me.

"Hey there, Nikki," Mr. Bukowski said when he saw me.
"What's up?"

"Um," I said. "Um..."

"Yes?"

"Um, well...you know the family tree project?"

"Yes."

"I..." I rubbed my hands up and down the sides of my
jeans, feeling the little ridges of the seams. "I can't do it."

"Oh?"

I shook my head.

"Do you care to tell me why?"

My face was getting hot. "My father...um...my father
was a sp—"

Booker was suddenly standing beside me. "Mr. Bukowski,
can I talk to you about the family tree project?"

Mr. Bukowski rocked back in his chair. "Booker, did you
notice I was talking with Nikki?"

"Oh, uh, sorry." Booker glanced at me, then looked back
at Mr. Bukowski. "Should I talk with you later?"

"That depends," Mr. Bukowski said. "Are you here to tell
me you can't do the assignment?"

"Yes, sir."

Mr. Bukowski shook his head, took off his glasses,

wiped them with a tissue slowly, then put his glasses back on, stared at the surface of his desk, and muttered under his breath, "Why didn't I think about this? Must be getting old." He looked up at us. "Neither of you lives in a family with two biological parents, right?"

Booker and I nodded.

"Hey, I'm sorry, guys. I obviously didn't think this assignment all the way through. Apparently even great teachers like me make stupid mistakes." He laughed and stood up. "I hope you didn't spend too much time worrying about it."

"Just all night," Booker said.

"Really?" Mr. Bukowski looked at me.

I nodded.

"Oh, darn. I truly am sorry." He picked up a pencil and beat a little rat-a-tat on his desk. "Okay, let's see, how about if you pick a topic related to genetics that interests you? Write a report or do a poster-board display or a PowerPoint. Sound good?"

We both nodded, even though, duh, who would ever say writing a report sounded "good"?

"And, hey," Mr. Bukowski said, "I'm sure there are other kids who want to do a different kind of project. Remind me in class if I forget to mention it, okay?"

The first bell rang.

I still had to get to my locker before homeroom, so I

walked fast, nearly trotting, zigging and zagging through the packs of kids in the hallway, but Booker stayed beside me.

"I know what you should do your project on," he said.

"Yeah?"

"Your eyes."

I stopped. Which made four kids slam into me, two of whom had to cuss me out before they shoved past.

I crossed my arms. And stared at Booker.

All my life people had been saying stupid stuff about my eyes. Like, "What's wrong with your eyes?" or "Hey, your eyes are different colors." Or my favorite, "Wow, did you know your eyes are different colors?" Like maybe I looked in the mirror every day and didn't notice I had one green eye and one brown eye.

When I was a little kid, I started squinting up my eyes as small as I could, hoping people would stop asking me about them. But then they asked why I was squinting, so I gave that up and accepted the fact that I had two different-colored eyes and people were going to say stupid stuff about them because, I guess, people like saying stupid stuff.

"You think weird eyes are genetic?" I said.

Booker shook his hair back from his face. "Well, eye color's genetic, I guess. Just like hair color and, I dunno, the way your chin looks, the shape of your nose, all that stuff."

I couldn't help putting my hand on my nose, which was

a little pointy. Like my mom's. "Maybe I should do my report on noses."

"Huh-uh. You should do it on your eyes." Booker glanced around the hallway, then down at the floor, then looked straight back at me. "And your eyes aren't weird," he said. "Just different. Just…special."

He spun away from me, disappearing into the mob of kids in the hall.

And I stood there, staring after him, thinking, *Did he just say that? That my eyes are special?* And then the second bell rang and I realized I was late for class.

5

Hustle Your Butt Off

For the rest of the week, every time I looked at Booker during science, he seemed to be hiding behind the long fringe of hair hanging across the side of his face.

Not that I looked at him all that often or anything.

Really.

Otherwise, it was a regular school week—writing prompts, Pearl Harbor, homework. And that stupid genetics project hanging over my head.

Also it rained a lot, like it always does in March, which meant I couldn't go out in our driveway after school to practice my pull-up jumper from just left of the free throw line, the shot I wanted Coach Duval to see. So instead, I brought my basketball into the kitchen to work on my ball-handling.

I cleaned it first to make sure it wouldn't leave little dotted ball tracks all over the floor, because, well, even though Mom had never actually told me I couldn't play basketball in the house, I didn't see any reason to make it obvious.

On Friday night, after dinner and after Sam and I cleaned up the kitchen, I plopped down on the sofa next to Mom. "Can you take me to the tryout tomorrow morning?"

Mom looked up from a book that, from its cover, seemed to be about worms and compost piles. "Are you talking to me?" Mom said.

"I'm trying to."

She set her book on her lap, and I repeated my question.

"Sure," Mom said. "But don't you want to go with Adria and Mr. Lawson? Usually you like to go with them."

I shook my head. "If I make the team, you'll need to be there to get all the information. If I don't make the team..."

Mom smiled. "I don't think you need to worry about that. You've always made the team."

"Mr. Lawson was always the coach."

"Isn't he still the coach?"

"No."

Mom sat back against the sofa cushions. "I didn't realize that."

"That's because you never listen when I talk about basketball."

"Yes, I do."

"Yeah?" I picked up a throw pillow and punched it into shape. "What kind of team am I trying out for?"

Mom closed her book, holding a finger in her place. "I'm not that clueless. A basketball team."

"Uh-huh, what kind of basketball team?"

"Are there different kinds of teams?"

I whacked Mom's leg with the pillow. "See? I've only told you about this five or six times. It's a *club* team. It's way better than county league, and way harder to make the team."

Mom sighed. "I'm sorry, Nikki. I don't mean to be so distracted."

"I know." I punched the pillow back into shape again and balanced it on one corner against the arm of the sofa. "Are we starting a compost pile?"

"Hmm?"

I pointed at her book.

"Oh, maybe. Did you know that some worm species can double their population in three months?"

"No, actually I didn't know that, Mom. But, wow, that's fascinating."

She laughed and whacked my leg with her book.

"Tryout's at ten o'clock tomorrow," I said, standing up. "I

want to get there early, okay? And can Sam go to Jeffrey's or someplace? I don't want him bugging me."

"I'll see what I can do."

Coach Duval looked up at the clock on the gym wall when Mom and I pushed through the big doors on Saturday morning. "You know the tryout doesn't start for half an hour?"

I nodded. "I want to warm up my shooting. Is that okay?"

"Sure. Need a ball?"

"I brought one."

"Okay, go to it." He walked over to Mom and they talked for a few minutes. I hoped she wasn't telling him about worms.

I jogged onto the court and stood up close to a basket to do my warm-up shooting, right arm down at my side, left arm doing all the work, going through my whole routine, three swishes from each spot, taking a step away from the basket, and three swishes from each spot again.

Other girls and parents came in, and other balls bounced and banged off rims of other baskets, and then a man's voice said, "Who's your shooting coach?"

I kept shooting, counting swishes.

"Who's your shooting coach?" the man's voice said again, louder this time.

I turned.

Kate's dad stood behind me, with Kate beside him. "Wow," she said, "you have really nice form."

Her dad glared at her, then turned his hard gaze back on me. "Who's your shooting coach?"

"Um." I felt truly ant-like with Kate's giant dad staring down at me. "Adria's dad has always been my coach."

He frowned and exhaled a quick, exasperated breath. "Who's Adria's dad?"

I looked around the gym, saw Adria and her father coming through the door, and pointed. "The man in the Dickinson College sweatshirt."

Kate's dad looked where I pointed, cocked his head, then looked down at me. "He's that girl's father?"

I nodded.

"I thought he was your father."

I stared up at him.

It wasn't the first time someone had made that mistake. Since Mr. Lawson had always been our basketball coach, he and Adria and I spent a lot of time together, which meant a lot of people saw us together, and a lot of those people, when they looked at us, saw what they expected to see. I mean, I had straight light brown hair and the kind of white skin that tans easily. Mr. Lawson had straight blond hair and the kind of white skin that never tans. And Adria had dark curly hair and golden-brown skin. Like her mom.

But if you actually looked at us, really looked at us, instead of just skimming across the color of our skin, you'd realize that Adria looked exactly like her dad—long, oval face; high forehead; straight, sharp jaw. My face was round—round cheeks, round chin, freckles across the bridge of my nose. I looked nothing like Mr. Lawson.

I was glad Adria wasn't standing with us, because it ticked her off when people thought her dad was my dad. Kind of ticked me off, too. "He's not my father," I said.

"Hunh." Kate's dad turned and walked toward Mr. Lawson.

I bounced my ball, trying to remember where I was in my shooting count.

"You want to keep shooting?" Kate said. "I'll rebound."

"Sure."

Shooting went a lot faster with Kate rebounding, especially since I only missed a couple of shots. Then we switched and I rebounded for her. She didn't miss any.

"Hey, you guys." Adria hopped onto the court, still tying one shoe, her long, skinny arms sticking out like wings. "Can I shoot with you?"

Kate said, "Sure," and I said, "No way," and Kate looked at me like she couldn't believe I said that.

Adria grabbed my ball and shot it in a lazy, sloppy way. The ball clanged off the rim.

"Brick," I said, and Adria and I cracked up.

Kate caught the rebound and tossed the ball back to me. "I guess you guys are friends."

"Since kindergarten," I said. "We've always played on the same teams."

"You're so lucky. I've never played on a team with my friends," Kate said.

I rotated my ball around my waist. "The man who gave out the tryout numbers said you always play with older girls."

Kate nodded. "I begged my dad not to make me this year. Last year I played on a ninth-grade team and all the girls hated me. Most of them wouldn't even talk to me when we were off the court."

"I bet you were better than them," I said.

"I don't know." Kate bounced her ball. "You guys are already so much nicer than anybody on my last team. I really hope we all make this team."

"I don't think you or Adria need to worry," I said. "But there are a lot of good guards. I'm keeping my fingers crossed."

"Okay, listen." Kate stepped closer to Adria and me, and dropped her voice down to a whisper. "My dad said I shouldn't tell anyone this, but..." She glanced toward the parents. "He asked Coach Duval what he's looking for at try-outs. And Coach said he's looking for good skills and team play, but more than anything else, he's looking for hustle. He said he doesn't care how good a girl is—if she doesn't hustle her butt off, he doesn't want her on his team."

A whistle blew.

"Line up, ladies," Coach Duval called. "Same as last Saturday. Layups. Right hand first."

"Let's hustle our butts off," Kate said.

And then, for the next two hours, that's exactly what I did. Hustled my butt off.

All through the layups and drills I went all out, as fast as I could, even running between skill stations instead of walking like most of the girls, even retrieving other girls' loose balls. When we started to scrimmage, and Kim-Ly stole the ball from one of my teammates and flew up the court, I raced after her, fought off a bigger girl for the rebound, and took an elbow to the eye in the process. And when the "Dude" girl spun away from me with a slick move, I scrambled after her and dove to bat the ball free from behind, hitting the floor on my elbows and knees and getting back up with floor burns on both elbows.

My calf muscles cramped, and a blister the size of Virginia grew on my heel, and my lungs ached and burned, but I kept going, pushing harder and harder, telling myself to move my feet and get my backside down and attack the hoop and *hustle, hustle, hustle*, until my lungs felt like they might catch fire and explode.

And then, finally, Coach Duval blew his whistle and

motioned us over, and even though I thought I might collapse in a puddle of sweat if I didn't lie down right then, I ran over, elbowed my way between two giraffes, and planted myself right in front of Coach Duval.

"This is the hardest part of any tryout," he said, "because I have to let some of you go. Every one of you played well, and I've seen lots of talent and lots of effort, but I can't keep thirty girls on a basketball team. So I'd like these girls to step over to the registration table."

He looked down at his clipboard. "Kate Nyquist, Adria Lawson, Taj Turriago, Maura O'Brien, Kim-Ly Tran, Jasmine Taylor-Jones, Linnae Rubalow, JJ Packer, Autumn Milbourne." Coach Duval paused, running his finger down his clipboard.

I was having trouble hearing by that point, because my ears had started to ring and my throat was closing up and tears burned so hot in my eyes that Coach Duval was a tree-sized blur in front of me.

But then he said something else, and even though his voice sounded like it was underwater, floating toward me slow and deep, what he said sounded like "Nikki Doyle."

Then a hand grabbed my arm and pulled me back through the tall girls, and I took a breath, finally, and it almost sounded like a sob, and the hand belonged to Adria, and she was saying, "We made it! Nikki, we made it!" She kept pulling me away from the big group standing around Coach Duval, all silent and still now, toward the small group on the other side of the gym, where girls laughed and hugged, and the girl who called everybody "Dude" jumped around, high-fiving and fist-bumping so hard she almost knocked over a couple of girls.

I couldn't help feeling sorry for the girls in the big group, all gathering up their stuff now, finding their parents, wiping their eyes, trying to get out of the gym as fast as they could, but I also couldn't help feeling fantastic.

I'd made it!

I'd hustled and hustled until I thought I might die, and I'd made it.

"Ladies." Coach Duval's deep voice cut through our noise. "Welcome to the Action. We've got the makings of a fine team here, so I hope you're all ready to work hard. Go get your parents. We've got things to talk about."

Kate's dad and a couple of other parents were already walking over, and the parents who weren't were at least standing up. Except my mom, of course. She still sat in her folding chair, her head bent over her book.

I jogged across the court, calling, "Mom, Mom," then finally said, "Carolyn!"

She looked up.

"Mom, I made it!"

I could tell from the way she looked at me, which was totally blank, that her head was still inside the book, and I was afraid she was going to say she just needed to finish a paragraph. But finally she kind of woke up and smiled, stood up, and we hurried back across the gym.

"First things first," Coach Duval said. "Practice will be Tuesday and Thursday nights, seven o'clock to nine." He kept talking—tournament schedules, team parents—but I was only half listening. I was way more interested in checking out my new teammates.

Besides Kate and Adria, there were two other tall girls. One was Taj, the girl who was such a good shot-blocker. She had copper-colored skin and wore her hair in natural curls, short on the sides and longer on top, which made her look even taller than she was. The other tall girl, Jasmine, wore long box braids that she'd gathered into a thick ponytail. She was the girl who'd elbowed me in the eye when we both went up for a rebound, but she'd said she was sorry and asked if I was okay when we came off the court and even offered to get me an ice pack, which I thought was really nice, considering we were competing for a spot on the same team.

The next-tallest girl was Autumn. She had reddish-brown hair twisted into a loose, floppy bun on top of her head and the kind of pinkish-white skin that flushed deep red from exercise, making her look like she had about the worst sunburn you ever saw. She was also the only girl on the floor wearing nail polish—bright pink to match her pink T-shirt and shoelaces.

The guards were me (yes!); superfast Kim-Ly; Maura, the bouncing "Dude" girl with the wild red hair; Linnae, the girl with the cornrows and wicked jump shot; and JJ-the-bulldog-girl. She had the same kind of coloring I had—white skin that tanned easily. Our hair was different, though. Mine was light brown. Hers was blue.

Mom sucked in a sharp breath.

"What?" I asked in a whisper.

"Eight hundred dollars," Mom whispered back. "Aren't you listening?"

"I know it's a lot of money," Coach Duval was saying. "But it covers a lot. Game uniforms, practice uniforms, rental fees for our practice gym, and registration fees for ten tournaments. Tournaments are on weekends, usually two games on Saturday and two on Sunday. A couple of tournaments will be out of town, so we'll have some additional costs for hotels."

Parents started asking questions, but Coach Duval held up his hand. "I'll tell you what. I'd like the girls to try on the sample uniforms over at the registration table. There's a form for you to write down what size you need and what number you want on your jersey, because god forbid I have jerseys printed up with numbers you don't like."

Mom grabbed my elbow and pulled me away. The other girls ran over to the uniforms, and the parents closed in around Coach Duval.

"Nikki," Mom said, her voice barely above a whisper. "I don't have an extra eight hundred dollars just lying around. Plus hotel costs!" Her forehead crinkled into lines of concern. "Your other teams were always sixty or seventy dollars. And you only had one game each weekend."

"Those were county-league teams," I said. "This is club ball. It's different."

Mom rubbed her forehead. "Did you know it would be so expensive and take so much time?"

I shook my head. But that wasn't quite true. When I'd signed up, I'd read on the club website that there would be at least ten tournaments, and some of them might be in places like Philadelphia or Norfolk, so we'd have to stay overnight, but that sounded so fun I didn't think about how much it might cost.

Mom frowned and kept rubbing at the worry lines on her forehead. She looked at the parents, all asking questions, nodding, smiling big *I want you to like me* smiles at Coach Duval. She looked at the girls, all holding up uniforms, laughing, shouting out the numbers they wanted. Then she looked straight at me.

"I'm so sorry, Nikki," she said. "I can't afford this. You can't play on this team."

Ultimate Sacrifice

Mom headed toward Coach Duval. "We need to tell the coach you won't be able to play on the team so he can call back one of the other girls."

"No!" I grabbed her arm. "Please, Mom, please. I have to play on this team."

"Why?"

"Because it's the best club program. The high school coach said so."

"I'm sure there are other good teams." Mom started to walk away, but I pulled her back.

"What if all the club teams cost this much?" I said. "They all play in tournaments."

"Then you won't play on a club team."

"But I have to! I have to play club if I want to make the high school team."

"Then maybe you won't make the high school team." Mom threw her hands in the air, her voice tight. "For goodness' sake, Nikki. It's just basketball."

I started to cry. "Please, Mom."

She stroked her hand down my arm. "Nikki, I'm sorry, but you have to be reasonable. We can't afford this team."

I pulled at the sleeve of my T-shirt, trying to use it to wipe at my tears. "I haven't spent the Christmas money Grandma and Grandpa gave me," I said. "They always send me birthday money, too. We can use all that. And maybe I could ask them—"

"No. You will not ask your grandparents to help pay for a basketball team."

"I could get a job."

Mom sighed. "Nikki, you're not even fourteen yet. You have to be sixteen to get a job."

"I could walk people's dogs or pick up dog doo in their yards or...or...Please, Mom, I'll do anything. I won't ask for new clothes. I won't eat as much. I..."

Mom rubbed the worry lines on her forehead and stared at the ceiling. She tapped her foot, looked over at Coach Duval, then back at me. "I'll give you until Monday night to find a way to earn some money," she said. "And I'll take a look at our budget. Perhaps there's something we can cut. But if you don't figure out something by Monday night, we have to tell the coach you can't play. We can't let it go longer than that."

I grabbed the bottom of my T-shirt and wiped my face. "Can I try on a uniform?"

Mom nodded. "I'm afraid I don't see much point in that, but go ahead."

Most of the other players were already gathering up their stuff to leave, talking and laughing, but Adria still stood at the registration table. "What happened?" she said as I picked up a jersey to try on.

"My mom doesn't want me to be on the team. She didn't realize it would take a lot more time than county league." I wasn't sure why I didn't tell Adria the truth—it wasn't any secret that her family had more money than mine—but somehow I didn't want to say that this team cost too much.

"My dad can drive you to practice and games if your mom doesn't have time," Adria said. "He'll be going to all of them anyway. He can't wait to see how Coach Duval does stuff." She held out the form with the uniform sizes and numbers. "I saved number twenty-three for you. That JJ girl wanted it, but I wrote it down with your name first."

"Thanks," I said. Twenty-three was Mia McCall's number, the number I always wore. Now all I had to do was figure out a way to wear it on this team.

I spent the rest of Saturday afternoon making flyers for my new dog-walking/dog-doo-cleanup service, then went around my neighborhood handing them to neighbors. Sam came along to "help," which meant it took about twice as long as it needed to, because he kept doing stuff like dropping his stack of flyers, so we'd have to chase after them while they blew down the street.

All our neighbors smiled at us and said the flyers looked "real nice," but only one of them said she might be interested in having me walk her dog.

Which meant the bus ride to school on Monday morning was an ordeal.

All Adria wanted to talk about was the Action. How *incredibly cool* it was going to be to play on a team with so many *great* players, and how much she *loved* Kate, because you'd expect somebody as good as her to be stuck-up, but Kate wasn't stuck-up at all, and how, since Kate and Taj were both taller than her, Adria might *finally* get to be a forward instead of a center like she always had to be in county league, and on and on and on.

Lunch was the same.

So was the bus ride home.

And the more Adria talked about the Action, the more and

more and *more* I wanted to be on that team. Not only because of how amazingly fun it would be to play with those girls. And not only because I *needed* to play on a club team if I wanted to be good enough to play in high school. But also…also if Adria was on that team and going to practice and playing in weekend tournaments and being friends with all the Action girls—if Adria was doing all that stuff, and I was doing none of it…I couldn't stand to even think about that.

Which meant I absolutely *had* to think of a way to pay for the Action. And I had to think of something fast.

A lot of my friends made money babysitting, and I'd done some sitting for our neighbors. But I hated it. Little kids are so annoying, with their sticky hands and goopy faces and always wanting you to read the same book over and over and over. Still, if it would mean I could play on the Action, I'd babysit forever. The problem was, people always wanted sitters on weekends, and if I was playing in tournaments every weekend, I wouldn't have time to babysit.

"What would you do?" I asked Mia McCall when I got home from school.

But Mia didn't have a lot of ideas. And anyway, she'd probably never had to think about how to earn enough money to be on a basketball team. Her mom understood about basketball. Her mom hung a hoop on their back door when Mia was a little bitty kid. She even moved to different states and changed jobs so Mia could play on better teams. Mia's mom got it.

Why couldn't my mom get it?

I pulled off my jeans and stepped into my favorite old grubby sweats. I had two hours before Mom got home, two hours to figure out some way to pay for the Action, so I headed outside to shoot hoops and think.

I tossed up some random shots, then I started my regular warm-up routine, standing in front of the hoop, the ball balanced on my left hand at eyebrow level, powering up with my legs, extending my arm, releasing the ball at the top of my stroke. *Shoot like you're letting a bird fly from your hand*, Adria's dad always said. *Not like you're throwing a rock at the basket.*

But that day, the ball might as well have been a rock. Or a brick. Because no matter how hard I tried to relax and just shoot, the Action and money and Mom and every unfair thing on earth stayed right at the front of my thoughts, like a giant standing between me and the hoop.

Which meant my shooting sucked.

The ball kept grazing the rim or bouncing back at me, so I had to keep going and going, shooting six or eight or ten one-handed shots from each spot before I swished three. Which meant my thinking sucked, too, because instead of thinking about how to pay for the Action, I kept thinking about how bad I was shooting.

And when I started working on my midrange jumper, my shooting got even worse, the ball flying everywhere except inside the hoop. I ran to catch it before it crashed into the azaleas that lined our front walkway and jumped over our neighbor's little hedge when the ball ricocheted onto their lawn, but I couldn't run it down before it bounced out into the street in front of a school bus.

I waited until the bus rumbled past, then ran across the street to grab my stupid ball and stomped back up my stupid driveway.

The bus stopped at the corner, the door opened, and the safety patrol stepped out and held up her flag. A couple of moms walked toward the bus, taking the hands of little kids as they jumped down the last big step. Bigger kids got off and fanned out toward their houses. I knew a lot of them. They were kids I'd gone to school with all through elementary school, kids Sam went to school with now.

I tossed my ball back and forth between my hands, watching the kids....

And that's when it hit me.

Sam didn't get off that bus because he went to after-school-care at his elementary school. But what if he didn't go to after-school-care? What if he got off that bus and came home, and I took care of him so that Mom didn't have to pay for after-school-care?

That would save a lot of money.

A lot of money that might be enough to pay for the Northern Virginia Action.

But, oh my god, could I do it? Could I spend every afternoon with Sam rocketing around me, bellowing in my ear, pestering me to help him build a starship with Legos or play some dumb video game? I squeezed my eyes shut—it would be awful. I'd probably go insane. But if it meant I could play on the Action, I'd take care of Sam every day for the rest of my life.

I tossed my ball in the air and whooped and jumped around. And even though I had a bunch of homework and should have gone inside to work on it, there was no way I could sit still and think about anything besides the Action, so I kept shooting and shooting until Mom and Sam finally got home.

I waved at them and ran toward the car before Mom even got into the garage, yelling, "I figured out how to pay for the Action!"

Mom parked and got out, looking at me over the roof of the car.

"I'll take care of Sam after school so you won't have to pay for after-school-care."

"Excuse me?" Mom laughed. "I must not be hearing you right." She reached into the car and got her purse. "Let's go inside."

So we trooped into the kitchen, me bouncing behind Mom, and Sam bouncing behind me. Mom set her purse on the counter, turned on the lights, and got a glass of water. "I seem to recall the last time we talked about you taking care of Sam after school, you were dead set against it."

"I know," I said. "But I've changed my mind. If taking care of Sam would save enough money for me to play on the Action, that's what I want to do."

Mom crossed her arms. "And have you thought about what taking care of Sam actually means?"

"Yes."

"Tell me what you think it means."

"It means I'd have to meet him at the bus stop and fix a snack and help him with homework."

"Every day. Not just when you feel like it."

"I know."

Mom shook her head. "Nikki, think about how irritated and angry you get with Sam all the time."

"I won't get angry!"

She almost laughed.

I grabbed Sam's shoulders. "We can do this, can't we,

Sam? Don't you want to come home on the bus instead of staying in after-school-care?"

"Can we ride bikes?" Sam bounced from one foot to the other. "Can I play with Jeffrey and Omar sometimes?"

"If your homework is done." I turned back to Mom. "See? I can do this."

Mom raised an eyebrow. She turned away, opened the refrigerator, and took out the casserole she'd made the night before.

"Sam, let's promise," I said. "I won't yell at you, and you won't bug me on purpose, okay?"

Sam nodded so hard it looked like his head might fall off. "I promise."

But Mom frowned. She turned on the oven and leaned against the counter. "What happens if we try it and it doesn't work? Have you thought of that? Because you won't be able to change your mind. There are children on the waiting list for after-school-care. If we take Sam out, another child will take his place. He can't go back."

"I won't change my mind."

"You'll still have your own homework to do. Plus all that basketball. You won't have time for anything else."

"I don't want to do anything else. All I want to do is play on the Action." I took a slow, pre-free-throw breath. "Please,

Mom. I told you I'd do anything to be able to play on the Action, and I meant it. I can do this. I can take care of Sam. I'll do a good job."

"It's really that important?"

"It's more important than anything."

Mom sighed. She shrugged off her jacket and hung it in the closet, then kicked out of her hideous clogs and stared at her feet, wriggling her toes around.

I chewed on my lip.

Sam bounced.

"I don't get it," Mom said at last. "I don't get how playing on this team, or any team, could possibly be so important to you. It's the last thing I would have wanted to do when I was your age." She shook her head. "I don't know where you got the sports gene, Nikki. You sure didn't get it from me."

She took hold of my shoulders and looked straight at me. "I'm serious now, Nikki. You cannot change your mind if we make this decision. No matter how frustrated you might get with Sam. No matter what else might happen."

"I know."

"And your grades cannot slip. School comes first. For both of you."

"I know."

Mom kept looking at me, looked over at Sam, then back

at me. She shook her head. "I hope we don't regret this." She looked hard at me for another minute, then said, "All right."

I whooped. I grabbed Sam's hands and we spun around the kitchen, chanting, "Action! Action! Action!" And even though I was still sore and bruised from the tryouts, I didn't even care when I bashed my hips into the counters, because I'd never been so happy in my whole entire life.

Roadkill

Our Action practice was in the same high school gym as the tryouts. It didn't seem quite as big as it had during tryouts because now the bleachers were pulled out from the walls. It had the same gleaming wood floor, though, and the same warm, musty smell. The parents who stayed to watch practice climbed up into the bleachers, but all of us girls sat in a big clump on the floor, tying our shoes and pulling our hair back and all that stuff.

Adria pulled a brand-new pair of shoes out of her gym bag—bright white high-tops with little pink and blue flecks along the sides of the soles. Taj and I each grabbed one.

"Whoa," I said. "These are so light. When'd you get them?"

"Dad took me shopping last night," Adria said. "To celebrate making the team."

"Man, these are pretty." Taj turned the shoe around in her hands. "Looks like somebody dipped them in ice-cream sprinkles."

Adria laughed. "They better not melt when my feet start to sweat."

Autumn held up her hands to show us her lime-green nail polish, which JJ said looked "girlie" but all the rest of us said looked cool. Then Maura stood up—"Dude, you guys, check this out"—and spun a ball on the tip of one finger, tossed it up a few inches, and caught it, still spinning, on another finger. Kim-Ly and Jasmine clapped and hooted.

By then, we all had our shoes on, ready to go, except for Linnae. She still sat on the floor, fighting with a complicated pair of ankle supports. "My mom's making me wear these," she said, wrapping a long Velcro strap over and under and around her foot and ankle. "She thinks I'll turn an ankle and die."

"Ohmygod, don't let my mom see those," Jasmine said. "She always thinks I'll get hurt. She wants me to quit basketball and join the chess club."

Kate said her dad would kill her if she quit basketball and joined the chess club, and Maura said, "Dude, chess? Really?"

And we probably would have kept right on like that all night if Coach hadn't blown his whistle.

"I'm not one to waste practice time with a lot of talking," he said. "But I want to go through a couple things before we start. So let me ask you something. How many of you were point guards on your other teams?"

I raised my hand. So did Linnae, Maura, Kim-Ly, and JJ.

"And how many of you were centers?"

Kate, Adria, Taj, and Jasmine raised their hands.

"Okay, great. We've got five point guards and four centers. Autumn, looks like you'll play all the other positions."

We all laughed.

Coach chuckled, too. "You see where I'm going with this? All you guards have been the best ball-handlers on every team you've played on. You bigs have always been the tallest. But we don't need five point guards or four centers. We need shooting guards, wings, forwards. So this is where you all take a big step up. Most of you will play positions you haven't played before. All of you will learn new skills. You might struggle, you might not be happy with me. But my job isn't to make you happy, right? My job is to teach you to be better ball players."

Coach paused, looking around at us. "You know who John Wooden was?"

Most of us shook our heads.

"One of the greatest basketball coaches of all time," Coach Duval said. "Led the UCLA men's team to ten national championships. He knew a whole lot about what it takes to excel. So I want you to hear something John Wooden said, and if you find yourself struggling to learn something new or change the way you've always done something, I want you to remember this: 'Do not let what you cannot do interfere with what you can do.'"

Coach Duval paused again, and we all stared up at him. *Do not let what you cannot do interfere with what you can do?*

But he didn't explain what that meant. He clapped his huge hands and said, "Okay, we've got two weeks to get ready for our first tournament. Let's have some fun. Let's win some games. Let's get to work. Line up along the baseline."

So we all ran over to the end of the court. Coach had really specific warm-up exercises he wanted us to do. First ankle flips, which are like a funny way of skipping; then Frankenstein walks, swinging our legs way up in front of us; then "over-unders," walking sideways up and down the length of the court, pretending to step over a fence, then duck under it; then skipping backward; then defensive slides, which are kind of like skipping sideways.

Then we ran sprints up and down the court three times,

then line drills—sprinting from the baseline to the free throw line, back to the baseline, up to half-court, back to the baseline, up to the opposite free throw line, back to the baseline, up to the opposite baseline, then all the way back to the first baseline. Even Kim-Ly was sucking wind.

Next came what Coach called core work. First planks, which were essentially bracing in the up position of a push-up, then sit-ups. But get this: We did our core work *while dribbling a basketball*. Half the team collapsed on their first attempt at holding a one-armed plank and dribbling the ball with the other hand. The rest of us collapsed every time Coach blew his whistle for us to switch hands.

It occurred to me that he might be insane.

Finally we stopped for a water break, and Coach zipped open his ball bag. "Everybody know the Rainbow Drill?"

Between gulping water and gasping for air, I nodded. So did most of the other girls.

"If you don't know it, watch the other girls, then join in." He pulled a bright yellow ball out of his bag, and since I was standing next to him, he tossed it to me.

I caught it, and nearly fell forward when its weight hit my hands.

Coach laughed. "Sorry, Lefty. I should have warned you it was a heavy ball."

I rolled the ball in my hands. It was stamped 3 LBS, which

probably doesn't sound very heavy, and it wouldn't be heavy, I guess, if I were holding a kitten. But a regular basketball weighs about one pound, which I knew because I'd once weighed my official WNBA ball on Mom's kitchen scale. So that's what I'd been expecting when Coach tossed the yellow ball to me.

He pulled another yellow ball out of his bag and tossed it to Kate, who was ready for it and didn't almost fall over. We formed two lines behind the baseline, one on each side of the basket, and ran the Rainbow Drill, each of us running out a few steps, curving around in front of the basket—that's the rainbow part—catching a pass, and laying the ball up, then getting in the other line, running out and curving around the other way, catching another pass, and laying the ball up with the other hand.

"Count the makes," Coach called. "Start over after a miss."

Normally this is a fun drill, because the whole team gets into a rhythm, and everybody's counting and getting more excited with the more layups you make in a row. But with a ball that weighs three times as much as a regular ball, it takes a while to figure out how much force you need to launch the ball off your hand, and by the time you figure it out, your arms ache so bad you might as well be heaving a bowling ball at the basket. Our counting went like this:

"One," miss, miss, "one," miss, "one, two," miss, miss, miss, "one." It was pathetic.

After about ten hours of that, Coach Duval blew his whistle and called for another water break, but we all stood there, our arms too tired to even pick up a water bottle.

Coach kind of chuckled. "You might hate those yellow balls now, but you'll love them by the end of the season, when you see how much stronger you are. How many'd you make in a row?"

"Five," Kate said.

"Next week you'll keep going until you make ten in a row. Fifteen the week after that. Then twenty. By next year, you'll be making a hundred, no sweat."

Now I knew Coach was crazy. The same thought must have occurred to Adria, because she shot me a look that screamed, *Help!*

We both shot the same look at her dad, who was sitting up at the top of the bleachers, talking with other parents. He'd said he wanted to see how Coach Duval ran practice, but now Mr. Lawson seemed way more interested in his conversation than in the torture going on down here on the floor.

Kate's dad was watching, though. So was JJ's mom. They were the only parents sitting at the bottom of the bleachers, their attention focused like laser beams on what we were doing. Kate's dad, Mr. Nyquist, wrote stuff in a little notepad, and Mrs. Packer reminded JJ to *get intense.*

Finally, Coach put away the yellow balls and tossed the regular orange ones to us. They felt like balloons after the heavy balls, and we all had to laugh about that. But Coach whistled us quiet and set us to work on ball-handling and catch-and-shoot drills.

We stopped for another water break, and unbelievably, we still had almost an hour to go.

"All right, basic offense," Coach said. "We've got some good height on this team, so we'll take advantage of that and run a pass-and-cut pattern to work the ball into the bigs for easy inside shots. We'll run other plays, too, but we'll learn this one first."

He split us into two groups and showed us where to stand at the beginning of the play, then walked us through the pattern, working the ball around and in, over and over, a little faster each time.

Learning plays was always easy for me—Adria's dad said it was because I was good at math and patterns and stuff like that—but learning this play wasn't easy. And it wasn't because it was complicated.

It was because of where Coach told me to stand when we

started the play. Out behind the three-point line, on the left side of the basket, way down by the baseline.

Not at the top of the key with the ball in my hands.

Not the point guard.

Not the floor general.

Not…important.

I'd just heard Coach say a lot of us would play positions we hadn't played before, but I hadn't thought anything about it. He couldn't mean me. How could he? I'd *always* been the point guard. On every team I'd ever played on. Coach couldn't want me to play a different position.

But he did.

And he didn't seem the least bit interested in stopping practice to explain it to me, even if I'd had the guts to ask. Which meant I was still stumbling around, not sure where to move or when to move, even though everybody else had the pattern down.

And then it was time to scrimmage, and big surprise, it was even harder to run the play with a defender on you.

Especially if the defender was JJ.

Every time I had the ball, she charged up in my face hollering, "Ball, ball, ball," and her mom yelled, *"Intense, JJ. Get intense!"* And the more *intense* she got, the more she whacked at me, trying to steal the ball.

Coach blew his whistle and told her to take it easy, which she did for about a minute.

After we'd gone up and down the court five or six times, I managed to break free from JJ. I cut across in front of the hoop and called for the ball. Linnae's pass was high, so I jumped to catch it, but the second my hand touched the ball, a JJ-shaped torpedo exploded into me. I flew about three feet and skidded across the floor.

Coach blew his whistle. "I like your hustle, JJ, but that's a foul. You okay, Nikki?"

I had a giant floor burn all along the inside of one knee, but I nodded that I was okay, and tried to bounce up.

"Good effort, good effort," JJ's mom called, and I started to say, "Thanks," thinking she was talking about my terrific effort to scrape myself up off the floor.

What was I thinking?

Her laser-beam eyes focused only on JJ.

I grabbed the ball and was about to pass it in to Adria, but JJ leaned up in my face and said, "Man, your eyes are really weird," and even though I should have been ready for that, since she'd done the same thing to me in tryouts, I jerked and passed the ball straight to Taj, who wasn't on my team, and JJ laughed and said, "Nice pass," and Coach blew his whistle and said, "You've got to make better passes, Nikki. Do it again."

JJ kept laughing, and I wanted to throw the ball at her face, but instead I lobbed it to Adria, who turned and made a quick jump shot that banged off the backboard and dropped through the net. I wished I were still in kindergarten so I could stick out my tongue at JJ, but instead I ran, sort of, down the floor to get back on defense.

Maura brought the ball up the floor and passed it to JJ, and I got my butt down and my hands up. And since we were supposed to be running the pass-and-cut pattern, and JJ was supposed to be looking to pass the ball inside, when she backed up and straightened up, I straightened up, too. And that's when JJ dropped her shoulder and drove forward, going full speed toward the basket, right into me. No, actually, right *over* me, because after my back hit the floor, the sole of JJ's shoe hit my arm, pinching my skin against the floor as she barreled on by.

"JJ!" Coach hollered. "That's a foul! Nikki had her feet set."

"Great effort!" Mrs. Packer called. "Really intense!"

Adria, Kate, and Kim-Ly bent over me.

"Are you okay?" Adria said.

I nodded, grabbed her hand, and let her pull me up.

"I think JJ's actually trying to hurt you," Kate said.

Kim-Ly brushed floor dust off my arm. "JJ wants to be a starter. She's trying to intimidate the other guards."

"She's doing a pretty good job," I said.

"Yeah, well, you can't let her," Kim-Ly said. "I played with her last year, and she tried the same thing on me. You have to give it right back."

"But she's fouling me."

"So? Foul her back." Kim-Ly grinned. "Last time I checked, fouls don't count in practice."

I looked at Adria. She shrugged, eyes wide, like, *Yeah, maybe nobody played like this in county league, but guess what—this isn't county league.*

Coach blew his whistle and told us to get some water, and then we were right back to work. And now, in addition to a big, raw floor burn on my knee, my back hurt where I'd hit the floor and my forearm burned where JJ'd stepped on it. My lungs burned, too, each breath sharp and raspy, and my legs were so heavy I might as well have been running through mud.

For the first time in my entire life, I just wanted practice to be over.

The scrimmage kept going, though, faster and faster, it seemed, while I got slower and slower. I tried my best to stay away from the ball so that maybe JJ would stay away from me, but then, wouldn't you know it, there I was, wide open at the top of the key.

Kim-Ly zipped a pass to me and cut toward the hoop. I

looked to pass the ball back to her, but Maura had her covered. I looked for Jasmine under the basket, but Kate had her covered. I looked for Adria and Linnae, but they were covered, too, and then here came JJ crashing toward me, and *I had to get rid of the ball*. I was a long way from the basket, and I never shot from way out there, but I had to get rid of the ball before JJ hit me again, so I lifted my chin, squared my shoulders, and shot.

The ball sailed up in a high arc, then dropped, barely grazing the rim, and fell through the net.

Adria threw her hands in the air like a football referee signaling a touchdown. "Threeeeee!" she called, running across the court to slap my hand.

I looked at my feet. Sure enough, I'd shot from behind the three-point line.

Coach blew his whistle. "All right, Lefty," he said. "That's what I want to see. You looked in to pass the ball to the cutter or the big for an easy shot, but they were covered. You were open, you were in your range, so you took the shot."

I almost said that I wasn't in my range, that I never shot from outside, that I was just trying to not get flattened again. But then I saw JJ glaring at me, so I decided to keep my mouth shut. I'd never made that shot before, but JJ didn't need to know that. And now that I thought about it, Coach didn't need to know it, either.

"Almost done," Coach said.

Almost? I looked at the clock. Three minutes to nine. Couldn't we end three minutes early? After all we'd done? Just three minutes?

But no.

"Line up along the baseline," Coach said.

So we lined up, then one by one walked out to shoot a free throw. On made shots, we clapped. On misses, we all sprinted to the opposite end of the court and back. Jasmine made her shot. So did Linnae and Autumn. All the rest of us missed. So after everything we'd done—the line drills, the planks, the heavy balls, the scrimmaging—we ran seven more up-and-back sprints to end practice.

"Have to make your free throws, ladies," Coach said.

As if we hadn't figured that out.

And then finally, *finally*, we were done.

I flopped down next to my gym bag, leaned back against the wall, and grabbed my water bottle.

Adria sat down next to me, breathing hard and groaning, and Kate dropped down next to her.

"We should change our team name," I said.

Adria and Kate looked at me.

I took a long drink of water. "Roadkill," I said. "The Northern Virginia Roadkill."

Kate started to laugh. She laughed harder and harder

until she fell over sideways and lay there, laughing, gasping for breath.

Adria and I laughed, too, laughing at how hard Kate was laughing mostly, even though laughing made my aching stomach muscles ache even more.

JJ's mom went over to talk with Coach Duval, and other parents headed toward the gym doors, calling to their daughters to hurry up. Kate and Adria and I untied our shoes and gathered up our stuff.

Mr. Nyquist stepped around Kate, bent down, and dug a basketball out of her gym bag. "Keep your shoes on," he said, straightening back up, towering over us. "Twenty-five free throws before you're done. Twenty-five *makes*. Not that garbage you were all chucking up at the end of practice."

Kate rubbed her hands across her face, leaving a streak of sweaty dirt. "Can't I skip it? Just for tonight? That was a killer practice."

Mr. Nyquist bent back down, sharp and quick as a hawk, his face an inch from hers. "One excuse leads to another. Pretty soon you're an average player, sitting on the bench. Is that what you want?"

Kate looked at her hands. "No."

Mr. Nyquist stood up. "Let's go, then."

Kate retied her shoes. "Wasn't that a nice three-pointer Nikki made?" she said.

"Who?"

"Nikki." Kate pointed at me. "Wasn't that a nice shot?"

Mr. Nyquist looked at me. "You make that shot a lot?"

I almost said no. But something stopped me. Something about the way he asked the question, the way he looked at me. Like he knew I'd never made that shot before. Like he could guarantee I'd never make it again.

I shrugged. "Sometimes."

It wasn't exactly a lie. I mean, I'd just made one, hadn't I?

Mr. Bukowski Wins the Game

It took me three tries to get my foot up on the first step of the school bus the next morning, my thigh muscles screaming at me every time I tried. Mrs. Patel, our bus driver, gave me a funny look when I grabbed the handrail to pull myself up the steps. When I finally made it to a seat and tried to sit down, those same muscles flat-out refused to cooperate, so I pretty much fell onto the seat, scraping the inside of my knee in the process. And even though I was wearing the oldest, softest pair of sweatpants I owned and had two huge bandages covering my floor burn, I still yelled, "Ow!"

All the kids on the bus turned to stare at me, and Mrs. Patel caught my eye in the big rearview mirror.

"Are you all right?" she asked.

I nodded.

"What happened?"

"Basketball practice," I said. "I'm a little sore."

Two stops later, when Adria hauled herself, hand over hand, up the steps, Mrs. Patel said, "Let me guess. Basketball practice?"

Adria nodded. "My legs don't want to move." She dropped into the seat beside me. "I may never walk again."

"Tell me about it. You think everyone else is this sore?"

"Kate texted me this morning that the only way she could get out of bed was to fall out onto the floor, then pull herself up holding on to her dresser." Adria laughed. "I thought she was in better shape than us, since she usually plays with older girls, but I guess not. I don't know how we're going to survive tonight."

"We don't have practice tonight," I said. "Practice is on Tuesday and Thursday, remember? This is Wednesday."

"Tonight I'm going to this strength-and-conditioning workout with Kate." Adria shifted her backpack on her lap. "Her dad told my dad about it, and my dad wants me to go. He says I need to improve my vertical leap so I'll be a better rebounder."

"Oh," I said.

"It doesn't sound like fun, though. It sounds like practice

last night, except without the basketball. Just the work. You want to go? We can give you a ride."

Yes, I wanted to go. I didn't know what it was, but I knew that Adria, my best friend, was going. And she was going with Kate, our new friend, who would now be *better* friends with Adria, and I definitely wanted to go. But I also knew exactly why I couldn't. Taking care of Sam after school might save enough money to pay for the Action, but there was no way I could ask Mom to pay for anything else.

That's not what I said to Adria, though. To Adria, I said, "I don't think so."

"Yeah, I don't want to go, either." Adria slid down in the seat and rested her head against the back. "But I guess I'm going. I'll tell you what it's like if I'm alive tomorrow."

We sat in silence for a couple of stops, watching kids board the bus, clomp down the aisle, and drop into seats.

"You think Coach was just trying us out in different positions last night?" I said. "You think he's going to move us back to our regular positions?"

"I don't know." Adria glanced sideways at me. "Like he said, he can't move everybody back to their regular positions."

"He's got to move me back, though. Your dad's always said I was the best point guard in all of county league."

"Yeah, but, you know, he's my dad."

"What do you mean?"

"I mean, of course he said we were the best. He's my dad."

"Adria, what are you saying? We both made the all-star team three years in a row. Everybody thought we were the best."

"Yeah, but..." Adria fiddled with the zippers on her backpack. "Remember how we always said a lot of girls in county league were good athletes, but they weren't really basketball players? They just played basketball in the winter to stay in shape for soccer or lacrosse."

"Yeah."

"So what I mean is, well..." She sat up and turned in the seat to look at me. "Have you really watched Maura play? She's an incredible ball-handler. We've never seen anyone who could do a spin dribble like her. Or pass the ball behind her back."

I leaned against the window. "Yeah."

"And Kim-Ly is so fast. She can push the ball up the court faster than anyone."

"She doesn't shoot very well, though," I said. "Or drive to the hoop."

"So, see? That's probably why Coach wants you to be a shooting guard. You do those things way better."

"Yeah, maybe," I mumbled, but that wasn't what I was thinking. What I was thinking was, who cared if I was a better shooter than Kim-Ly or Maura? All shooting guards did was stand around and wait for the ball to come to them. Point guards led the team. They made everybody else better by running the right plays and getting the ball to the right person. That's why Adria's dad said point guards were the most important players on the floor.

And I'd always been the point guard.

"Hey, I'm playing a new position, too," Adria said. "I've never played forward before. I've always been a center."

"But you *want* to play forward."

"Still, I have to learn a lot of new things," Adria said. "It's kind of scary." She looked at me sideways. "It'll be fun, though, don't you think?"

I bunched up the sides of my sweatpants with my fingertips. "I don't know."

The bus slowed, pulled into our school parking lot, and stopped. Adria and I grabbed the back of the seat in front of us and pulled ourselves up. We hobbled down the aisle, shuffling along with the other kids.

Adria was in front of me, and when she got to the steps, she crow-hopped down the first two, leaning on the handrail and jumping down on one foot, then bringing the other foot down on the same step. I tried to do the same thing, but the kid behind me said, "Move it," and gave me a shove that knocked me into Adria.

She stumbled down the last step and took two awkward steps before catching her balance. But just as she straightened up, I staggered out of the bus and crashed into her again. She fell forward, hitting the asphalt on her hands and knees. All the kids getting off our bus laughed, and all the kids getting off the other buses laughed, and I grabbed Adria's arm to help her up.

"I'm sorry," I said about eighteen hundred times, and Adria said, "It's all right. It's not like you did it on purpose."

Which proved what I already knew—Adria was a really nice person, and I was a jerk.

Because, you know, maybe I didn't reach my hand out fast enough when she lurched forward, maybe I didn't try quite hard enough to catch her before she went down, and maybe that was because...because some people get to go to strength-and-conditioning classes and improve their vertical leap and hang out with a new friend and play forward instead of center like they always wanted to. And other people, well, other people have to be shooting guards.

Things didn't get a lot better after that.

For one thing, I had to haul myself up a long flight of stairs to get to my first class, and when I came back down to the first floor for my second class, the stairs had somehow grown to be twice as long. I hung on to the handrail, crow-hopping down each step, my thigh muscles screaming, and the kids behind me hollering at me to hurry up and get out of the way. And then, oh boy, I got to climb all the way back up to the second floor for third period.

By the time I limped into science, I truly felt like road-kill. I climbed onto my lab stool, propped my elbows on the table, dropped my head into my hands, and groaned.

"What happened to you?" Booker said.

I peeked sideways at him. "Basketball practice. I'm a little sore."

"What position do you play?"

I stared at him now. Had he somehow figured out the worst possible question to ask? "Guard," I said. Not point guard. Just plain old, nothing-special guard.

Booker shook his hair back from his face. "Looks like you play floor." He pointed at the inside of my right forearm, where JJ's heel print stood out in vivid purple and red, complete with the little zigzags of her shoe tread. "How'd that happen?"

So I told him all about JJ *getting intense* and showing *great effort*, which turned out to be funny in the retelling, especially about JJ's mom with her laser-beam eyes, and especially when Adria leaned over from her lab table and threw in how mad JJ looked when I sank the three-pointer at the end of practice. But that also wasn't funny, because it reminded me that Adria was a nice person and I wasn't.

"Wow!" Booker rocked back on his lab stool. "You can shoot threes?"

For a second, I thought about telling the same not-quite lie I'd told Mr. Nyquist. "Uh, well, actually," I said, "that was the first one I ever made."

Booker grinned. "You picked the right time to sink one."

"Nikki and Booker!" Mr. Bukowski said. "Do you plan to chat all morning or are you ready to join us?"

"Sorry," we said together.

Mr. Bukowski started his lecture—Gregor Mendel and his pea plants and the beginnings of genetics—and we all opened our notebooks to take notes. Then Mr. Bukowski handed out a worksheet with these charts called Punnett squares and explained how we were supposed to use them to figure out what pea plant offspring would look like, based on the dominant and recessive genes of their pea plant parents.

Instantly, the room filled with noise, everybody talking and sharpening pencils and shuffling papers around. Mr. Bukowski wandered through the classroom, helping kids and answering questions.

When he got to Booker and me, he said, "You've told me your genetics project topic, haven't you, Booker?"

"Yes, sir," Booker said.

Mr. Bukowski nodded. "Okay, good." He turned to me. "How about you, Nikki? Have you thought of a topic?"

"Um…" My face got hot. I didn't want to tell Mr. Bukowski that I hadn't thought about it at all, but finally I said, "Well, not really."

"Any ideas?"

Booker spun around on his stool to face Mr. Bukowski. "Don't you think Nikki should do her project on her eyes?"

Mr. Bukowski looked at Booker, his eyebrows raised. "Gee, Booker," he said. "I believe I was asking Nikki for *her* ideas."

"Sorry." Booker turned and looked at his paper, then spun back around. "But Nikki's eyes are really interesting, don't you think? There has to be some kind of genetic thing going on to make someone's eyes come out two different colors, doesn't there?"

Mr. Bukowski adjusted his glasses. "Well, Booker, at the risk of insulting Nikki by talking *about* her instead of *to* her, yes, there is some kind of genetic thing that leads to heterochromia iridis, which, as you can probably guess, is the scientific term for the coloring of Nikki's eyes. But it could be that Nikki doesn't find her eyes all that interesting. It could be that after thirteen years, she's gotten used to them and wishes people would stop talking about them."

"Oh." Booker looked from Mr. Bukowski to me, then back, then back again. "Sorry, I didn't mean to…I mean, I wasn't trying to…I mean…Sorry, Nikki." He spun around, whipping his hair across his face, and hunched over his worksheet.

"It's okay, Booker," I said. "It doesn't bother me." Which, you know, was a total lie, because I hated it when people talked about my eyes. But it was hard to be annoyed at Booker.

Mr. Bukowski patted Booker's shoulder. "We're all glad you're so enthusiastic about science."

Booker nodded his head about a quarter of an inch and scrunched up his shoulders.

"Now," Mr. Bukowski said, "have you come up with any ideas for your project, Nikki? Any questions about genetics you'd like to find answers to?"

I shook my head. "No, but—" I remembered something my mom said. "Mr. Bukowski, is there a sports gene?"

"A sports gene?"

"Yes."

"You mean a single gene that makes people good or bad at sports?"

"Um, well, I don't know what I mean. My mom said I must have inherited 'the sports gene,' but not from her."

"Ah." Mr. Bukowski chuckled. "I suspect your mother was using that expression more as a figure of speech than as a scientific reality. But, of course, we do inherit our body types from our parents—the length of our legs, the width of our shoulders, and so on. And the size and shape of our bodies certainly affects our innate ability at sports. You don't see people who look like me playing professional football, for example, do you?"

How could I answer that? I mean, obviously I couldn't say, *No, you look like an Albert Einstein bobblehead, and Albert Einstein bobbleheads don't play pro football.* One, that would be mean. And two, it would be stupid, duh—Mr. Bukowski graded my work. I thought for a minute. "You could be a field goal kicker."

Mr. Bukowski looked at me, his mouth half open like he was about to say something, then he smacked the lab table with the flat of his hand, bent over, and shouted these great big "HA-HA-HA" laughs.

All the kids in class turned to look at Mr. Bukowski laughing so hard, which was a pretty funny thing to see all by itself, but it was even funnier if you were also trying to picture him in shoulder pads and tight little football pants, running up to kick a field goal.

He finally stopped laughing and stood up. "Field goal kicker," he said. "Can't believe I never thought of that. You think I'm too old to start?"

"Um," I said.

"Never mind, never mind." Mr. Bukowski took off his glasses, wiped them on a handkerchief he pulled out of his pocket, put them back on, glanced at my worksheet, pointed at one of my answers, and said, "You might want to recheck that." Then he looked at me. "In any case, I think you've asked an interesting question, one that's certainly worth exploring. Why don't you do a little research, see if you can narrow your topic, then we'll talk again. One way or another, you've got to have your topic by the end of the week, okay? Remember, this is half your grade for the quarter. You need to get busy."

He tapped the lab table with his knuckles, readjusted his glasses, and cleared his throat. "Field goal kicker," he said. "Can't wait to tell my wife about that." He leaned forward, looking around Booker's hunched-up shoulders at his worksheet. "Good work, Booker," he said, then moved on to the kids at the next lab table.

You know that sound people make when they're trying not to laugh, trying to hold their mouths shut tight, but finally can't hold it in anymore? That sound you can't spell, but if you could spell it, it would be something like *Ppppbbbbfffftttt*?

Well, the second Mr. Bukowski walked away, that sound exploded from the mouths of Booker and the other two kids at our lab table, Sunil and Laura. Which, of course, made me laugh, which, also of course, made my abs shriek with pain.

"Ow, ow, ow," I said, holding my stomach. "It hurts to

laugh." And I told them about Coach Duval's evil basketball-dribbling sit-ups and planks.

Which made them laugh harder.

Then Booker cupped his hands around his mouth to make his voice sound like a sports announcer, except not loud like a real sports announcer, and said, "The kick is up! It's up and it's good! Mr. Bukowski wins the game!"

Which made us all laugh even harder, which meant—big surprise—none of us finished our worksheets. Which meant—another big surprise—extra homework that night.

Booker

I should have started on my homework as soon as I got home from school that day, because even without the science worksheet I hadn't finished in class, I had a ton of work to do. Plus I *had* to come up with a topic for my genetics project. But it was my last week of after-school freedom before I started taking care of Sam, so instead of digging into my homework, I dumped my backpack on my bed, threw a fist pump at Mia, and headed out to the driveway.

I worked on ball-handling for a while, dribbling two balls at once, crossing them back and forth, then sitting on the driveway and dribbling fast with just my fingertips, because maybe if I got better at all that, Coach would see I should be a point guard. Also it helped my muscles loosen up.

But you can only spend so much time dribbling before it gets boring, so I did my regular shooting warm-up, the ball poised on my left hand, my right hand behind my back, powering up with my legs, extending my arm, holding my follow-through, and...*swish*. One.

I corralled the ball and did it again, but this time the ball touched the rim before falling through. Didn't count. I did it again. *Swish*. Two. And again. *Swish*. Three.

A lot of girls hated form-shooting. Even Adria. She thought it was stupid. But I liked the way it made me focus on one thing and work to get that one thing exactly right. And I loved *feeling* the shot—the energy rushing up from the balls of my feet, through my ankles and legs, right up my spine to my shoulder and forearm, and out through the tip of my index finger. Like a zing of electricity whipping through me. Like finding "the zone" when I was playing a game, every thought and distraction falling away.

I caught my ball again and kept going. Three swishes in front of the hoop, then three on the right side, three on the left, then back in front of the hoop, a step farther back, with the ball poised on my left hand, and powering up, and letting it fly, and...*clang*. Didn't count. *Clang*. Didn't count. *Swish*. One.

"You always shoot one-handed?"

I spun around. Booker stood at the end of the driveway, holding the handlebars of his bike.

"Where'd you come from?"

He looked over his shoulder. "Uh, the street?"

"I mean, what are you doing here? I mean...Geez, you scared me."

"Sorry." Booker swung his leg off his bike and walked up the driveway. "So do you always shoot like that? One-handed?"

"No, it's just the way I warm up." I picked up my ball from where it had rolled onto the grass.

"Oh. Why?"

"Why, what?"

"Why do you do that?"

"So I'll have good shooting form."

"Oh." Booker squinted up at our old hoop.

I rotated my ball around my waist. "Do you play basketball?"

"Yeah," Booker said, which made sense, because he was at least a head taller than me. And skinny, really skinny. "I like soccer and baseball better, though. I like being outside." He rolled his bike back and forth. "My folks haven't had a chance to sign me up for any teams here yet. Since we just moved."

So then we stood there being awkward, not saying anything, until I finally said, "How'd you know where I live?"

"I didn't. But I live a couple of blocks away and I was out riding around. I saw you out here." He looked at the street, up at the hoop, then back at me. "How come you're not doing a family tree?"

"What?"

"A family tree. You know, for the genetics project."

"Oh, well..." I shrugged. "I'd rather do something else."

Booker laughed. "You're kidding, right? You'd rather do some big research report instead of calling up your relatives and asking them what kind of earlobes they have?"

I spun the ball on my finger. "Yeah, well... maybe. What about you? Why aren't you doing a family tree?"

"Me?" Booker kicked at the front tire of his bike. "I'm not in touch with my relatives."

"Why not?"

Booker crossed his arms, letting the bike tilt over against his hip. He shook his hair back from his face. "You really want to know? Or just making conversation?"

"I want to know," I said. "Since you brought it up."

"I guess I did, didn't I." He glanced at his watch. "Okay, well, my parents are in prison and—"

"*What?* Oh no! What happened?"

Booker jammed a hand into his pocket. He stared down at the driveway and pushed a pebble around with his foot. "My parents were drug dealers. Addicts, too."

"Oh, gosh. Um, how old were you when they went to jail?"

"Kindergarten."

"So what happened? Did you go to live with relatives or something?"

"No. They were all into the same thing. Drug dealing and stuff."

"Who took care of you?"

"My kindergarten teacher." Booker pushed his hair back from his face. "We lived in this little town up in the mountains where everybody knew what everybody else was up to. So my teacher came over to my house to talk to my parents one day because I guess I wasn't showing up at school much. When she got there, my parents were passed out in the living room and I was trying to cook dinner." Booker smiled his half smile. "I wasn't much good at making dinner when I was six."

"I'm not very good at making dinner now."

Booker laughed. "Yeah, me neither. So anyway, Mom, I mean my teacher—she was my teacher then, but she's my mom now—called the cops and took me home with her."

"So that's where you stayed?"

"Yeah. My teacher and her husband got custody of me, then finally got to adopt me after a couple of years. And then they got worn out with people looking at us funny and asking them about 'that drug-dealers' kid,' so they looked for jobs outside of that town and finally found some here."

"Wow," I said, which under the circumstances was a pretty lame thing to say, but, you know, what wouldn't be a lame thing to say?

So then we stood there for another minute not saying anything, until finally I said, "I'm sorry that happened to you, Booker."

He looked down and frowned, kicked at his bike tire again. "Yeah, it wasn't much fun." Then he shrugged and looked back up. "Guess you can't pick your parents, though, can you? So what's your story?"

I bounced my basketball a couple of times. After what Booker had told me, my story sounded...well, dumb. Not very important. But it was still so embarrassing. I mean, how was I supposed to say *sperm donor* in front of a boy? In front of anyone? "I, um..." I took a deep breath. "You can't tell anyone, okay?"

Booker laughed. "Who would I tell? I've only lived here a couple of weeks. I hardly know anybody."

"Okay." I bounced my ball a few more times, then said as fast as I could, "My mom wanted to have kids but she wasn't married so she went to a doctor and did this thing called artificial insemination with um, um, um...spermfromadonor."

"Really?"

I nodded.

"Wow, that's really interesting."

"Interesting? Are you kidding me? It's gross. It's probably the most embarrassing thing in the entire world."

"Really? Well, yeah, okay, I guess I can see how it might be embarrassing. But still, it's really interesting. I wonder how doctors figured out how to do that. I wonder how they keep the sperm alive and what kinds of tests they do to make sure it's okay, and—"

I stared at him. Did he really just say *sperm*? Like it was a normal thing to say? My cheeks burned.

"You don't think it's interesting?" Booker said.

I shook my head.

"Oh, uh, sorry." His cheeks suddenly got red, too. "I get kind of wound up about science stuff." He rolled his bike back and forth. "I really like Mr. Bukowski, don't you? He's the best science teacher I've ever had. You like him?"

I nodded.

Booker looked at his watch. "Oh man, I gotta go. Gotta get my chores done."

He swung onto his bike, waved, and pedaled like crazy down the street.

My Paper Dad

I tried to keep shooting after Booker left, but I couldn't focus. I kept thinking about how I'd feel if Mom were in prison. It made me have this kind of ache inside.

So I gave up and went in to tackle my homework. I grabbed my backpack and headed into Mom's "office," which was actually supposed to be the dining room. We didn't need a dining room, though. We needed a place for Mom's books. She'd lined the walls with bookcases and arranged the books in perfect Library of Congress order, which I knew because Adria's mom arranged their books by shape and color, and she and Mom had this running "argument," poking fun at each other for arranging their books the "wrong" way.

I sat down in front of the computer to type in my answers

to some "free response" questions for history. It didn't take long to knock them out, but then I had to print them, and there was no telling how long that would take, since Mom bought our printer when dinosaurs roamed the earth.

I turned it on, giving it a friendly little pat for encouragement, and checked the paper tray. Empty. I pulled open the top desk drawer to look for paper. None there. None in the second drawer, either. None in the big file drawer... Wait—something caught my eye. My name on a folder.

I pulled the drawer all the way open and looked closer. The tab at the top of a folder said *Nikki, Donor*. I reached for it, but the second my fingers touched the folder, I pulled them back. And sat there, staring at the folder tab.

Nikki, Donor? Was it really something about my father?

Was I not supposed to see it?

But... but I had to see it.

I grabbed the folder, accidentally pulling up the one behind it, too. Its tab said *Sam, Donor*. So I grabbed both folders and ran upstairs to my bedroom, swinging the door shut behind me, even though, obviously, there was nobody else in the house.

I sat down cross-legged on my bed, dropped Sam's folder next to me, and slowly, slowly opened my folder....

And there he was.

My father.

Five or six sheets of paper, forms and typed pages, held together with an orange paper clip.

I lifted the corners of a couple of pages, peeking at them, looking for a picture. But there wasn't one. And no name. Just "Donor 3658."

I pulled off the paper clip and started reading.

The first form was basic information:

Height: 5'11"
Weight: 175 lbs
Hair Color: Dark Brown
Eye Color: Brown.

Wait, what? Mom had blue-gray eyes. I always thought my father must have had one green eye and one brown eye. But his were plain old brown? So where did I get mine?

I scanned down the rest of the form. Blood type: A. Didn't wear glasses. But nothing about whether or not he was left-handed.

My eyes burned. I wanted to know what I *got* from my father, what I inherited from him, how we were connected. This wasn't telling me anything important. I picked up the folder and banged it down against my legs. The papers jumped and spilled sideways.

I looked up at Mia, and even though I knew she couldn't

really, truly talk to me, I still heard her tell me to calm down, take a deep breath, keep reading. Maybe I'd find a connection.

A lump had come up in my throat and I swallowed hard, trying to push it down, squeezed my eyes shut for a moment, then gathered up the spilled pages.

The next page turned out to be more interesting than blood types and glasses. It was titled "Education, Hobbies, and Activities." It said my father majored in biology at the University of Virginia, then went to the University of Maryland and was "a PhD candidate" in something called "entomology." Then it said he liked to run and he'd been on the track teams in high school and college, too, and that he also liked hiking and camping and kayaking.

"My father likes outdoor stuff," I said to Mia.

Cool, she would have said if, you know, she could actually talk to me.

I kept reading.

My father also liked fly-fishing, whatever that was. He liked listening to jazz (boring) and reading biographies (really boring). And he could ride a unicycle and juggle.

Ride a unicycle and juggle? I bet none of my friends' dads could do that. Adria's dad couldn't. Or, well, I'd never seen him do it, and if you could ride a unicycle and juggle, wouldn't you show all your kids' friends? I bet Kate's dad couldn't do it, either.

The next section was called "Staff Analysis," and it said that everybody liked my dad. It said he had a "ready smile, a pleasant manner, and a lively sense of humor." It said he was "attractive, physically fit, and knowledgeable on many subjects." It said he brought flowers to one of the staff members when he heard that her father died.

I turned to the last page. It was titled "Donor's Statement." It said: "I've always considered myself to be a fortunate person. My father served in the US State Department, so I grew up in five different countries and learned to speak three languages. It was great to make friends in so many different places and learn about how people live in other parts of the world. I hate sitting still. That's one of the reasons why I chose to study entomology. It keeps me outside, moving around a lot. I hope to have a family someday, but for now I'm glad to help other people create families of their own."

And that was it.

My dad, in black and white.

I pressed my fingertips against the page, tracing the words "a family someday...families of their own." A real person wrote that. Not just some embarrassing sperm-donor freak. A person.

My father.

I scooped up the folder and pressed it against my chest,

my eyes burning again, and lay over on my side, curling up, hugging the folder. Hugging it so hard my arms hurt.

I don't know how long I lay like that. Maybe I fell asleep, I don't know. All I know is that I heard voices—Mom and Sam— then a tap at my door, then Mom standing in my doorway, her gaze flicking from my face to the folders to my face again, and Sam launching onto my bed, hollering, "Nikki, guess what!" and Mom saying, "Sam, go look in the linen closet in my bathroom. I think you'll find a new box of Legos on the second shelf," which sent Sam rocketing out of my room.

Mom sat down on the edge of my bed, smoothed my hair back from my face, and said, "Nikki, I'm so sorry you found this on your own."

I frowned up at her. "Why didn't you show me?"

She stroked my hair. "I was waiting for the right time." Her voice caught. "I waited too long, didn't I?"

"Yeah, you did."

"Have you read the whole file?"

I nodded again. "He sounds like a nice person." My voice caught, too.

Mom smiled a small smile. "That's why I picked him." She kicked off her hideous clogs. "I haven't looked at that file in a long time. Can we look at it together?"

I sat up and bunched up my pillows against the headboard. Mom swung her legs up on the bed, and we leaned back against the pillows with our knees bent, the folder open across our laps.

Mom straightened the pages, then turned them slowly.

I pointed at "entomology." "What's that?"

"The study of insects," Mom said.

"Insects?"

Mom nodded.

"People study bugs? Eeeewwww."

Mom shrugged. "Different people like different things."

"Yeah, but bugs?"

Mom laughed, pointing at the juggling and unicycle riding. "I'd forgotten about that."

"I wish there was a picture," I said.

"That would be nice, wouldn't it? But donors are meant to be anonymous."

"I wish he had one brown eye and one green eye."

Mom patted my hand.

"I wish I knew him."

Mom shifted, turning onto her hip so she could wrap her arms around me and pull me over against her, hugging me tight. We sat like that for a long time.

"Mom?" I said at last.

"Hmm?"

"Do you think I could ever meet him?"

She sighed and stroked her hand across my hair. "I don't know, Nikki. Apparently there are registries and organizations to help people find donor parents. When you get older, you can try to find him if you want to."

"Why can't I try to find him now?"

Mom held me tighter. "Nikki," she said, "I don't know if you're old enough to understand this, but when you go hunting for someone who intended to be anonymous, you have to be prepared to find someone who has no interest in knowing you. I think that would be a difficult thing to prepare yourself for at any age. But at thirteen, I think it would be impossible. Beyond impossible."

We sat like that for a long time again. We sat like that while I thought about how it would feel to walk up to a man with brown hair and brown eyes who had lived in five countries and could ride a unicycle and juggle, and say, *Hi, I'm Nikki, your daughter.* And how it would feel if he said, *Not really*, and walked away. And the more I thought about it, the more I decided Mom was right. It gave me that achy feeling inside again—the same feeling I got thinking about Mom in prison.

"Mom," I said at last, "why didn't you want to get married and have a regular family?"

She sat up a little more and pulled her arm out from behind me, like maybe it was going to sleep squished between my shoulders and the headboard. "I did want to get married," she said. "But the man I wanted to marry didn't want to marry me."

"Why not?"

"That's a very long story." Mom stretched her legs out, tapping her feet together. "He was a lovely person. Wonderful, really. Smart, kind. But every time we talked about getting married and having a family, he said he wasn't ready. After six years, I realized he'd never be ready. I was thirty-three by that time. I had a good job and I wanted to have children. I didn't want to wait any longer."

She spread her hands and sort of shrugged. "Maybe it's not the best way to have a family, but..." She closed her eyes, her mouth curving down in a sad arc, her worry line creasing her forehead.

You know, it's hard to see your mom looking sad. Even if she sometimes bugs you by wearing hideous clogs and getting lost in books and being clueless about basketball, even if you're maybe a little bit mad at her for not showing you your father's donor file before, it's hard to see your mom looking really, really sad. So even if you still wish you had a family with a mom *and* a dad, you don't say that.

At least I didn't.

I said, "It's okay, Mom. I like our family the way it is."

Mom smiled. "I do, too, Nikki."

"And besides, if you'd married that guy, the guy you wanted to marry, then I would have gotten half my genes from him, and then I wouldn't be me, would I?"

"No, you wouldn't."

"And if this guy was my actual dad," I said, pointing at the folder, "if he was my real, in-person dad, not just my paper dad, we'd always be going hiking and camping and searching for bugs and stuff, and he'd probably make me be on a track team, and I wouldn't get to play basketball."

"You might learn to juggle, though," Mom said.

"Or ride a unicycle."

We both laughed.

"Hey, I just thought of something." I shuffled back through the pages. "How tall did it say he is?"

"It's right here." Mom pointed. "Five foot eleven."

"Oh."

"Is that a problem?"

"Well, you know, I wish he was tall."

"Five foot eleven is fairly tall. Taller than average."

"It's not six feet, though," I said. "I know there's only an inch difference, but six feet sounds a lot taller."

"I suppose," Mom said.

"How tall are you?"

"Five foot five. That's about average for US women, I think."

"I bet it's not average for women who play basketball."

"Probably not. You could find out."

"How?"

"Look at the rosters of the professional women's teams," Mom said. "I'm sure they list the height of each player. You could certainly measure the girls on your team and figure out the average height of eighth-grade basketball players."

I thought about that for a minute. They might think it was weird, but... "Maybe that could be my science project." I told Mom about the genetics project, how I couldn't do a family tree, so I had to do a report and I wanted to do something about sports.

I sat up straighter. "I could measure the girls on my team, then I could measure the girls in my science class to see how tall they are. Then I could compare them."

Mom nodded. "That would be interesting. I'm not sure if it relates directly to genetics, though."

"Oh, right." I thought some more. "I know! What if I found out how tall their parents are, too? I could make graphs that show the girls' heights and the parents' heights, and compare the basketball families to the non-basketball families."

Mom smiled. "I think that's an excellent idea."

Fortunately, when I told Mr. Bukowski my idea the next morning, he thought it was "an excellent idea," too. Unfortunately, he also wanted me to research what scientists had discovered about the "heritability" of height.

Oh boy, more homework.

More Trouble

Coach Duval thought my science project sounded like a good idea, too. He also said we couldn't take time out of practice for me to measure the girls, so I should bring my tape measure to the first tournament and do my measuring between games. That sounded fine, except that the tournament wasn't until the next weekend—not the weekend that was two days away—and my project was due on the Monday right after the tournament. And since the tournament was in Baltimore, which would take over an hour to drive to, and we had two games on Saturday and two on Sunday, that meant I'd only have Saturday and Sunday nights to make my graphs and complete my project.

Fortunately Mr. Bukowski did give me class time to

measure the girls in my science class, but he made me go out in the hallway because when I tried to measure the girls in the back of the classroom, each time a girl walked back there to get measured, all the other kids turned around to watch instead of doing their own work.

There were only thirteen girls in the class, so you'd think it wouldn't take long to measure them, but you'd be wrong about that.

They all had to do a lot of giggling and goofing around, for one thing. Then Lindsey Welsh refused to take off her shoes because her toes were "too ugly," until I pointed out that we were standing in the hallway by ourselves and no one else would see her toes and I *promised* not to tell anyone what her toes looked like. Then Mary Katherine Pentangeli made me measure her three times, insisting she was only five foot one, even though the tape measure clearly showed she was five foot two, because, as everyone knew, she liked Joey Martinez, the shortest guy in our class, so she wanted to be supershort, too. I had to tell her I wasn't going to put girls' names on my graphs, just their height, and I also had to *promise not to tell anyone* how tall she was.

I gave all the girls a questionnaire to take home and fill out with their parents' heights, which they all did, except Mary Katherine, who *promised* to text me her parents' heights. I gave the same questionnaire to the girls on my basketball team, but Linnae and Autumn were the only ones who gave them back to me at the next practice. Everyone else had forgotten to take them out of their gym bags.

This project was turning out to be a lot more trouble than I'd expected.

Taking care of Sam was a lot more trouble than I'd expected, too, though since I'd spent eight years living with him, I don't know why I was surprised.

Monday, my first official day of taking care of him, wasn't too bad. I hung out in the driveway shooting until Sam's bus rumbled past, then I dribbled the ball down the street toward the bus stop. Before I made it past two houses, the bus stopped, the safety patrol stepped out, and Sam exploded out the door. He flew up the street, his backpack slamming into his hips, his voice coming out in sharp bursts—"Nikki! Nikki! Guess what! Jeffrey got sent to the office for talking back to Miss Spraig. And Taylor got in trouble for not doing her homework. And Mr. Olivera said we don't get to play dodgeball at recess anymore because Jack threw the ball really hard at Kritika and she fell and broke her arm. And—"

By that time he'd run right up against me, and I was covering my ears with my hands because he was yelling loud enough to be heard in five states.

"What's wrong, Nikki?" Sam said. "Do your ears hurt?"

"You're kind of loud."

"Oh, sorry." He dropped his voice to a whisper and we walked home. Or actually, I walked. Sam jumped and spun and skipped backward. "Kritika got a chartreuse cast. Isn't that a great word? *Chartreuse.* But I didn't get to sign it yet, because her Sharpie ran out of ink and I couldn't find mine, so Taylor was going to let me use hers, but then she got in trouble...."

He kept going like that all the way up the driveway and into the garage, until it occurred to me that if we tried to do homework right away, he wouldn't be able to sit still long enough to get anything done, so I told him to drop his backpack and get on his bike, and we rode our bikes up and down the street five or six times.

So after Sam ran his battery down, we went inside, and I made popcorn and poured us some juice, and we sat down at the table with our backpacks. Sam showed me his assignments, and I told him to get started on the hardest one first and to ask for help if he had trouble. And since he had mostly math homework, which he's good at, he only had to ask for help a couple of times, so he got his work all done, and I got mine half done before Mom got home, and we all felt good.

Tuesday was pretty much the same thing, Sam yammering a mile a minute all the way up the street, filling me in on the third-grade news. Then Booker rode by on his bike, so Sam and I got on our bikes, too, and we rode up and down the street with Booker, and that made Sam extra happy, because he got to tell Booker about Kritika's chartreuse cast, which Sam finally got to sign, and all the other superexciting stuff that happened to him that day. I tried to tell Sam that Booker didn't care about that stuff, but Booker said it was okay and told Sam about his own third-grade teacher who kept frogs and snakes in their classroom. And then when Mom got home, Sam just had to tell her about Booker and his third-grade teacher's snakes, and Mom looked at me hard and said, "You know you're not allowed to have friends here before I get home, Nikki." And I had to say, "He wasn't here-here. He was just riding by, so we rode up and down the street with him a couple of times."

But, you know, if I'm totally honest, I have to say that we rode up and down with Booker a few more times than we really needed to, which meant I didn't get all my homework done before basketball practice and still had math to do when I got home at nine thirty, feeling like roadkill again.

Wednesday, Sam had to start working on a report on George Washington, which meant he needed a lot more help with his homework. First of all, I had to explain to him that the Three Important Facts he'd written down (that George's mother's name was Mary, that he had a brother, and that his father died when George was a kid) were not actually very important and definitely not why we remember George Washington, and that Sam needed to read more than the first page of his book on George Washington to find out the important stuff.

Sam said the book his teacher gave him had too many big words, so then I had to read it with him and help him figure out the actual Three Important Facts, which meant we'd barely finished Sam's homework by the time Mom got home, and I hadn't started mine, which meant a long slog of homework ahead of me that night.

Thursday, Sam caught his foot on the step when he blasted out the door of the bus, skidded across the gravel at the side of the road, and got up with one cheek and both elbows pretty well shredded.

Oh boy.

Two of the moms at the bus stop rushed over to see if he was okay, but since Sam wasn't crying—because who wants to cry when all the kids at the bus stop are looking at you?— the moms told me to make sure I cleaned all the cuts well (*really?*) and walked off with their own kids.

It took a long time to get him all washed off and covered in Bactine and bandages, and by that time it was too cold to go outside in just a T-shirt, and Sam didn't want to pull a sweatshirt over his elbows, so we decided to play a video game for a little while before we started our homework. And since Sam beat me in the first game, we had to play another one, and unfortunately for us, we were still playing when Mom got home.

We both got in big trouble for that, except that Sam got in less trouble because he was all bandaged up and Mom felt sorry for him, and besides, I was supposed to be the Responsible One.

But worst of all, I hardly got *any* of my homework done before basketball practice, so when I got home after practice that night, I still had a page of algebra to do, another worksheet on Mendel and his pea plants, and a chapter on World War II to read in my history book. I fell asleep somewhere around the Battle of the Bulge, and Mom woke me up and told me to go to bed and try to finish my reading on the bus in the morning, and she hoped I'd Learned My Lesson.

And then, of course, in case my homework and my science project and taking care of Sam weren't hard enough, there was basketball.

That second week of practice, in addition to an extra set of sprints and line drills and a thousand more planks and sit-ups while dribbling, we had to keep running the Rainbow Drill with the horrible, heavy yellow balls until we made ten layups in a row without missing. On Tuesday, after we'd shot about a hundred layups and missed half of them, we got all the way to nine in a row before I missed, and everyone groaned, and I guess Mr. Nyquist didn't think I felt bad enough about that, because he slapped the bleachers and said, "Oh, for crying out loud, it's just a layup," not very loud, but loud enough for me to hear. It must have been loud enough for Coach to hear, too, because he turned and gave Mr. Nyquist a scary-looking frown. That made me feel a tiny bit better.

So then we shot about a hundred more layups before we finally made ten in a row.

You would've thought we'd just won the NCAA championship, the way we all jumped around and cheered and high-fived each other. Coach clapped his giant hands slow and loud and said he was glad he had a team that could tough out the hard stuff.

And then he proceeded to try to kill his team with more sprints and drills and scrimmaging, and then, of course, more sprints at the end of practice for every missed free throw.

Thursday's practice wasn't quite as hard because Coach said he didn't want to wear us out before our first tournament that weekend. But we still had to make those deadly ten-in-a-row layups with the horrible, heavy yellow balls and we still had to do the evil sit-ups and planks. And with my arms aching and my abs tight and sore, I still had to focus hard during our scrimmage to remember where I was supposed to be when my team was on offense, because I still wasn't a point guard.

And then, like I said, I had all that homework to do when I got home after practice Thursday night because Sam and I had made the Very Poor Decision to play video games after school.

On Friday morning I dragged myself out of bed, dragged myself onto the school bus—and still didn't finish reading about the Battle of the Bulge because I fell asleep with my head banging against the bus window—then I dragged myself up and down those endless flights of stairs at school. By the end of the day, when I finally dragged myself up our driveway and into the house, all I wanted to do was curl up on my bed and go to sleep. But, oh boy, in half an hour, Sam would launch from his bus like a fast-talking missile.

I looked up at Mia. "Are you ever this tired?" I asked her. "Are you ever so tired you hate everything?"

As usual, Mia didn't have a lot to say, but it didn't matter. I knew that anyone who played as hard as she did had to get really, *really* tired. But no matter how tired she got, no matter how much her muscles might ache, there was one thing I knew she never hated. She never hated basketball.

But standing there in the middle of my bedroom, just wanting to fall onto my bed and sleep forever and knowing I had to get up at six o'clock the next morning to make it to Baltimore in time for our first game, I wasn't so sure about me.

Clueless

Sam had soccer tryouts that weekend, so Mom needed to stay home with him instead of going to Baltimore with me.

"I'm sorry to miss your first games with this new team," she said Saturday morning. She stood behind me while I ate breakfast, brushing my hair and pulling it into a high ponytail, then weaving the ponytail into a tight braid, which was how I liked to wear my hair for games—a braid didn't stick to my neck when I got sweaty.

"You don't have to do that," I said between bites of eggs and toast. "I can fix my hair in the car."

"I know." Mom kissed the top of my head and kept on braiding. "You've done a good job with Sam this week."

"Except Thursday."

She laughed. "Except Thursday."

There was a knock on the side door, and Adria burst into the kitchen. "Ready?"

"Ready." I jumped up from the table.

Mom handed me the lunch bag she'd packed. "What does your dad always say before games, Adria?"

"Play hard. Have fun."

"Oh yes." Mom gave each of us a quick hug. "Play hard. Have fun."

"We will," we called, running out.

Adria and I spent the first fifteen minutes of the drive talking about how great our Action team was and how we were going to *kill* all the other teams.

Then Mr. Lawson said, "Do you remember your first basketball game?"

"In second grade?" I said.

Adria turned around from the front seat. "I remember our team name."

"The Hello Kitties!" we shouted together.

Mr. Lawson laughed. "I took a lot of ribbing about that from the other coaches. Especially from the woman whose team was named the Timber Wolves." He glanced at Adria, then at me in the rearview mirror. "Do you remember anything about our first game, though?"

I said, "Not really." And Adria said, "No."

"Well, here's what I remember," Mr. Lawson said. "The game was complete bedlam. All the girls, both teams, ran around in a pack, grabbing the ball back and forth, maybe dribbling, maybe throwing the ball at the basket." He glanced at us again. "But the three of us had already spent time working on your skills, remember? So, Adria, you knew how to bank the ball off the backboard to make a basket. It didn't go in very often, but it did sometimes. None of the other girls knew how to do that."

"Oh yeah!" Adria danced around in her seat.

Mr. Lawson glanced at me in the mirror again. "And, Nikki, the first time you put up a shot, I heard the other team's coach say, 'What the heck? That girl's actually shooting.'"

Adria turned to look at me. We both shrugged, and she turned back to her dad. "What do you mean?"

"What I mean is, all the other girls threw the ball at the basket," he said. "Just heaved it up with both hands, as hard as they could. You'd already begun to develop shooting form, Lefty."

"Had I, too?" Adria said.

Mr. Lawson shook his head. "Not as much, but like I said, you'd learned how to bank the ball off the glass."

Adria made a *hmph* kind of sound.

Mr. Lawson laughed, reached over, and patted her knee.

"Who won the game?" I said.

"We did," Mr. Lawson said. "Eight to two. You each made two baskets, and a girl on the other team, by some miracle, made one."

"Go, Hello Kitties!" Adria and I yelled.

We kept on like that all the way to Baltimore, laughing, talking about our county-league teams, remembering great plays we made and all those hours we spent practicing in the Lawsons' driveway, which also made me think about all the hours I'd spent out in my own driveway, shooting on our old, rusty hoop.

When we finally got to the sports center where the tournament was being held, Mr. Lawson dropped Adria and me off in front of the gym while he went to park. We grabbed the handles of the big gym doors, yanked them open, stepped inside...

And froze.

Ten full-sized basketball courts, lined up two-by-two, stretched out in front of us, with ten games going on, full tilt, all at the same time. Twenty teams in twenty sets of colors raced back and forth across the courts, balls booming off the floor, referees' whistles screeching, coaches yelling, parents cheering, and all that noise crashing up against the gym's high ceiling and roaring straight back down. More teams swarmed around the sides of the courts, filled the bleachers, and streamed past on the running track that circled the courts, with parents and coaches and little brothers and sisters streaming past, too, bouncing balls, hauling ice chests, laughing and shouting and hollering at the little kids to not run off and get lost. And even though it was only eight o'clock in the morning, the air inside the gym was already hot and thick with pizza and popcorn smells pouring out of the snack bar and sweat rising from the courts.

My gym bag slipped from my shoulder and hit the floor. "How are we going to find our team?"

Adria took a full minute to answer. "Maybe just walk around looking for blue-and-orange jerseys?"

"Or maybe wait for your dad?"

"Good idea."

So we stood there, watching and listening as all the people and colors and noise spun around us, until Mr. Lawson came in. He whistled through his teeth. "Looks like you girls have hit the big time. Come on, let's find your team."

We walked halfway around the gym before I heard someone call our names and looked up to see Kim-Ly, Maura, and Taj waving at us from the bleachers.

"Dude!" Maura hollered before we'd climbed up two steps. "Do you believe this?"

"See that red team?" Kim-Ly said. "I saw their jerseys. They're from North Carolina, and that green team over there is from New York. And see that huge purple group with

'Chargers' on their warm-up jackets? They're from Philadelphia. My cousin's on their tenth-grade team."

Jasmine and her parents came in, and Autumn climbed the bleachers holding up her hands, fingers spread, displaying her blue-and-orange fingernails, and her mom climbed up behind her, teetering on the narrow steps in a pair of hot-pink, pointy-toed high heels.

"Look what my mom got for us," Autumn said, dropping her gym bag on a bench and pulling out ten pairs of orange-and-blue-striped shoelaces.

"Dude!" Maura whooped, jumping down three steps to grab a pair, her wild red curls flying out around her head. "These are the coolest!"

We thanked Mrs. Milbourne, all talking at once, checking out Autumn's nails, relacing our shoes—all except JJ, who insisted on keeping her old, dirty white shoelaces because they were "lucky," and besides, the striped laces were "girlie."

Linnae came in with her parents. She sat down next to me and pulled a pair of padded elbow sleeves from her gym bag. "My mom's making me wear these," she said. "She saw you skin your elbows the other night, so now she thinks I'm going to get a floor burn and die."

"Ohmygod," Jasmine said. "Don't let my mom see those. She'll make me wear them, too."

Kate came in with her dad. She waved at us and started

up the bleachers, but her dad stayed down on the floor, talking to another man. Kate dropped down on a bench in front of Adria and me and groaned.

"Are you okay?" I said.

Kate shook her head. "See that man my dad's talking to? The guy with the white hair and green shirt?"

"Yeah," Adria and I said together.

"He's a college scout. He evaluates high school players and writes a newsletter that college coaches read. My dad recognized him when we came in and asked him to watch me play."

"But we're only in eighth grade," I said.

"Tell that to my dad. He says I need to"—Kate lowered the pitch of her voice to sound like her dad—"take every opportunity to get on the recruiters' radar."

"Why?" I said.

Kate looked back at me. "Because according to my dad, that's what it takes to get a full ride at a big-time D1 program."

I sat back. "What does that mean?"

Kate laughed. "Sorry. I forget everybody's family isn't totally obsessed with basketball scholarships."

And Adria said, "Oh, Nikki, you know. Division One colleges are the big schools like UConn and Tennessee that you see on TV. They give full scholarships. Full rides."

"Oh," I said. "Right." Even though I didn't actually know what they were talking about. I mean, I knew colleges gave sports scholarships. But there were different divisions of colleges? And you had to "get on the recruiters' radar" to make a college team? And Kate and Adria were both thinking about that? All I was thinking about, apart from the game we were about to play, was making my high school team.

"So, um," I said, "why's your dad so obsessed with all that?"

Kate pulled her shoes out of her gym bag. "He wants me to have"—she lowered the pitch of her voice again—"better opportunities than he had." She started relacing her shoes with the striped laces that Autumn had tossed to her. "My dad was a supergood player in high school," she said. "He got scholarship offers from a bunch of big universities. Syracuse, Indiana. Schools like that. But his parents wouldn't let him go that far away. So he played at this smaller college near where he grew up and never got to go to the NCAA tournament or be on TV or anything. He doesn't want that to happen to me."

I looked over at Kate's dad, still standing on the gym floor, talking to the recruiter guy, and I tried to picture Mr. Nyquist as a high school kid, being good enough to play basketball on a really good college team, but his parents not letting him go. And as scary as he was, it made me feel sad for him. I mean, I couldn't help thinking about how I felt when Mom said I couldn't play on the Action.

Kate pulled on her shoes. "Dad says the whole reason to be on a club team like the Action is that we'll play in show-case tournaments where college coaches will see us."

"We will?" I said.

"I guess so. I think they mostly watch older girls, but Dad hopes they'll come to watch me."

"My dad hopes the same thing," Adria said.

I wanted to say my mom hoped so, too, but how stupid would that be? Adria knew my mom was clueless about all this stuff.

And I'd just found out that I was clueless, too.

A Black Hole on the
Basketball Court

"Ladies," Coach Duval said. He'd been sitting a few rows in front of us, but now he stood up. "We're up next on Court Four. Let's get over there and warm up."

We all trooped down from the bleachers and Coach led us across the gym, showing the parents where they could stand or set up their folding chairs between the courts during the game. And all of us Action girls bounced around, jabbering, then lined up on the running track to do our ankle flips and Frankenstein walks and over-unders.

All except Kate. She stood by herself, bent over a trash can, throwing up.

I ran over to her. "You okay?"

She straightened up, took a drink from her water bottle,

swished the water in her mouth, and spit it in the trash can, then took another drink. "Just nervous." She glanced up into the bleachers where the recruiter guy sat.

"Don't look at him," I said. "You'll play great."

Kate took another sip of water. "I better."

The game clock on Court Four buzzed, ending the game on the floor, so we all ran over, dropped our gym bags behind our bench, grabbed the balls out of Coach's bag, and ran onto the floor to warm up our shooting. I don't think any of us put up more than a few shots, though. Balls from the courts next to ours flew over into our layup lines and whistles blew and game clocks buzzed on all the other courts, and the whole gym was one big, wild, blaring mess. I wanted to put my hands over my ears the way I did when Sam bellowed at me.

When there was a minute left of warm-up time, Coach called us over. "Okay, first game. We might have a few jitters, but we won't worry about that, right? You make a mistake, forget it and move on. Run the offense. Play tough defense. Talk to your teammates."

Maura bounced on the balls of her feet, Kate chewed on the side of her thumb, all the rest of us nodded.

"Starters for this game: Maura, JJ, Linnae, Adria, Kate. Looks like they've got some tall girls, too, so we'll start in our two-three zone on defense and try to keep their bigs out of the lane. All right, hands in. 'Action' on three. One, two, three."

"Action!" we yelled, and the starters trotted onto the court.

I sat down between Kim-Ly and Taj, not exactly happy to be on the bench. I'd always been a starter before. But I tried not to think about that and clapped for my teammates. "Go, Action!" I yelled.

And then, when Kate stepped into the circle at the center of the court for the tip-off, I gasped. So did Kim-Ly and Taj. Because the girl who stepped into the circle for the other team—wearing a bright purple Philadelphia Chargers jersey—was taller than Kate.

The ref blew her whistle and tossed the ball in the air. Both girls jumped, but Kate jumped higher and her hand found the ball first. She tipped it to Adria, who took it straight up the court for a layup and two easy points.

We all clapped and cheered, and the girls on the floor sprinted down the court to play defense.

"Hands up!" Coach called. "Move your feet."

The Chargers point guard, a girl with long, tight braids and a big number eleven on her jersey, brought the ball up. She stopped at the three-point line, and before Maura or JJ could close out on her, she picked up the ball, shot, and drained a three-pointer. The Chargers parents clapped and cheered.

"Uh-oh," Kim-Ly said. "I hope she can't do that again."

But she could. And did. Two more times in the first five minutes of the game. The Chargers parents kept clapping and cheering, but we'd all gone dead silent—all except Kate's dad, who hollered, "For crying out loud, play some defense on her!"

"Time-out!" Coach Duval called, and we huddled around him.

"Okay, they've got a good shooter," he said. "So what're we going to do? Let her keep taking it to us? Fold up and go home? Or put a lid on her?"

Nobody said anything for a moment because, honestly, I think we were all in shock. I mean, here we were in the first game of our first tournament, and not only did the other team have a giant bigger than our giant, they also had a point guard who could drain threes like they were nothing.

"Well?" Coach said.

"Put a lid on her," Adria said.

"All right, then. Everybody take a deep breath and calm down. Switch to man-to-man defense. Maura, pick up their point guard at half-court and stick on her like a tick. If she gets past you, JJ slides over and picks her up. Kate, don't let their big get around you. All right, 'Action' on three. One, two, three."

"Action!" we all yelled, maybe not quite as loud as we had before, and the starters ran back onto the court.

Maura brought the ball up and signaled for the other girls to run the offense, but they ran through the whole rotation without getting a single open look at the basket.

"Be patient," Coach yelled. "Keep running it."

On the second rotation, Kate popped open underneath, Adria zipped a pass to her, and Kate pivoted around the Chargers big and hooked up a shot. It tapped the backboard and dropped through the net.

"All day long!" Mr. Nyquist's voice boomed out. "All day long, Kate! Keep calling for the ball!"

Our man-to-man defense started to work. With Maura right up in Number Eleven's face, the girl got rattled and made some bad passes that led to turnovers. She was still fast, though, and she managed to get past Maura again. JJ slid over to pick her up, but it was a JJ kind of slide—she slammed into the girl and sent her flying.

The ref blew her whistle and called a foul, and JJ's mom yelled, "Come on, Ref. That wasn't a foul. Let the girls play."

But a minute later, when Number Eleven got by Maura again, JJ "slid" into her so hard the girl hit the floor and skidded three feet.

The Chargers coach leaped up. "Intentional foul! You can't let that go, Ref! That was flagrant!"

"Bull!" JJ's mom hollered. "It wasn't flagrant. Let the girls play!"

"Subs!" Coach Duval yelled, loud enough to be heard over all the other yelling. "Autumn, you're in for JJ. Kim-Ly, go in for Maura. Nikki, in for Linnae. Check in at the scorer's table."

The ref motioned us in, a whistle blew, play started.

I didn't.

From the corners of my eyes, I saw teams streaking past on the courts on either side of ours, parents waving their arms and cheering, more teams warming up on the running track at the end of the court. Whistles blew on all ten courts, and I couldn't tell which came from our game and which came from the others.

So when the Chargers point guard passed the ball to the girl I was supposed to be guarding, I was still standing there, rooted to the floor, trying to figure out which shouts and whistles to pay attention to. Of course the Chargers girl blew past me, heading for the hoop. Kate stepped over to stop the girl's layup, but whacked her arm and got called for a foul.

The ref signaled two free throws.

"For crying out loud!" Mr. Nyquist's voice exploded from the sidelines. "Wake up, Twenty-Three!"

I think I stopped breathing.

Adria grabbed my arm. "Nikki, focus!"

"I can't."

"You can! We're all having trouble. It's so loud and there's so much stuff going on. You have to screen it out."

"I can't."

"You *can*!"

The girl I was supposed to guard missed her first free throw.

"I've got to line up to rebound," Adria said. "The ball and the hoop, remember?" It was what her dad always said if we were struggling—*just focus on the ball and the hoop.*

I rubbed my fingers along the sides of my shorts, scrunching the fabric with my fingers, silently chanting, "The ball and the hoop," while the girl I was supposed to guard sank her second free throw. Adria grabbed the ball and stepped out of bounds, ready to pass the ball back in to Kim-Ly, but the Chargers coach yelled, "Press," and the Chargers closed in. Autumn, Kim-Ly, and I cut back and forth, trying to shake our defenders, but we couldn't get open.

"Time-out," Coach Duval called.

We ran over and grouped around him.

"Okay, we haven't had time to work on a press break yet, so here's what we're going to do." Coach picked up his clipboard and looked straight at me. "Nikki, that long pass you threw to Kate during tryouts—can you make that pass again?"

I was still having trouble breathing, let alone talking, so when I didn't say anything, Adria said, "She can make it."

"Yeah?" Coach looked at both of us now.

"She can make it," Adria said again, and I tried to nod.

"Okay." Coach drew out the play, telling each of us what to do. "Got it? Good. 'Action' on three. One, two, three."

"ACTION!"

The other girls headed back onto the floor, but Coach clamped his hand on my shoulder. "You okay?"

"I got really distracted."

"Yup," he said. "It happens in a place like this. So now you know what it's like. Forget about all that and just play ball." He gave me a pat on the back that was more like a shove. "You got this, Lefty. Go get 'em."

I ran to the baseline. The ref blew her whistle and handed me the ball. I held it up, slapped it, and yelled, "Go!"

The girl guarding me jumped up and down, waving her arms, yelling, "Ball, ball, ball," right in my face, which usually annoyed the heck out of me, but actually helped me this time, because I had to work so hard to see around and over her I forgot about all the other stuff going on in the gym.

Kim-Ly and Linnae cut toward the sidelines, drawing their defenders with them, Adria took three steps backward, then spun and ran straight toward me, her hands in the air, and Kate did the opposite, running toward me from half-court, taking a stutter-step, then sprinting toward the other end of the floor. I faked a pass to Autumn, then cocked my arm back and fired a pass, high and fast, straight toward the spot where Kate was headed. The ball bounced a few feet ahead of her; she caught it as it rose off the floor, and without even breaking stride, she jumped to lay the ball up and in.

Adria grinned, pointing at me. From the sidelines, Maura shouted, "Dude!" And Kate trotted back down the court, clapping her hands.

In every other game I'd ever played, the rest of the world would have dropped away, and I would have been there with just the ball and the hoop and my teammates, in the zone. But in this game, the whole world stayed right there. Loud and nerve-racking and wild.

I tried to drive to the basket for a layup, but the Chargers big swatted the ball away. Then I forgot where I was supposed to be and missed a pass I should have caught. And then, when I was about to throw the ball in from the end line, my defender leaned up in my face and said, "Eeeewww, what's wrong with your eyes?" I jerked and threw a bad pass, and a Charger grabbed the ball and took it straight to the hoop to score.

Coach subbed me out.

At halftime, we were behind by eight points, which, considering all the dumb stuff I did and considering that the Chargers center was a beast under the hoop, getting a ton of rebounds and blocking every shot that came near her, eight points behind was maybe not too bad.

Things got better in the second half. Kate seemed to figure out the Chargers big and got around her for some close-in shots, Kim-Ly got out on a couple of fast breaks, Taj made a pretty baseline jumper, and Adria made four free throws in a row. And then, when I got back in the game, I came around a screen near the free throw line—the spot Mr. Lawson taught me to shoot from—caught a pass from Jasmine, jumped and shot, and the ball arced up away from me and swished through the net.

The Action parents clapped and cheered, and Coach called directions, and we were all feeling good.

With a minute to go, we were down by one and we had the ball. We ran all the way through our pass-and-cut pattern without anybody getting an open look, but finally I popped open near the free throw line again, and Kim-Ly fired a short, sharp pass. I caught the ball and turned, and here came the Chargers giant girl right at me. I pump-faked to throw her off, then jumped and shot, and the ball flew up...hit square in the middle of the big girl's hand and smashed straight back down to the floor.

The buzzer blared, ending the game. And that's when I saw Kate, wide open under the basket, with the Chargers center drawn off her to stop me.

Oh boy.

Kate was right there. Right there under the basket with

no one on her. And I hadn't seen her, hadn't even looked for her, hadn't passed her the ball.

And we lost.

Somewhere behind me a voice roared, "Oh, for crying out loud!"

Was it possible to sink through the floor and disappear? Because that's what I wanted to do.

We lined up and slapped hands and said "Good game" with the Chargers, then we grabbed our gym bags and followed Coach Duval to the bleachers.

"So, we did some things well. We did some things not so well," he said. "Bigs, we have to be more aggressive on rebounds. Guards, we need to do a better job taking care of the ball. And, everybody, we need to work harder on defense. But we stayed aggressive, we fought back hard, and for the most part we kept our heads in the game. All good. Lots of great things to build on."

He checked his watch. "Our next game is at one o'clock, so we have a couple of hours to get something to eat and get some rest. Okay, hands in, 'Action' on three. One, two, three."

"ACTION!"

Parents stepped over and said stuff like, "Not too bad for the first game" or "We'll get the next one" or "Nice job, Coach," except JJ's mom, who said, "We would've won if the refs called a fair game."

Adria leaned over and said, "I'm going to the snack bar with my dad. You coming?"

"I'll be there in a minute," I said. "I want to put on dry socks so I don't get blisters." And sit there and feel bad all by myself.

I mean, you know, I'd been playing team sports since I was seven years old. Which meant I'd played long enough to know that nobody ever won or lost a game all by herself.

But still. Not making that last shot. And worse than that, not seeing Kate *wide open* under the basket. Plus all the other dumb stuff I did.

I unlaced my shoes.

Down on the floor in front of me, Kate's dad stood next to the recruiter guy with the white hair and green shirt. Kate jumped down from the bleachers to join them. I was paying more attention to my shoes than to them, but we were far enough from the noise on the courts that I couldn't help hearing their voices.

"Hey, thanks for watching Kate play," Mr. Nyquist said.

"No problem," the other man said. "Always like to see the young kids. See who's coming up."

"So?" Mr. Nyquist said.

"So, yeah, Kate, you played a nice game," the recruiter guy said. "Good fundamentals. You run the floor well. You don't want to let your coach keep you playing center all the time, though. You look at the rosters of the top college programs, girls your size play wing and forward. You need to be six five, six six to play center at the big schools. Think you're still growing?"

Mr. Nyquist and Kate answered at exactly the same time. Mr. Nyquist said, "She's definitely still growing," and Kate said, "Oh god, I hope not!"

The other man laughed. "Too tall for all the boys, huh? Well, don't worry. They'll grow. Hey, listen, I gotta watch another game. Keep up the hard work, Kate."

"Before you go," Mr. Nyquist said, "you have any tips? Things Kate should work on?"

"Well, sure," the other man said. "The main thing is, you want to start developing a perimeter shot so college coaches will see you can play on the wing. But here's the deal, Kate. Small girls have to be something really special to get noticed. Girls your size with good skills, good attitude, coachable, you'll get plenty of attention." He chuckled. "You know what they say: You can teach a girl to dribble, but you can't teach her to be tall."

By that time, I'd taken off my shoes, changed my socks, dropped my shoes into my gym bag, and shoved my feet into my slide-on sandals. I stood up.

I guess Kate, her dad, and the other man hadn't noticed me sitting there, because when I stood up, they all turned and looked at me. I smiled, gave a dumb little wave, and started walking away.

"Hey, Twenty-Three." It was the recruiter's voice.

I turned back.

"Heck of a pass."

"Wasn't that a great pass?" Kate said.

Mr. Nyquist scowled.

"Coach set up that play for Nikki," Kate said. "She can make that pass every time."

"Yeah?" the white-haired man said. "Don't see many girls your age with the upper-body strength to make that pass. Not with any kind of accuracy. You play softball?"

"I used to," I said.

"Give it up?"

I nodded.

"How come?"

"Um." I glanced at Kate, who smiled back at me, then I glanced at her dad, who stared at the floor, scowling worse than ever. "Softball's kind of slow."

The white-haired man laughed. "Yeah, I gotta agree with you there. I'll tell you what, though. You might wanna reconsider. Arm like that, not to mention on a lefty. Might turn some heads."

"Oh," I said, which was a totally lame thing to say. But what was I supposed to say?

The man chuckled some more. "Anyway, nice pass. You got a pretty shot, too. Just need to stay out of the trees."

"Um, okay," I said. "Thanks." Which was also a dumb thing to say because I didn't know what he was talking about—*stay out of the trees*? I gave another little wave and headed for the snack bar.

"If she's smart, she'll take your advice and go back to softball," Mr. Nyquist said behind me. "Good arm, but the girl's a black hole on the basketball court."

"Dad! Shh," Kate said.

"Oh, come on," he said. "You know I'm right. Anybody can see a girl like her doesn't belong in this league."

Genetics Stinks

I didn't join Adria and Mr. Lawson in the snack bar right away, because first I had to find a bathroom and lock myself in a stall.

A black hole on the basketball court. A black hole. A Black Hole.

Was I really, truly that bad? I mean, right before the game I found out from Kate and Adria that I knew nothing about college basketball. Was I clueless about club ball, too?

You know I'm right, Mr. Nyquist had said to Kate. Did she? Did she know I didn't belong in this league? Did everybody?

I stood in the stall, shaking, pressing toilet paper to my eyes, blowing my nose about a thousand times, trying not to sound like I was crying, because I couldn't stand the thought of every girl who came into the bathroom thinking I was a stupid crybaby on top of thinking I was a Black Hole.

But as much as I wanted to, I couldn't stay in there forever—Adria had already texted me, asking where I was and if I was okay. (*Yeah. In the bathroom*, I replied). So finally, when I couldn't hear anybody else in there with me, I got myself together, left the stall, and stood in front of a sink, splashing cold water on my face until my whole face was red, not just my eyes and nose. Then I found Adria and Mr. Lawson and sat down with them. I pulled my lunch out of my gym bag and tried to look normal.

"You okay, Lefty?" Mr. Lawson said. "You look like you don't feel well."

So much for trying to look normal. "I have a headache," I said, which was true, but obviously not why I felt bad.

"Dehydration." Mr. Lawson fished a blue Gatorade out of the little cooler he'd brought along and handed it to me. "Drink the whole thing. It's hot in here, and you girls have never played a game at that pace before. You need to stay hydrated." He handed a yellow Gatorade to Adria. "You too," he said.

So I drank the Gatorade and tried to eat some of the turkey sandwich Mom had packed for me, and Adria and Mr. Lawson talked about her footwork, and when we got up to leave, Mr. Lawson patted my shoulder and said, "Don't worry, Lefty. The next game'll be better."

Which should have made me feel better, because it meant Mr. Lawson had noticed me struggling in the first game and was trying to give me a little pep talk. But it actually made me feel worse, because it meant that even Mr. Lawson, who'd spent the last six years teaching me to play basketball and the last three years telling me I was the best point guard in all of county league, even he thought I played like a Black Hole.

And on top of that, the next game wasn't better. It was worse.

Because in addition to all the noise and the screeching whistles from the other courts and the game moving twice as fast as a county-league game, now I was also scared. Scared of doing more stupid stuff that would make my team lose. Scared of making my teammates hate me. Which made me play even worse.

And when I was on the bench, I sat there feeling like I might throw up, and instead of bouncing around in my seat, clapping and cheering and chomping at the bit to get back in the game, I sat there hoping Coach wouldn't put me in. A hope I'd never, ever, *ever* had before.

And then, when I got home, I realized I'd spent so much time feeling awful between games, I'd completely forgotten about my genetics project and hadn't measured my team-mates. Which meant I could only do some of the work on my big poster-board graphs on Saturday night and would have to finish the whole huge project Sunday night.

Ugh.

Sunday morning, before I left for the tournament, I wrote *measure* across the back of my hand with a black marker. Then, between the first try-not-to-be-a-Black-Hole game and the second try-not-to-be-a-Black-Hole game, I reminded the girls about my project, and we all went over to the side of the gym so I could measure them. Kate and Adria helped, Adria pulling the tape measure up along the wall, and Kate laying a ruler flat across the top of each girl's head and marking the spot where the ruler hit the tape measure.

Just like in class, it took longer than I thought it would, because most of the girls had their hair in ponytails or buns that got in the way of the ruler, so they all had to pull out their elastic bands and grumble about having to spend a bunch of time fixing their hair again. Plus about half the girls didn't take their basketball shoes off between games, so they all had to grumble about taking their shoes off to be measured.

Kate was last. She took off her shoes and stood up against the wall, and Taj laid the ruler on Kate's head, stretching up on her tiptoes to make sure it was level.

"What do you think you're doing?" Mr. Nyquist's voice said behind me.

I spun around.

He glowered down at me.

"It's okay, Dad," Kate said. "Nikki's just measuring us."

He shifted his gaze to her. "Put your shoes on."

"I will as soon as Nikki finishes—"

"Put your shoes on now." Mr. Nyquist didn't raise his voice, but he might as well have roared, because his words hit hard and sharp as a knife.

Kate stepped toward her dad. "I'll put them back on in a minute. As soon as—"

"Now!"

Her eyes teared up. She dropped her head, swiped the back of her arm across her eyes, grabbed her shoes, and shoved her feet into them.

Mr. Nyquist dropped his hands into the pockets of his khakis and rocked back on his heels. "You're a basketball player, Kate. The only height that matters is your height on the court. And on the court, you have your shoes on."

"This is just for my science project," I said, my voice coming out in a squeak. "I'm not putting girls' names on my charts. Just their heights."

Mr. Nyquist didn't even glance at me. In fact, he turned sideways so his back was toward me, still looking at Kate. "Don't ever let anyone measure you with your shoes off," he

said. "Not unless they've already offered you a scholarship."
Then he walked away.

Kate, Adria, Taj, and I stood there for a moment, not
moving, maybe not even breathing. Then Kate stepped back
against the tape measure and whispered, "Subtract an inch.
Measure me like this and subtract an inch."

Which we did. And subtracting an inch, Kate was still six
foot two.

And I was still five foot four.

Playing four basketball games in one weekend is a lot, especially if you've never done it before. So even if you're trying
your best to not be a Black Hole and not get in the way of the
girls who belong in that league, it's still four games of sprinting up and down the court, playing tough defense, diving for
loose balls, fighting for rebounds, and colliding with JJ-like
players on the other teams.

By the time I poured myself out of Mr. Lawson's car on
Sunday evening, every muscle and tendon and ligament and
every other thing in my whole entire body was groaning,
begging me to take a hot shower, gobble down dinner, and
fall into bed.

But that wasn't going to happen. I had my genetics project to finish.

Which meant that when I limped into science class Monday morning, I was tired, I was grumpy, and I was all-around ticked off.

Because here's another thing about being left-handed. If you're left-handed, it's really hard to write stuff left-to-right, the way we do in English, and not smear every letter with the side of your hand as you move along. So if you want your work to look good, you have to be careful and go slowly, holding your wrist up away from your paper. When I was little, it always took me ten times as long as everybody else to do my classwork because I couldn't stand it if my writing wasn't perfect.

But after playing four basketball games in one weekend, not to mention already having a sore wrist from one of the times I hit the court diving for a loose ball, I didn't want to go slowly.

I wanted to be done.

Which meant my big height charts, my charts that were worth half my grade for the quarter, looked like dog doo.

And then, on top of all that, I was also major-league bummed out about what I'd learned about the "heritability" of height.

And oh yeah, if all that wasn't enough, I was a Black Hole on the Basketball Court.

But I guess none of that stuff had happened to Mr.

Bukowski over the weekend, because he grinned and rubbed his hands together. "Okay, people, who's first?" He looked around the room. "No volunteers? Really? Well, let's see. Sunil, why don't you start us off?"

Sunil mumbled, "Why me?" But as it turned out, he didn't have any reason to be nervous, because he'd done a PowerPoint presentation that he projected up on the class-room screen, and instead of just making a chart, he'd taken pictures of all his relatives' ears, or had them email him pictures of their ears. And when you look at a whole screen full of ears, without any faces attached to them, it's pretty weird and interesting. Especially since Sunil's little cousin had decorated her ear with pink and silver glitter, and his great-aunt's ear hung down about an inch because she'd worn huge gold earrings all her life, and his grandfather had the top part of his ear cut off in a car accident. So it was a pretty interesting project to look at. Or it would have been if I hadn't been so grumpy.

Mary Katherine Pentangeli's project would have been interesting, too. She'd drawn her family tree on a giant piece of butcher paper that she rolled out and taped up across the entire whiteboard, because that's how much space she needed to fit her family. Each of Mary Katherine's parents had five or six brothers and sisters, and each of them had at least two or three children, which meant Mary Katherine had thirty-two cousins and eight cousins-once-removed because some of her cousins already had their own children. Plus all four of her grandparents were still alive, and they each had five or six brothers and sisters, and each of them had a couple of kids and a bunch of grandkids, which meant Mary Katherine had eighty-seven second cousins. And somehow she'd managed to get in touch with almost all of those people to find out what kind of earlobes they had.

Obviously, Mary Katherine was going to get an A on her project.

And just as obviously, Kyle Moffett was not, because he stood up and showed us a piece of binder paper with three squares drawn on it. One was labeled *Mom, Dangling*. One was labeled *Dad, Attached*. And one was labeled *Me, Dangling*.

"What about your brother?" Mr. Bukowski said.

"My brother?" Kyle said.

"Yes, your brother, who was in my class last year and is now in ninth grade. Remember him?"

"Oh, yeah." Kyle looked at his paper, like maybe he expected his brother's square to magically appear. "He had a baseball game last night, so I didn't get to see what kind of ears he has."

"Mmm," Mr. Bukowski said. "Sounds like maybe you waited a little too long to start your project?"

"I kind of forgot about it."

"Uh-huh. Well, any effort is better than none, I suppose."
Mr. Bukowski looked around the room. "Okay, let's see. Nikki,
what have you got to show us?"

Oh boy.

I climbed off my lab stool, limped to the front of the
classroom, and set my three big charts on the tray beneath
the whiteboard, leaning them up against Mary Katherine's fabulous family tree. The graphs looked even worse in
the sharp fluorescent light of the classroom than they did
at midnight in our kitchen, and I had a momentary urge
to turn them around so nobody could see how messy they
looked, but just as quickly I realized it would be impossible
to explain my project without the graphs, so I frowned at
them and turned to face the class.

"Um, well, I researched the genetic links to height," I
said. Then I told the class about what I'd learned—how scientists call height a polygenic trait, because your height is
controlled by a bunch of different genes, but is also affected
by whether or not you get enough to eat when you're a kid
and stuff like that, but that genes are the most important
part because they account for 90 percent of your height, and
all the other stuff accounts for only 10 percent. So what that
means is, if both your parents are tall, but you don't get a

whole lot to eat while you're a kid, you'll still grow up to be pretty tall. But if both your parents are short, even if you get plenty to eat, you'll still grow up to be short.

So then I showed the class my graphs. And what the graphs showed was that in our class, the tallest girl (Adria) was five foot ten, the shortest girl (Minh Bui) was four foot ten, and the average height of the girls was five foot two. The average height of the moms of the girls in the class was five foot four and the average height of the dads was five foot ten.

In other words—which I didn't share with the class—my mom and my dad were each an inch taller than the average mom and dad in the class, and I was *two whole inches taller* than the average girl.

But on my basketball team, the average height of the girls was five foot six, from Kate at six foot two to Kim-Ly at five foot three. The average height of the moms was five foot seven, and the average height of the dads was six foot two.

Which meant that I was two inches *shorter* than the average girl on my team, my mom was two inches shorter than the average mom, and my dumb old paper dad was *three whole inches shorter* than the average dad.

And what all *that* meant was that even though I might be *slightly* tall compared with girls who didn't play basketball, I would never be *actually* tall. Not compared with basketball players. And even though Mom might say stuff like, *Don't worry, Nikki, you'll grow more,* I now knew I'd never grow enough, and there was absolutely nothing I could do about it because height was 90 percent genetics. And Genetics Stinks.

But, you know, I didn't mention that to my class.

"Very interesting, Nikki," Mr. Bukowski said. "So one might conclude, from looking at your graphs, that height is a desirable trait for basketball players. In fact, one might conclude that people of average height are at a distinct disadvantage on the basketball court." He chuckled, then said, "It's like a person my size who wants to play football, isn't it? He'd better learn to kick field goals if he wants to make the team."

I wanted to say, *Gee, Mr. Bukowski, thanks for pointing that out.* But I didn't. What I said was, "Um, yeah," which was pretty lame, but it was the best I could do.

"Interesting project, Nikki," Mr. Bukowski said. "Your charts aren't up to your usual standard of neatness and attention to detail, but an interesting project."

I grabbed my charts and started hobbling back to my lab stool, but Mr. Bukowski said, "Leave your graphs, Nikki. Remember, we're going to display the projects in the science hallway?"

Oh yeah.

Great.

Adria got up to give her presentation. She had a PowerPoint, like Sunil, and also like Sunil, she'd included pictures of her relatives. But Adria had pictures of whole faces, not just ears, and since all the people in her mom's family had skin that was various shades of brown and tan and all the people in her dad's family had skin that was so white it probably glowed in the dark, her PowerPoint slides looked interesting, too. Plus, instead of showing which of her relatives had attached or dangling earlobes like most of the kids in class, Adria showed which ones could roll up the sides of their tongues and which ones couldn't—which is also an inherited trait—so Adria stood up in front of the class with PowerPoint slides full of people sticking out their tongues. Everybody thought that was hilarious, and even though I was still grumpy and ticked off, I couldn't help laughing, too.

Some more kids got up to give their presentations, and some were good and some weren't, and then Mr. Bukowski called on Booker.

Booker shook his hair back from his face. "I wrote a report, Mr. Bukowski. I don't have charts to show or anything."

"That's all right," Mr. Bukowski said. "Tell us what you learned."

Booker got up slowly and walked to the front of the classroom. He set his report on the counter where Mr. Bukowski demonstrated experiments and stared down at it. "I did my report on the genetic links to drug addiction."

He turned the first page of his report, then turned the

next page, then started talking. And I couldn't help thinking about him standing in my driveway, telling me about how he got wound up about science, because after he started talking, he kept right on, talking faster and faster, all the way to the end of the class period, telling us about the three different "alleles" of the "mu-opioid gene" and the "alteration of dopamine receptors" and the development of the "prefrontal cortex" and how all that relates to addiction in teenagers and on and on with a bunch of other eight-foot-long science words that got Mr. Bukowski so excited his nutsy Einstein hair just about vibrated right off his head.

"Terrific!" Mr. Bukowski said when Booker finished. "Fascinating report."

The bell rang, and Mr. Bukowski asked Booker and Mary Katherine to stay after class, and the rest of us charged out the door, heading for lunch, which is usually my favorite part of the school day, other than PE.

But that day lunch was an ordeal, because Adria was all fired up about my height charts.

"Boy, your graphs gave me a lot to think about," she said between bites of her sandwich. "You know how I've always felt like such a freak for being so tall?"

"Yeah," I said, with about as much enthusiasm as I'd say, *Yeah, that's a mud puddle*, hoping Adria would take the hint that I didn't want to talk about height anymore.

She didn't take the hint.

"Remember how I used to cry in third grade when boys called me Monster-girl?"

"Mm-hmm," I said.

Adria bit into an apple and crunched for a minute. "Now I get why my dad's bugging me to work on ball-handling. He says girls my size are guards in college. I didn't think he knew what he was talking about, but I guess he does. I'm two inches shorter than Taj and *four* inches shorter than Kate, and that girl on the Philadelphia Chargers team was taller than her. I'm a shrimp compared with those girls."

By that time, I was seriously considering pulling the ham out of my sandwich and throwing it at Adria. Fortunately Booker and Mary Katherine came rushing in and sat down next to us, which got Adria to finally shut up, and kept me from plastering my best friend with lunch meat and turning her into my ex–best friend.

"Mr. Bukowski wants us to enter our projects in a science contest," Mary Katherine said. "Can you believe it? Me? The girl who sucks at science? My dad's going to freak. Who knew having a gigantic family would turn out to be a good thing?"

"Do you actually know all those people?" I said.

"Most of them." Mary Katherine opened her lunch bag and pulled out a sandwich and corn chips. "You should see

Thanksgiving at my house. This year we had sixty-three people, not counting babies. If you didn't get food on your plate fast, it was gone."

"We had five people for Thanksgiving," Booker said. "My mom, my dad, my two grandmas, and me."

"I can top that," I said. "We had three. My mom, Sam, and me."

"How'd you eat a whole turkey with just three people?" Mary Katherine asked.

"We didn't. It was Sam's turn to choose what we had for dinner, so we had tacos."

That made Mary Katherine laugh so hard she almost spit her corn chips all over the table, which sounds like a bad thing, but was actually a good thing, because it completely got Adria off the subject of what a shrimp she was—at five foot ten—which meant I didn't have to lose my best friend that day.

15

In Case Being a Black Hole Wasn't Bad Enough

Taking care of Sam got a little easier that week. We decided that twenty minutes was probably the right amount of time to ride bikes or kick a soccer ball around before we started our homework. Or if Sam wanted to jump on his pogo stick, I'd spend the twenty minutes shooting. It rained on Wednesday and we decided that whenever it rained, we could play a board game or build Lego stuff for twenty minutes. But no video games.

Sam still yammered a mile a minute, which was still annoying, but making decisions together like that, coming up with our own "rules," made us feel like our own little team. And on Thursday, when Booker rode by on his bike and Sam and I joined him on our bikes, he kind of joined our team, too, because when Sam said, "We can only ride bikes for twenty minutes," Booker said, "That's cool. I've got to get my homework started, too."

And, you know, it was almost fun.

Or, actually, when Booker was with us, it was definitely fun. But otherwise, well, yeah—almost fun.

But if taking care of Sam got easier that week, school sure didn't. In history, we had a big end-of-unit test on World War II. And since I'd spent so much time on my genetics project, plus taking care of Sam, plus basketball, I'd hardly spent any time studying for the test. And—what a surprise—tests are a lot harder if you don't study.

My English teacher piled on the work, too, assigning an essay along with all the reading we always had to do, which kept me up late three times that week.

And if all that wasn't bad enough, I had to walk past my big height charts in the science hallway twice a day, which made me: one, cringe at how messy they were; two, worry about somebody asking me why I hadn't done a family tree like almost everybody else; and, three, remember that I'd never be tall because of my parents' stupid, not-tall genes.

Basketball practice didn't get easier that week, either. We had to make fifteen layups in a row with the heavy balls, for one thing. By the time we finished, my shoulders ached so bad I actually hoped my arms would fall off. Then we learned a new offensive pattern, and since I still wasn't playing point guard, I kept getting confused about where I was supposed to be. And since I also kept worrying about everybody thinking I was a Black Hole, I made more mistakes. During water breaks I stood apart, running the play in my head.

We had another tournament that weekend. Mom had planned to go, but Sam woke up with a fever Saturday morning, so they both had to stay home.

"Play hard. Have fun," they called as I ran out to get in the Lawsons' car.

And even though Mom didn't usually have a clue about what was going on during games, I was bummed that she and Sam wouldn't be at this tournament. It would have been nice having someone there cheering just for me.

But as it turned out, when we got to the gym where the tournament was held, I was glad Mom wasn't there. She would have hated it.

The gym was called Maryland Hoop Heaven, which made us all think it would be a big, fancy gym. But the people who named it must have had a weird sense of humor, because Maryland Hoop Heaven was an old supermarket that had been gutted of all the freezer cases and cash registers and stuff, and now had a fake wood floor with twelve courts marked out on it. The ceiling was low, so it was even louder than the gym we'd played in the week before, and the lighting was the old supermarket lighting, which made weird pockets of light and shadow all over the courts. And to top it all off, instead of a snack bar, there was a group of women over in one corner cooking hot dogs and hamburgers on a bunch of little George Foreman grills. Standing inside Maryland Hoop Heaven made you feel like you were swimming in hamburger grease.

"Eeeeewwww," Kim-Ly and Taj said as soon as they came in, and Autumn said, "I can feel my face breaking out."

Coach chuckled. "Welcome to club ball, ladies," he said. "Get used to playing in all kinds of places."

Dark and icky as the courts were, they didn't turn out to be a problem, because there weren't any teams in our age group nearly as good as the Philadelphia Chargers at this tournament. Which meant there weren't any teams nearly as good as us. We won all our games easily.

"What a waste of time," I heard Mr. Nyquist say to Kate after our last game on Sunday. "I don't know why I let you play on this team. You're not going to improve your game playing against competition like that."

But I thought it was okay, because: one, playing against easy teams, I didn't have to worry about doing something dumb and losing the game; and, two, since our bigs were almost always open under the hoop, I could keep passing the ball to them and didn't have to worry about taking a bad shot when somebody had a better one.

"Why aren't you shooting, Lefty?" Coach asked me once when I came out of a game.

"The bigs are wide open underneath," I said.

"All right, fair enough. But you can take a shot now and then. You don't have to be quite so unselfish."

"Okay," I said, even though, duh, I wasn't being unselfish. I was trying not to be a Black Hole.

"That was kind of a dumb tournament, wasn't it?" Adria said when she got on the bus Monday morning. "I hope we have better competition next weekend."

I shifted around in the seat to look at her. "That's not what you said on the ride home yesterday. You said it was fun to be on a team that won so much."

"I know, but—" She pushed up the sleeves of her sweater. "We won't get better if we play against bad teams."

"You sound like you've been listening to Mr. Nyquist."

Adria shrugged. "My dad talked with him a lot this weekend. They think we should play against ninth-grade teams."

The bus stopped and some kids got on, shuffled past us, and dropped into seats.

"Do you think Mr. Nyquist knows a lot about basketball?" I asked.

"My dad thinks he does." Adria pulled an elastic band out of her backpack and gathered her hair into a bun, pulling a few curls loose around her face. "Hey, you want to come to my house after school? Kate's coming over. She's going to teach me to do a reverse layup."

I stared at her. "Kate's coming over to your house? Since when are you such good friends?"

Adria laughed. "What are you talking about, Nikki? We're on the same team. We go to the same strength-and-conditioning class. I invited her over to hang out. Is that a problem?"

I sighed. "No, it's not a problem."

"So do you want to come over?"

"Yeah, I want to come over."

"Okay, good."

"But I can't."

"What? Why not?"

I pulled at a thread on the sleeve of my sweatshirt. "I have to take care of Sam after school."

Adria rocked back, squinting at me. "No, you don't. He goes to after-school-care."

"Not anymore." I pulled harder at the loose thread.

"Since when?"

"Since the Action. With all the tournament fees and travel costs and everything, I made a deal with my mom that I'd take care of Sam after school so we could save the cost of after-school-care."

"Oh," Adria said. "Well, poop. But I guess we're kind of in the same boat on that. My dad told me that since he's paying for all this, I should be scoring double digits every game. Yeah, right. Like that's the easiest thing in the world to do."

I knew what she was doing. She was trying to make me feel better.

But the thing was, I didn't feel better. "We're not in the same boat."

"What?"

"We're not in the same boat. Your dad wants you to score more. My mom couldn't care less if I play basketball. You're hanging out with Kate, going to strength-and-conditioning classes, learning to do reverse layups. I'm helping Sam multiply fractions and sound out big words. We're not in the same boat. We're not in the same ocean."

"Come on, Nikki," Adria said. "You're on the Action, same as me. Same as Kate. You're just feeling sorry for yourself."

"That's what you think?"

"Well...you think I *want* to go to strength and conditioning?"

"Don't you?"

"I...I don't know. I mean, it's fun going with Kate and all. But it's just a workout. There are all kinds of workout routines on the internet. You could do one of those if you want to." She pulled another curl loose from her bun. "You know what Coach said—you have to work hard if you want to get better."

"You think I'm not working hard enough?"

Adria drummed her fingers on her leg. "I don't know, Nikki. I mean...do you think you're playing well?"

"You don't think so?"

"Um." Adria looked at the floor. "You don't seem like yourself. You—"

"Mr. Nyquist says I'm a black hole on the basketball court."

Adria sat back up. "What?"

I nodded, expecting Adria to be as upset as I was about that. Expecting her to be outraged. To defend me against Kate's scary dad.

But that's not what happened. What happened was that Adria burst out laughing. "A black hole on the basketball court? What a weird, goofy thing to say."

The bus lurched to a stop in the school parking lot, and Adria got up, still laughing. But I sat there while the other kids got off the bus, looking out the window, watching my best friend disappear into the crowd of kids pushing through the heavy glass doors at the front of our school.

I didn't have a lot to say at lunchtime, but Adria didn't seem to notice. We were sitting near Mary Katherine Pentangeli and the group of girls she usually sat with, so Adria talked and laughed with them about boys and stuff. I ate my sandwich, then mumbled that I had homework to finish and went to the library and pretended to read a book.

Adria and I didn't have classes together in the afternoon, but on the bus ride home, she said, "Nikki, are you okay? You're so quiet."

For a moment I thought about saying, *I can't believe you laughed about the black hole thing. It really hurt my feelings.* But in the same moment I realized what a dumb, little-kid thing that would be to say.

So instead I said, "Just tired. It takes a lot of energy to deal with Sam. I'm trying to save up." I smiled to show I was joking around. Even though I wasn't.

"You sure you can't come over?" Adria said. "Sam can come, too. He could play video games, or I bet Mom would let him paint or something while you and Kate and I shoot around."

I shook my head. "I promised my mom I'd help Sam get his homework done every afternoon."

"Kate and I could come over to your house for a little while."

I shook my head again. "You know my mom doesn't let me have anyone over before she gets home."

"Oh yeah," Adria said. "Well, poop."

And I said, "Double-poop," which almost made it seem like things were okay-normal.

But I think we both knew they weren't.

When I got home, I sat on my bed and looked at Mia McCall, soaring high above the court, muscles straining, every part of her focused on the ball and the hoop. So confident. So in control. I wanted to talk to her about Adria. About Mr. Nyquist. About being a Black Hole on the Basketball Court.

But how could I?

She was Mia McCall. How could she possibly understand?

I decided to go outside to shoot, thinking it might make me feel better—or at least make me forget how bad I felt—but when I got out there, all I could think about was Adria in *her* driveway with Kate, learning to do reverse layups. So after one lame shot that didn't even hit the rim, I grabbed my ball and sat down at the end of the driveway to watch for Sam. I pulled my sweatshirt hood over my head, because even though it was April, it was still chilly. Especially if you were sitting on cold asphalt, being miserable, instead of running around doing reverse layups with your new friend.

What was going on? I mean, how could Adria *laugh* about Mr. Nyquist saying I was a Black Hole? She was my *best friend*. Had been my best friend since the first day of kindergarten, when we walked into the classroom, clinging to our mothers' hands, wearing identical Hello Kitty T-shirts. How could she not understand how upset I was?

But...but if Adria laughed about it, did that mean she

thought Mr. Nyquist was right? He'd said, *You know I'm right*, to Kate. Did everybody really, truly think I was that awful?

I pulled my hood tighter and rubbed my hands across my face.

How had this happened?

How could I all of a sudden be so bad at basketball? I'd been a really good point guard. I *knew* I had been. The *best* point guard in county league, Adria's dad had said.

But then a bad thought occurred to me, and I heard Adria's voice on the bus the morning after the first Action practice—*Of course he said we were the best. He's my dad.*

And then an even worse thought came into my head, because I heard Adria say, *Remember how we always said a lot of girls in county league were good athletes, but they weren't really basketball players? They just played basketball in the winter to stay in shape for soccer or lacrosse.*

So...so maybe I was only a good basketball player compared with those girls. Compared with soccer and lacrosse players. Not *actually* good.

Just like I was kind of tall compared with the girls in my science class, but not *actually* tall. Not compared with girls who played basketball.

I bit on my bottom lip and stared so hard at my basketball it turned into an orange blur.

"Hey, Nikki."

I looked up.

Booker rode his bike into our driveway and got off. "What're you doing?"

"Waiting for Sam."

"Yeah, but how come you're not shooting?"

I could have said, *I'm too tired* or *My hands are too cold,* but what was the point of that? "I'm a black hole on the basketball court."

Booker laughed, just like Adria. But then, unlike Adria, when I didn't laugh, too, he stopped and sat down next to me. "What are you talking about?"

I tossed my basketball back and forth between my hands and didn't say anything.

We sat like that, both quiet, until Booker said, "What's wrong, Nikki?"

I shook my head. "Everything."

"Oh good, that's specific. Easy to solve."

I glanced at him. "You're real funny."

"I try to be." He smiled. "But really, Nikki, what's going on?"

I sighed. "I suck at basketball."

"Yeah, right," Booker said. "That's why you're on that big club team with Adria."

"Well, some people think I don't belong there."

"What people?"

"Adria, for one. She told me on the bus today that, basically, I suck and I need to work harder. And Kate's dad said I'm a black hole."

"Somebody's dad called you a black hole?"

"Not to my face. But I heard him."

"Geez, what a jerk."

"Yeah, he's not exactly the nicest dad in the world. The thing is, though, he knows all about basketball. He got scholarship offers from all these big basketball schools. And he had this recruiter guy watch Kate play in our first game. He knows what he's talking about."

Booker tapped his foot against the driveway. "Maybe."

"Well, the recruiter guy must know what he's talking about or he wouldn't be a recruiter."

"Yeah, so?"

"So after he watched our game he said I had a good arm and I should play softball."

"Oh, well, okay, why don't you play softball, then?"

"I hate softball!"

Booker leaned away from me, eyebrows raised.

Oh boy.

"I'm sorry," I said. "I didn't mean to yell at you. I just . . . I love basketball. I really, *really* love basketball. And I wanted to play on this team so bad and I *need* to play on this team to be good enough to make varsity in high school. But that recruiter guy? He said coaches always want tall girls, but small girls have to be really special for a coach to notice them. I always thought I was special because I was a left-handed point guard. But I'm not even good enough to play point guard on this team. Now I'm just a regular guard or a wing or something, and I'm terrible at that. Kate and Adria are talking about playing in college, and I'm not even going to be good enough to play in high school."

We sat there for a few minutes, staring at the street, not saying anything.

Then Booker said, "You could be a field goal kicker."

"Booker, come on. You don't kick field goals in basketball."

"No," he said. "But players do other special stuff. Like shoot three-pointers."

"I can't shoot three-pointers."

"You made one in your first practice."

"Oh, yeah, one. The only one I ever made in my life."

"So?" Booker said. "You made one. You can make more."

"No, I can't. That was luck. I've never been an outside shooter."

"So? Learn how."

"What?" I yelled. "How am I going to *learn how*? Who's going to teach me? I don't have a dad who played in college. We don't have the money for me to take extra classes like

Kate and Adria. I've never been an outside shooter. I can't just *decide* to turn into one!"

Booker looked at me, not smiling his half smile, not shaking his hair back from his face. He got up. "Okay, well, whatever. I gotta go." He swung onto his bike, then turned back. "You know, Nikki, you could probably find people to help you if you wanted to. But, like, you'd have to want to. Say hi to Sam for me."

Then he was gone.

And I sat there.

I threw my basketball onto the lawn, pulled my knees up in front of me, and covered my face with my hands.

Oh. My. God.

In one day—One Day—I'd found out my best friend might not actually be my best friend anymore and I'd screamed at my new friend. My new friend who was the only boy who had ever said anything to me like, *Your eyes aren't weird. Just different. Just…special.* And now he was gone.

And then, wouldn't you know it, here came Sam's bus rumbling down the street. It stopped at the corner, the door opened, and Sam exploded from the steps, hitting the ground running, bellowing, "Nikki! Nikki, guess what!"

And wasn't that the perfect way to end this perfectly horrible, awful, *excruciating* day?

Working on My Lying

Sam blasted up the street, hollering out all the amazing stuff that happened in third grade that day, but when he got to our driveway, I was still sitting there with my legs folded up in front of me, my elbows on my knees, and my hands cradling my face.

He skidded to a stop. "What's wrong, Nikki? You look sad."

I rubbed my face. "It's been a bad day."

"You want to ride bikes?" he said. "It might make you feel better."

"No."

"You want to jump on my pogo stick?"

I shook my head.

"I could rebound for you."

"I don't want to shoot."

Sam shifted his weight back and forth. Then he reached out and patted my head. "You want me to make some popcorn? I know how."

I couldn't help smiling at that. "Sure."

So we went inside and Sam put a bag of popcorn in the microwave and I made sure he set the timer right.

"You want to play a board game?" he asked.

I shook my head.

"Okay, I'll get some Legos." He started up the stairs, then turned back. "I hope you have a better day tomorrow, Nikki."

"Thanks," I said. "It couldn't be a lot worse."

And I guess it wasn't. Worse, I mean. Nobody told me I was terrible at basketball, and I didn't scream at anybody and make them hate me. But it wasn't a lot better, either.

For one thing, on the bus to and from school and all through lunch, Adria yammered on about how much fun she had learning to do reverse layups, even though she wasn't good at it yet, and how funny Kate was when her dad wasn't around. And no matter how many times I said stuff like, "Oh" or "Hunh," or even looked out the window, she didn't seem to get that I didn't want to talk about this stuff. How could she be so oblivious?

And Booker—Booker sat sideways on his lab stool, his

back toward me, all through our science class. He didn't talk to me between classes and he didn't ride his bike over after school.

And then, oh yeah, there was Action practice.

I might be a bad player, but I was still on the team and still had to go to practice, so when Mom got home from work Tuesday night, I asked her if she could take me. I told her Adria and her dad were coming from someplace else and couldn't pick me up. I told Adria that Mom wanted to see practice.

Boy, I was getting good at lying.

But I really, *really* needed someone there who didn't think I was a Black Hole.

Sam had to come, too, of course. He brought a book to read and some Legos to play with, but before we'd gotten half-way through our warm-up, he was down on the floor by the side of the court, watching us, trying to copy our exercises.

"Is that your little brother?" Linnae asked me. "He's so cute. Look at him over there Frankenstein-walking with us."

"You wouldn't think he was cute if he was your brother," I said, which, considering how nice Sam had been to me the day before and considering that he and I were now kind of our own little team, was a pretty crummy thing to say. But, well, yeah, I was feeling crummy.

"Hey, I'd take a little brother any day," Linnae said. "I've got two older brothers who think it's funny to tease me until I cry."

Coach blew his whistle, which meant it was time for sprints and line drills and planks and sit-ups, so talking was done.

And then, out of the corner of my eye, I saw Coach walk over to Sam and squat down to talk to him. Then Mom jumped down from the bleachers and went over to talk with them, too. I expected Sam to stay in the bleachers after that, but then there he was setting out orange plastic cones for us to weave through in ball-handling drills, and there he was digging horrible, heavy yellow balls out of Coach's ball bag, and there he was standing at the baseline, "helping" us count our twenty makes in a row while we ran the Rainbow Drill with the heavy balls.

"Is that your little brother?" Autumn said, and Kim-Ly said, and Jasmine said. "He's so cute."

"Dude!" Maura said to Sam every time she ran past him, slapping his hand.

We did defense drills and rebound drills, learned a new press break, scrimmaged for half an hour, then shot our free throws.

I made mine. So did Kate, Adria, Kim-Ly, and Autumn. Which meant we only had to run five up-and-back sprints at the end of practice, when we were all tired enough to fall down where we stood.

I didn't drop onto the gym floor next to Kate and Adria and laugh about being the Northern Virginia Roadkill when we finished, though. I sat on the bottom row of the bleachers to take off my shoes. Linnae and Maura sat down next to me, and Sam ran over to yammer a million miles a second about how much FUN he had and how much he LOVED our team and LOVED COACH DUVAL and LOVED coming to practice and COULDN'T WAIT to see us play in the tournament on Saturday.

"You can be our mascot," Linnae said.

Sam hopped back and forth from one foot to the other. "What's a mascot?"

"It's like a lucky charm, dude." Maura threw Sam a fist-bump. "You can bring us good luck."

"Unlikely," I said, and Maura and Linnae cracked up.

When we got in the car after practice, Mom said, "It was nice of your coach to let Sam help."

I turned and looked at Sam in the back seat. "You owe me, big-time."

He grinned.

Mom pulled out of the parking lot. "I can see why you've been so tired lately. That was quite a workout."

All I could do was laugh.

"Does Coach Duval always push you that hard?"

"Yeah. Sometimes harder."

Mom shook her head. "It's certainly more exercise than

I'd enjoy." She glanced over at me and smiled. "But if you're having fun on this team, all that hard work must be worth it."

We drove in silence the rest of the way home. Even Sam was quiet, which I thought was a miracle until I realized he was asleep. But the whole way home, and all through my shower and brushing my teeth and getting ready for bed, Mom's words kept bouncing around in my head—*hard work, worth it, fun.*

I got into bed and looked over at Mia. "Have you ever wondered if the hard work is worth it?" *Would it be worth it even if you weren't a good player? Even if people said you were a Black Hole on the court?*

But Mia couldn't answer that, of course. No one would ever, ever, *ever* say that about her.

I went to sleep still thinking about that stuff. I woke up thinking about it, too. And I kept right on thinking about it all through that week.

I wanted to talk to Adria about it, because that's what we always did—talked to each other about things that bothered us.

But I couldn't.

She'd already told me I wasn't working hard enough. Plus she was having all that fun doing extra work with Kate. How could I ask her if she thought the work was worth it? She'd laugh at me again.

Talking to Sam about it was out. I mean, we might be almost-having-fun together after school, but who would ask a third grader for advice?

And Mom? Talk to her about the trouble I was having on the Action? After *begging* her to let me play on this team? After making the Ultimate Sacrifice so we could afford it? Yeah, right.

I had other friends, but they weren't the kind of close friends I'd talk to about important stuff. And the other girls on the team—I didn't know them very well, yet. Plus what if they all thought I was a Black Hole?

So who, then? Booker?

He'd kept his back to me in our science class all week.

But on Friday, I decided I couldn't stand having him mad at me anymore, so right before the bell rang for lunch, I leaned toward him and said, "I'm sorry I got so upset and yelled at you."

He was already shoving books into his backpack, but he stopped and turned toward me. "Thanks. I thought you were still mad at me."

"Mad at you?"

"Yeah. Usually when somebody yells at you, you figure they're mad at you."

"But I wasn't mad at you. I was, um..." I twisted the hem of my T-shirt around my finger.

"You were mad, and I happened to be there," Booker said.

"Yeah." I looked up at him. "I was mad, and you happened to be there. That makes it even worse that I yelled at you, doesn't it?"

Booker pushed his hair back from his face. "It happens to everybody sometimes, I guess."

I picked up his science textbook and handed it to him. "I'm sorry I was such a jerk."

Booker nodded. "Thanks."

The bell rang and I thought maybe Booker would walk to the cafeteria with me and maybe I could talk with him some more, but as soon as we got out of the classroom, he headed toward a big group of guys. There was no way I was going to follow him over there.

But at least Booker and I had made up. Or sort of made up. I wasn't sure if he still wanted to be my friend, but at least he didn't seem to hate me.

That was a good thing.

The other good thing was that, since Sam was so excited about seeing the Action play, Mom was planning to take me to the tournament that weekend.

Which meant I didn't have to make up more lies about why I couldn't go with Adria and Mr. Lawson.

Are We Having Fun Yet?

The tournament that weekend was called a one-day run. Only two games, both of them on Saturday. The gym wasn't as big as Maryland Hoop Heaven or the Baltimore sports center—only six courts with six games going on at the same time. But there were still plenty of players and coaches and parents and little kids filling the bleachers and the sidelines. Plenty of noise, too. Whistles screeching, parents cheering, balls booming off the floor. And even though the air didn't smell like hamburger grease, it was still hot and thick and sweaty.

Mom took hold of Sam's hand as soon as we stepped inside. "Oh wow," she said. "I'm beginning to understand what you meant about this league being different from county league."

"This gym's small compared with the last two," I said.

"Wow," Mom said again, but Sam pointed in five different directions, talking nonstop about how tall this girl was or that girl was and could he have some popcorn and—LOOK!—there was a team with chartreuse uniforms, and on and on.

We found my team and climbed up the bleachers. Autumn pulled out ten new pairs of shoelaces. Each pair had one orange lace and one blue lace. We shouted "Thank you!" to Mrs. Milbourne, who sat down on the bottom bleacher bench instead of climbing the stairs in her lime-green heels, and started relacing our shoes. Except for JJ, of course, because her old white laces were "lucky." Linnae pulled a mouth guard out of her gym bag and said, "Do you believe my mom's making me wear this? She saw a girl get popped in the mouth last week, so now she thinks I'm going to lose a tooth and die." And Jasmine said, "Ohmygod, don't let my mom see that. She'll make me wear one, too."

Adria came in with both of her parents, and Mrs. Lawson ran up the bleacher steps to hug me.

"I don't know what I think about this new team taking up all your time," she said. "I truly haven't seen you in forever."

I laughed. "Well, maybe not for a month."

"Seems like forever." She gave my braid a little tug and sat down next to my mom.

Adria sat down next to me, then Kate and her dad came in, and Kate climbed up the bleacher steps to sit with us. She opened her gym bag and pulled out a pair of shoes that looked exactly like Adria's.

"You got them!" Adria grabbed one of Kate's shoes and held it up.

"What?" Taj grabbed the other shoe. "More ice-cream sprinkle shoes? Okay, I am going to work on my dad about a pair of these shoes. They are *so pretty.*"

"You should get some, too, Nikki," Adria said. "We can all match."

"That brand never fits me," I said. Which saved me from saying there was no way I could ask Mom for a new pair of basketball shoes.

Then Coach stood up and said, "Game time, ladies," which saved me from needing to say anything else.

We clomped down to the floor, then ran through our warm-ups, and halfway through our Frankenstein walks Kate threw up in a trash can. Nobody else seemed to notice, but I ran over to see if she was okay.

"Is that college scout guy here again?" I asked.

Kate shook her head. "No." She took a long drink of water. "Just regular nervousness, I guess. I'm okay now."

I glanced at her dad. He was setting up a video camera a few feet from the sideline.

The horn on the game clock blew, so it was time for us to get on the court to run our shooting drills. Then the horn blew again, and it was time to start the game. We grouped around Coach and he named the starters—Kate, Jasmine, Autumn, Kim-Ly, me. Me? The other starters ran onto the court, but I stood rooted to the floor.

"Nikki?" Coach said. "You going to play today or what?"

"Sorry." I ran onto the court.

The ref blew her whistle and the game started, and I guess Coach must have listened to Mr. Nyquist and Mr. Lawson about signing us up to play tougher competition, because even though the other team didn't have anyone as tall as Kate or Taj, they had something else.

Half of them were as fast as Kim-Ly.

The other half were faster.

We spent the whole game scrambling to keep up, while the girls on the other team ran our legs off. If we could get the ball to Kate or Taj when they were close to the basket, they scored pretty easily. But it was hard to get a clean pass in to them, because the girls on the other team were so fast they could guard us really close. And if they intercepted a pass or got a rebound and sprinted toward their basket, it didn't matter how many times Coach or Kate's dad or JJ's mom yelled, "STOP THE BALL," the only one of us who had a prayer of catching them was Kim-Ly, and she spent so much time racing up and down the court she was sucking wind before we were five minutes into the game.

That didn't seem to matter to Sam. His high-pitched, little-kid voice kept calling, "Nikki, run faster," which made a bunch of people on the sidelines laugh but didn't help me one bit, because, duh, if I *could* run faster, I would.

But, double-duh, I couldn't.

Plus I was still trying not to be a Black Hole, not get in anyone's way or take a dumb shot when someone else might have a better one, and still over on the left side of the floor on offense—not up at the top of the key with the ball in my hands—feeling weird and out of place and useless. So I kept passing the ball as soon as it came to me, not looking to score, not even when Coach hollered, "Nikki, drive the baseline!" when I had an open lane to the hoop.

The score stayed close, mostly because Kate and Taj could shoot over their defenders. Coach subbed us in and out a lot, trying to keep fresh legs in the game, but midway through the second half, my legs turned to Jell-O, and no matter how hard I told myself to hustle and keep pushing, my legs flat-out refused. All the other Action girls must have had Jell-O legs by that time, too, because they were all dragging their feet. Even Kim-Ly walked the ball up the court instead of sprinting like she usually did, and JJ stopped bashing into people.

With a few minutes to go, we were completely gassed, and

the other team pulled away. They ended up winning by eight points.

When the horn finally blew to end the game, we slapped hands with the other team, then collapsed onto the bleachers around Coach.

"Well, other than getting run into the ground, you did okay," Coach said. "Played tough defense. Hit the boards hard for rebounds. Kept looking for the open man on offense." He looked around at us. "So, what did we learn from this game?"

"Don't play teams full of superfast guards," Kate said, and everybody laughed, including Coach.

"Yeah, that's one approach," he said. "What else?"

"We need to be in better shape," Adria said.

Coach nodded. "You ready to run more sprints in practice next week?"

We all groaned, but we all nodded, too.

"All right, then. 'Action' on three," Coach said. "One, two, three."

"ACTION!"

Everybody headed out for lunch.

I took off my shoes and changed my socks and stepped into my slide sandals.

"You want to come to lunch with us?" Adria said. "Kate and her dad are coming. We're going to a deli down the street that Mom likes."

I shook my head. "We packed our lunch."

"Okay. I'll see you later, then." She followed Kate out of the gym.

Mom and Sam and I went outside to eat lunch at a picnic table with Kim-Ly's family and Taj's family. It was nice to be outside, away from the noise and heat and smells inside the gym. And it was fun to be with Kim-Ly and Taj. Like Adria and me, they'd been friends since kindergarten, so they had all kinds of goofy jokes and stories they told about each other. But I couldn't help thinking about Adria and Kate and what they might be talking and laughing about.

After lunch we gathered back together in the bleachers, the parents in one big group and us girls next to them. I sat next to Autumn, who held up bottles of orange and blue nail polish and offered to paint everyone's nails. Maura and Linnae jumped up, shouting, "Me first!" and hurdled the bleacher benches, racing toward Autumn, throwing their hips into each other, laughing and shrieking, until Maura slammed her shin into a bench and let out a howl, and Coach said, "Ladies, let's don't have a broken leg up here in the bleachers. Save the competition for the court."

Kim-Ly pulled a pack of playing cards from her gym bag, and she and Taj played a game called Spit that involved a lot of slapping the cards down on the bench between them, and Maura hollered, "Dude, you guys, quit bouncing the bench around! You're messing up my nail job!" Jasmine lay down on a bench with her head on her gym bag and big headphones clamped over her ears, and said, "Ohmygod, I am *so* tired. Wake me up at game time, you guys, okay?" And JJ stood on the floor, dribbling the ball back and forth between her legs, watching the nail painting.

Adria and Kate came back in with their parents. They wanted their nails done, too, but Autumn said the polish wouldn't have time to dry before our next game.

"Hmph," Adria said, digging her shoes out of her gym bag, and Taj said, "Oh man, I love those shoes!"

And then there was Coach, standing up, saying, "Let's go, ladies."

We ran our warm-up—during which Kate threw up into a trash can. Then the horn on the game clock sounded, so we ran onto the floor to do our shooting drills. But before we got halfway through, shouting erupted from the scorer's table.

We all turned to look.

It was hard to understand what was going on at first. Both referees, Coach Duval, and the other team's coach stood together, and it seemed like the other team's coach was mad about something, waving his arms around and pointing at our team. We finally figured out that he didn't believe Kate or Taj were eighth graders. He wanted to see their birth certificates.

Coach Duval pulled a binder out of his ball bag and leafed through it to the copies of the birth certificates we all had to give him when he registered our team with the league. He took out two of them, and right about then the game clock blared, signaling it was time to start the game.

The refs glanced at the birth certificates for about ten milliseconds, handed them back to Coach Duval, and headed onto the court, ready to start. But the other team's coach grabbed the papers, put on a pair of glasses, and studied them, trying to figure out if they were fakes, I guess.

All this time Kate's dad and JJ's mom were shouting stuff like, "Start the game!" "They're all the right age!" "Forfeit if you're afraid to play our girls!"

Until finally Mr. Nyquist yelled, "For crying out loud! Why would I want my daughter to play down? She should be playing against high school girls instead of wasting her time against a kindergarten team!"

That sent the other team's coach charging toward Mr. Nyquist, at which point Mr. Nyquist—all six-and-a-half feet of him—stood up out of his folding chair to tower over the other team's coach. The refs sprinted across the court to get between them, their hands pressed against each man's chest, pushing them apart, and Jasmine's dad jumped over a chair to take hold of Mr. Nyquist's arm and walk him away.

And then we all just stood there, staring at each other—everybody except Kate. She sat on our bench with her eyes squeezed shut and her hands over her ears.

I looked at Mom. She stood next to Adria's mom, her eyes wide, her arms wrapped tight around Sam, like she was ready to grab him up and run in case a riot broke out.

The refs called both coaches to the middle of the floor and talked to them, and after that, Coach gathered all us girls together and herded us over to our parents. "I know tempers can get short sometimes," Coach said, "but we need to all calm down. Any more outbursts, the refs won't bother with technical fouls. They'll throw us out of the gym. And we don't want to be that team that gets thrown out of gyms, right?"

Mr. Nyquist started to say something, but Coach held up his hand, frowned one of his scary-looking frowns, and said, "How about we just let the girls play?"

So what all that meant was that by the time we finally started the game, we were so far behind schedule the refs made us play with a running clock—not stopping the clock for fouls or free throws or the ball going out of bounds. And as it turned out, that was a good thing, because not only was the other team not tall and not fast, their coach hadn't taught them how to stay low and get their hands up on defense or to do much of anything on offense except dribble the ball around and try to drive into the lane, which was impossible because Kate or Taj or Adria or Jasmine was always between them and the basket.

At halftime we were ahead twenty-eight to three. Which meant nobody wanted this game to go on any longer than it had to.

During halftime Coach drew up a couple of new plays on his clipboard and told us we had to run through them five times before anyone took a shot, and then, about half-way through the second half, he took out all our bigs and kept them on the bench for the rest of the game, and even with all that, we won forty-four to ten.

But none of those forty-four points came from me, even though Kate called out a couple of times, "Nikki, take that shot!" and Adria yelled, "Shoot, Nikki!" I was still completely focused on not making mistakes and not doing stupid stuff and not getting in somebody else's way.

After the game, we all lined up and slapped hands with the other team and said, "Good game," like usual, but you could tell that those girls just wanted to get out of the gym as fast as they could.

We followed Coach to the bleachers and grouped around him. "Wow, not much of a game," he said. "I don't know how that team got into our bracket. Somebody's mistake."

He set his ball bag on a bleacher bench and turned so he was kind of including the parents in our team meeting.

"Okay, listen up. We're heading into the big tournaments now. The tournaments that count toward who gets to play in the national championships. No more easy wins. Some of the games are going to get tense. Some are going to be more physical than you girls are used to. And we're all going to get wound up tight sometimes, me included. So we need to take care of each other, right? Because, like I said before, we don't ever want to be the team that gets kicked out of a gym."

He looked around at all of us and turned to look at the parents. "Right?"

We all nodded and the parents nodded, too, then Coach turned back to us.

"We've got two weeks before the next tournament," he said. "Two weeks to get ready to play some of the best teams in our region and show them what we've got. You ready for that?"

We all nodded harder.

"All right. 'Action' on three," he said. "One, two, three."

"ACTION!"

A couple of parents clapped and a couple others came over to talk to Coach, and everybody gathered up their stuff and headed out. Mom and Sam went to get the car.

I pulled off my shoes, dropped them into my gym bag, and put on my slide sandals to walk outside. When I got up, Coach was still standing at the bottom of the bleachers.

"Nikki," he said when I got down to the floor, "are you having fun?"

"What?"

"Are you having fun playing on this team?"

"Um..."

We walked a few steps, Coach obviously shortening his stride to stay beside me.

"Let me put it a different way," he said. "Why aren't you shooting?"

Oh boy. What should I say? *Because I'm a Black Hole on the Basketball Court and I don't want to get in the way of girls who actually belong in this league?* "Um, well, I guess I haven't been open."

"You've been open," Coach said, "and in your range."

That kind of hung there between us for a minute while we walked toward the gym doors.

"Seems like something's spooked you, Nikki. What are you afraid of?"

"I'm, um...I'm afraid of doing stupid stuff and taking bad shots and making us lose, like I did in the first game." The words tumbled out in a rush before I could stop them. "In county league I could drive to the hoop or shoot from the lane, but I can't do that now, because the girls on these teams are so much bigger and faster. Well, except for this last team."

"So why didn't you shoot in that game?"

"I . . . I don't know." I looked up at him. "But also, I've never been a shooting guard before. I've always been a point guard. It's always been my job to get the ball to the open player."

Coach stopped short. "Really?"

I nodded.

"Hunh." He boosted his ball bag up on his shoulder. "You came in early to the second tryout and stood there form-shooting all by yourself, nobody making you do it. I figured, here's a pure shooter."

"I wanted to be as good as I could be at the tryout."

Coach smiled. "You were good, Lefty. You competed real hard."

We started walking again and pushed through the big gym doors, the sharp afternoon sun making me squint.

Mom swung our car into the traffic circle in front of the gym, tooted the horn, and waved.

Coach waved back, then put his hand on my shoulder. "Here's the deal, Nikki. I see you working hard on defense. And defense is important—don't get me wrong. But if you don't attack just as hard on offense, the other teams'll figure out real quick that they don't need to guard you and they'll go double-team Kate or whoever has a hot hand. Then we're playing four on five. Can't win like that. And these big tournaments we're heading into, we get into the second day, it's win or go home."

I rubbed my hands up and down the sides of my shorts but didn't say anything.

"You understand what I'm saying?" Coach said. "If you won't compete, you're letting your teammates down, and I can't put you on the floor. You'll be spending all your time on the bench next to me. That what you want?"

I tried to swallow the lump in my throat. "No."

"All right, then." Coach shifted his bag to his other shoulder, opened a side zipper, and pulled out a pair of sunglasses. "Club ball is a big step up from county league. Can't play the same way you always played. Seems like you've figured that out. So now you need to take the next step. You remember at the first practice I talked about John Wooden? Remember who he was?"

I nodded. "The UCLA coach."

"Right. So I want you to listen hard to what he said. 'Do not let what you cannot do interfere with what you can do.'"

I stared up at him. "I don't know what that means."

"Think about it." Coach waved at Mom again. "'Do not let what you cannot do interfere with what you can do.'" He patted my shoulder and put on his sunglasses. "See you Tuesday."

I stood there, watching him walk away, until Mom tooted the horn again.

"What was your coach talking to you about?" she said when I got in the car.

I turned in my seat and tossed my gym bag into the back next to Sam. "Just stuff."

Mom pulled out of the parking lot. "Nikki," she said, glancing at me, "are you enjoying this team?"

And Sam said, "How come you didn't score any baskets?"

And for once, I was glad Kate's dad was one of the parents watching our game, because instead of answering Mom and Sam, which I really, really, *really* didn't want to do, I said, "Wow, Mr. Nyquist sure got mad about the other coach wanting to see those birth certificates."

"That man is unhinged," Mom said. "Does he always act like that?"

And Sam said, "Whose dad is he?"

So we talked about Mr. Nyquist and Kate and basketball scholarships and stuff like that all the way home, and I didn't have to say anything about Coach benching me if I didn't start playing better.

That didn't stop me from thinking about it, though.

18

Mia Takes On LeBron

On Sunday morning I woke up to the smell of pancakes, which is the most wonderful smell in the entire world to wake up to, and it would have made the morning perfect if I hadn't also woken up with the same thought I'd gone to bed with the night before: *What if Coach benches me?*

"Oh good, you're up," Mom said when I padded into the kitchen. She got up from the kitchen table, where she'd been reading—big surprise—and turned on the stove. "Sam has a soccer game this morning, so we need to leave soon. I was thinking I might have to put the pancake batter in the refrigerator and let you make your own pancakes when you got up."

"I can make them if you need to get ready."

"I have a little time yet," Mom said.

I got a glass of juice and stood next to her while she poured pancake batter into the pan. I loved seeing the little bubbles pop on the surface of the batter, so I kept standing there, watching. But I wasn't really thinking about pancakes. I was thinking about my talk with Coach.

"Mom," I said, "you know when I got in the car after the games yesterday you asked if I was enjoying playing on the Action?"

"Mm-hmm." Mom slid a spatula under the pancakes and flipped them.

"Why'd you ask that?"

She turned but didn't say anything for a minute, just looked at me with her worry lines creasing her forehead. Finally she said, "Nikki, I've always loved watching you play basketball, because you look so happy when you're playing." She rubbed at her worry lines. "No, not just happy. Joyous. You've always looked like basketball filled you with joy. But that's not the girl I saw on the court yesterday." She reached over and tucked a stray piece of hair behind my ear. "Yesterday I saw a girl who didn't look happy at all."

I bit down on my bottom lip and willed myself not to tear up.

"Is your coach mean to you girls?" Mom asked. "Does he yell at you when the parents aren't around?"

I shook my head. "No. He pushes us to play better and he tells us if we're doing something wrong, but he doesn't yell at us."

"The girls, then? Is someone bullying you?"

"No. Well, JJ's kind of mean, but it's just because she plays rough. And she's rough to everybody, not just to me."

Mom picked up her big coffee cup—the one Sam and I gave her that had ASK A LIBRARIAN—SHE'LL FIND THE ANSWER printed on the side—and poured more coffee into it. "What about you and Adria? I noticed her spending a lot of time with that tall girl. Did you two have a falling-out?"

I stared at the floor and didn't say anything.

"I think that answers my question."

I sighed. "It's not really a falling-out. It's just, well, Adria and Kate are going to an extra training class together and hanging out at Adria's after school sometimes, and I can't go over to Adria's, because, you know, I have to take care of Sam." I poked my finger at a pancake. "And Adria said some things that made me mad. I don't know. It sounds kind of dumb when I talk about it like this."

"No, it sounds like you're missing your friend." Mom patted my arm, then slid the pancakes onto a plate and handed it to me. "But you and Adria have been friends for so long, I'm sure you'll work it out."

I sat down to eat, hoping she was right.

"In any case," Mom said, "though I'm sorry you and Adria are having trouble, I'm glad it's not the team that's bothering you. You're working so hard in practice. You're sacrificing all your free time." She poured more batter into the pan. "I'd hate to think you weren't happy on this team."

Oh boy.

I bent over my pancakes so Mom couldn't see my face, because I knew I couldn't hide how totally *un*happy I was about the Action. I pulled her book toward me, looking for a way to change the subject. The book was called *Oranges*. "What's this book about?" I held it up.

"Oranges," Mom said.

"You're reading a whole book about nothing but oranges?"

"It's fascinating." Mom flipped the pancakes. "Did you know that oranges growing on the south side of a tree are sweeter than the oranges on the north side?"

"Umm, no, Mom. I didn't know that."

"I'm assuming that's only true in the northern hemisphere, though, where the south side of a tree gets more direct sunlight. I expect it's the opposite in the southern hemisphere."

"I've always thought so," I said.

Mom looked at me and we both cracked up.

"I'm sorry for you that you don't find oranges interesting," Mom said, still laughing.

Thunder exploded in the upstairs hallway, and Sam—in full soccer gear, cleats and all—vaulted down the stairs and crashed onto the kitchen floor, his feet shooting out from under him.

"Sam!" Mom ran toward him. "You don't wear cleats in the house! Are you hurt?"

"No."

"Did you dent the floor?"

Sam lifted his feet and looked at the floor. "I don't think so." He started to get up, but his cleats slipped against the floor again.

"Take those off!" Mom glared at him.

"Nikki, you wanna come to my soccer game?" Sam hollered, untying his cleats. "It's my first one."

"I'm sorry, Sam, I can't go today. I have to do homework. But, hey." I held out my fist, and he ran over to give me a fist-bump. "Play hard and have fun, okay?"

"Okay!"

Mom scooted back to the stove. "I'm going to finish cooking these last couple of pancakes, Nikki, then we need to go. I'm sorry to leave you such a messy kitchen."

I'd just stuffed a big bite in my mouth, so I half mumbled, "That's okay," and waved my fork at her. "Thank you for making them."

After Mom and Sam left, I cleaned up the kitchen,

then went up to my bedroom. I didn't start my homework, though. What I did was sit on my bed and think about being benched.

What was I going to do?

I'd busted my butt to make this team. And as Mom said, I was continuing to bust my butt in every Roadkill practice. I was giving up all my afternoons to take care of Sam. I was turning in messy science projects that I wasn't proud of, not studying enough for tests, skimping on other homework, too.

So here was the question: Was I having so much fun on the Action that it made all that stuff worth it?

I would have laughed, if I didn't feel like crying.

I slumped back against the wall. Was I having *any* fun?

Well, yeah, I loved hanging out with the team. I liked all the girls. Well, I wouldn't say I truly *liked* JJ, but now that she was bashing into girls on other teams, she didn't bash into me as much, so I was at least getting along with her.

And traveling to all those huge gyms was fun. Even practice was kind of fun, or at least funny sometimes, because it was so hard that a lot of the girls cracked jokes about it.

It was the basketball that wasn't fun.

The playing. And it was *playing* basketball that I'd always loved most. Being out on the floor with my teammates, zinging the ball around, flowing across the court like we were connected.

But I didn't feel like that playing on the Action. On the Action, I was a Black Hole and it was no fun at all.

I lay over on my side, grabbed my pillow, and hugged it.

What was I going to do? Working so hard and giving up my free time, and now maybe Coach was going to bench me? And it wasn't like I was all of a sudden going to grow a bunch and get super tall—I knew that from my stupid genetics project.

Maybe . . . maybe I should just quit.

Maybe I should give up on basketball.

Maybe I should do what that recruiter guy said and go play softball.

My chest ached—ached the way it had when I'd thought about what it would feel like if Mom were in prison or if my paper dad didn't want to know me.

I looked over at Mia. There was no point asking her what she'd do if she were in my place. No coach would ever say to her, *I can't put you on the floor if you won't compete.* And there was no way she'd ever, even once, thought about quitting because she was playing like a Black Hole.

"But what if you were?" I said to Mia. "What if you were in a new league where everyone was bigger and faster than you?"

But how could Mia answer that? She'd always been the best. The best player in the entire country when she was in high school. The best player in the country when she was in college. And now she was one of the absolute best players in the WNBA, which meant she was one of the absolute best players in the world.

There wasn't any league anywhere that Mia McCall could play in where she'd be going up against a bunch of players who were better than her.

Well, unless she played in the NBA.

"What would you do then?" I asked her. "What would you do if you were in the NBA, playing against men who were bigger and faster and stronger than you?

I stared up at Mia, really looked at her, at the concentration on her face, at the total effort that showed in every one of her straining muscles, at her complete focus on lifting the ball toward the basket and putting it through the hoop.

Then I tried to picture LeBron James standing between her and the basket with his arms up, ready to stuff her beautiful shot.

"What would you do then?" I asked her. "What..."

And then I knew.

Just as surely as I knew Mia was having fun leaping toward the basket, I knew that if she were playing against LeBron James and couldn't drive past him to the hoop, she'd have that same concentration on her face and that same effort in every muscle and...she'd shoot from outside. She'd shoot way before LeBron got anywhere near her.

She'd shoot from the three-point line.

And then I heard Coach, inside my head, say, *Do not let what you cannot do interfere with what you can do,* and I realized Mia knew exactly what that meant.

It meant that if LeBron were standing between her and the basket, she wouldn't let him shut her down. She'd figure out a different way to compete.

And then I heard another voice, that college scout's voice: *You've got a pretty shot, too. Just need to stay out of the trees.* And I finally got it—the trees, duh, the tall players. He meant I needed to shoot from outside.

And what did Coach say the day before? Not about benching me. The other thing—*Here's a pure shooter.* Was that why he didn't put me at point guard? Because he thought I was a good shooter?

Yeah, but still, an outside shooter? "I've never been an outside shooter," I said to Mia.

And then it almost seemed like Mia really did answer me, because I heard one more voice inside my head. Booker's voice: *Yeah, so? Learn how.*

I sat up.

How? How could I learn to be an outside shooter without

someone to teach me? Without some kind of special training program or a dad who played in college?

But then I thought of something else. Something I'd read in an article about Mia. Her dad did play basketball in college and even in the NBA, but he wasn't in her life when she was growing up. He wasn't there to teach her how to do a reverse layup or shoot a three. And even though her mom was athletic, she didn't play basketball in college. She played volleyball.

Obviously Mia had sports genes. She had great sports genes. But she didn't grow up with a dad who could help her... just like me.

I jumped up and ran downstairs to Mom's office, yanked open the file drawer where she kept my paper dad, and pulled out the file marked *Nikki, Donor.* I flipped through the pages until I found what I was looking for. My dad had been on the track team at the University of Virginia.

My Dad Ran Track in College.

He ran at UVA. Which meant he must have been a good runner. Maybe not good enough to be in the Olympics or anything, but still, really good.

So even though Mom might be totally, completely clueless about *everything* having *anything* to do with sports, my paper dad was an athlete. An athlete who was good enough to *Run in College.*

And I got half my genes from him.

And that meant that even though I didn't have a father who could show me how to do a reverse layup or shoot a three-pointer or take me to special training classes or ask college scouts to watch me play, I still had a dad—even if he was just a paper dad—who gave me something else.

I had a dad who gave me his sports genes.

Field Goal Kicker

Ten minutes later, I stood out in our driveway, trying to figure out where the three-point line would be if I were standing on a real basketball court. But wherever I stood, thinking maybe this was the three-point line, or maybe that was it, the basket looked way, way, *way* far away.

Finally I decided that wherever the three-point line might be, there wasn't any point trying to shoot from there until I warmed up, so I stood right in front of the hoop and did my regular routine.

When I finished that, I shot a few layups, then I went over to my favorite shooting spot, ten feet back from the basket, just left of center. And I stood there, bouncing my ball, thinking.

How was I going to do this? How was I going to get from here, shooting close to the hoop, to way back there behind me somewhere?

I took a step back from the basket, then another, and then I thought maybe that's what I should do—start shooting from my favorite spot, then step back and shoot from there, then keep stepping back and see how far I could get before I couldn't make a basket.

I sure wished Mia were here to help me out and tell me if that was a good idea. Or Coach. Or (duh) Adria's dad.

I started texting Adria—but stopped. Did I really want to tell her I was trying to learn to shoot from the three-point line? What if I couldn't do it? Would she laugh at me again? But I could really use some help. . . .

Wait, what did Booker say the day I yelled at him? After he said I should learn to shoot threes? He said I could find people to help me if I wanted help. Did he mean he'd help me? He said he played basketball. Maybe he was a good shooter. Maybe he *could* help me.

I found his number on my phone—we'd shared our numbers in science one day, in case, you know, we had to text about homework or something. I tapped his number, then immediately jabbed at my phone to stop the call—*Oh god, what was I doing? This was so stupid*—too late. Booker had already picked up.

"Hey, Nikki," he said. "What's up?"

I stood there frozen.

"Nikki?"

"Um," I said. "Hi."

Silence.

Then Booker said, "Nikki, did you call me for a reason or just to, like, breathe into the phone or something?"

"Oh, um, yeah, I was thinking...uh..."

"Yeah?"

I took a deep breath, then said as fast as I could, "I was thinking about trying to learn to kick field goals and I was wondering if maybe, um, you might want to come over and maybe help me?"

Booker laughed.

"Oh, right, yeah, it's a dumb idea. Sorry."

"No!" Booker said. "It's not dumb. I'm laughing about kicking field goals."

"Oh."

"So no more black holes, huh?"

I think I finally exhaled. "I don't know. I might still be a black hole, but maybe I can be one that kicks field goals."

"Okay," Booker said.

"Okay?"

"I'll help. Or I'll try to help, anyway."

"Really?"

"Yeah. I have to mow the lawn. Then I'll be over."

"Okay, um, thanks."

"Sure."

We hung up.

Oh.

My.

God.

What had I just done?

Apart from the fact that I wasn't allowed to have friends over when Mom wasn't home, and apart from the fact that I had no idea how to shoot a three-pointer and was going to look like an idiot, I had just called the boy who told me my eyes were special, and now he was going to think I liked him, which I didn't. I mean, I did, but *Ohhhhhhh*, why did I call him?

I threw my ball at the basket. It whammoed off the backboard, banged against the front of the rim, and fell through the net.

That made me laugh. If I could make a basket by hurling the ball at the hoop, maybe I could figure out how to shoot threes.

"Okay," I said to myself. "Don't think about Booker. Get to work." I looked up at my bedroom window. "Help me out, Mia, okay?"

I picked up my ball, stood at my favorite spot, bounced

the ball in front of me, caught it, squared my shoulders, and shot. *Swish.*

I grabbed my ball again, went back to my favorite spot and took a step back. Then I repeated what I'd done—bounced the ball, caught it, squared up, shot. The ball tapped the backboard and dropped through the hoop. I ran over to catch it, went to my favorite spot, and took two steps back. Then same routine—bounce, catch, square up, shoot. The ball hit the backboard, rattled on the rim, and bounced out. I grabbed it, went to the same spot, and did it again. Same result. I did it again. *Swish.* I corralled the ball, went back to my favorite spot, took three steps back and shot. The ball hit the back of the rim, bounced up, and came down through the net. I ran to get it, then took four steps back from my favorite spot and stopped.

I was pretty far from the hoop now, farther than I'd ever take a shot in a game. Or even in practice, if JJ wasn't about to run me over. I bounced the ball, caught it, squared up, and shot. The ball flew from my hand, sailing in a long, high arc, hit the back of the rim, bounced against the front of the rim, then bounced out.

I'd missed.

But I hadn't missed by much. My ball had hit the *back* of the rim. I collected my ball, went to the spot I'd just shot

from, took another step back, and shot again. Same result—
I missed. But not by much. And not because I couldn't shoot
that far.

Could I actually do this? Could I learn to be an outside
shooter?

I looked around at my asphalt "court." Where *was* the
three-point line, anyway? How far was it from the basket?

I ran into the house, plopped down in front of the computer
in Mom's office, and typed in, *How far is the three-point line?*

And what came up was—it depends.

Well, the screen didn't actually say, *It depends.* It said
for high school basketball the three-point line is 19 feet, 9
inches from the center of the basket; for college it's 20 feet,
9 inches; for the WNBA it's 22 feet, 1.75 inches; and for the
NBA it's 23 feet, 9 inches.

Great. So which one should I use? Obviously I wasn't in
the NBA or the WNBA or college, but I wasn't in high school,
either.

So then I looked at the court diagrams, and that made
it clear, because I could see right away that on a high school
court, the three-point line touches the small arc above the
free throw line, just like on the courts we played on.

I dug through the junk drawer in the kitchen, looking
for a tape measure, while our poor old printer chugged away.

Then I grabbed the diagram and ran back outside. I searched the shelves in the garage, moving gross, spiderwebby flowerpots and bags of plant food, until I found what I needed—Sam's bucket of sidewalk chalk.

I carried all my stuff over to the hoop, and that's when Booker rode up the driveway. He leaned his bike against a tree and shook his hair back from his face, sending a spray of tiny green flakes sparkling into the sunlight.

"You're shedding grass," I said.

"What? Oh, yeah, that always happens." He ran a hand through his hair, tossing more grass clippings into the air.

I rotated my ball around my waist. "You don't have to do this, you know. I mean, do you really want to help?"

"Sure."

"You don't think it's dumb?"

"No. Besides, you got me out of weed-whacking. I told my dad I needed to help a friend with a project. Dad thought that was 'super.'" Booker grinned and made little air quotes with his fingers. "My folks are worried about me making friends."

"Why?"

Booker shrugged. "I guess because I've only ever lived in one little town. They're afraid I won't 'fit in.'" Air quotes again.

"Were you worried about that?"

"Kind of. Not anymore. I like it here. Kids are cool. School's way better. A lot harder, but that's okay." He picked up the court diagram. "So what's the plan?"

"I want to mark the three-point line on the driveway. I need to figure out where the center of the basket is, then measure nineteen feet, nine inches from there."

"How accurate does it need to be?"

"As accurate as I can make it, I guess."

Booker looked up at the basket. "You know how to make a plumb line?"

I shook my head.

"Well, what you do is put two straight sticks across the top of the rim, then tie a piece of string where the sticks cross, and tie a weight to the other end of the string. It'll hang straight down and show you where the center of the basket is."

"How do you know that?"

"My dad's redoing the cabinets in our kitchen. I've been helping him." He shook more grass out of his hair. "You have a ladder?"

I nodded. "In the corner of the garage."

He went to get the ladder, and I ran inside to get scissors and a ball of twine. Then I ran back out to the garage shelves and reached behind the spiderwebby flowerpots for two bamboo plant stakes.

Booker was already up on the ladder.

I handed the plant stakes up to him and he set them on the basket rim. Then I tossed the string up, and he tied the end around the cross point of the sticks and dropped the string down through the net. I cut it off where it touched the driveway and tied that end around a piece of sidewalk chalk. When I let go, the string swung back and forth and back and forth until it finally stopped, and I used another piece of chalk to mark a big X on the asphalt right beneath the string.

"Too bad Mr. Bukowski isn't here," I said. "He'd be so impressed."

Booker climbed down. "Do you want to draw the whole three-point line? Or just mark a few spots?"

"Well..." I looked around at the driveway. "Maybe I should start with just a few spots."

Booker pulled out the end of the tape measure and held it down in the middle of the X, and I walked the tape measure away from the basket, right past my favorite spot, and out to nineteen feet, nine inches. I drew a thick chalk line on the driveway, then walked around in an arc, marking more spots.

I stepped behind my last chalk mark, turned, and looked at the hoop. "Whoa, the basket looks a long way off from here."

Booker stood up and walked the tape measure toward

me, letting it spool itself back into the case. "It won't look so far once you get used to it. It'll be just like that one-handed shooting you do right in front of the hoop." The end of the tape measure snapped in, and Booker turned to look back at the basket. "Or maybe not."

We both cracked up.

"Hey," Booker said. "If it was easy to shoot three-pointers, everybody would do it. Do you have a plan?"

"A plan?"

"How you're going to learn to do it."

"Not exactly." I told Booker what I'd done before—starting close to the hoop, then taking a step back after I made a basket at each spot.

"That sounds as good as anything," Booker said. "And probably better than standing out here, jacking up shots until one finally goes in."

We gathered up all the stuff we'd been using to measure, and just as Booker climbed back up the ladder to grab the plant stakes, Mom's car turned into the driveway.

Sam's head appeared out the passenger-side window, hollering, "Booker!"

"You better climb down," I said. "Sam's going to launch out of the car."

Before the car came to a full stop in the garage, Sam's door burst open. He yelled, "Nikki! Booker! I scored a goal!"

and zoomed out, his cleats clattering across the asphalt as he ran. Fortunately Booker had one foot on the ground when Sam jumped to hug him, so they didn't have far to fall.

"Sam!" Mom called, getting out of the car and hurrying after him. "Be careful."

That made me laugh. "You really think Sam will ever be careful?"

"No. But I keep hoping."

Booker stood up with Sam still clinging to one arm.

"Mom, this is my friend Booker," I said. "He's in my science class."

Mom smiled. "Hello, Booker."

"It's nice to meet you, Ms. Doyle." Booker reached out to shake Mom's hand, which was probably difficult with Sam hanging on his arm.

Mom looked up at the basketball hoop, then down the string to the X on the driveway. "It looks like you have some kind of engineering project going on."

"I needed to find the center of the basket so I could measure out where the three-point line would be," I said. "Booker knew how to make a . . . what did you call it?"

"A plumb line."

Mom smiled. "Quite ingenious." She looked back up at the hoop. "Are those my plant stakes?"

I nodded.

"Mmm. Well, please remember to put them away when you're finished. I'll need them in a few weeks when the peonies get taller."

"I will," I said.

"All right, I'll leave you to your project," Mom said. "Sam, please take off those cleats and put on your tennis shoes if you're staying out here. We don't need you slipping on the asphalt and cutting your head open."

Sam ran back to the car, hauled out his soccer bag, and sat at the edge of the garage to put on his sneakers, his mouth going the whole time. "Nikki, I scored a goal. The first one of our whole team. Then Omar scored two. He's really good. Everybody has to take a turn playing goalie, but being goalie is boring. All you get to do is stand there while everybody else gets to run around, and then—"

"Sam!" I shouted. "I'm glad you scored a goal. That's very cool, but Booker and I are doing something here. Could you get on your bike or jump on your pogo stick or something? You can tell us all about soccer in a little while, okay?"

"Okay!" Sam grabbed his pogo stick.

"Put your helmet on."

"Oh, yeah."

"And jump down there at the end of the driveway, okay? Not up here by the basketball hoop." I turned back to Booker. "I can't remember what we were doing."

Booker laughed. He climbed up the ladder and grabbed the plant stakes, pulled up the string, and tossed it all to me, then jumped down from the ladder and put it back in the garage.

I gathered up all the other stuff.

"Okay, let's go." Booker picked up my ball and tossed it to me. "I'll rebound."

"Really? You don't mind?"

He smiled his crooked half smile. "It's better than weed-whacking."

"Okay." I walked to my favorite spot, bounced my ball, squared up, shot, and—*clang.* The ball hit the front of the rim and ricocheted straight back.

"Uh, let me try that again." This time the ball went in the hoop but still skimmed the front rim, so I stayed in that spot and shot three more times before I swished one, then I stepped back.

Then I kept going like that, not stepping back until I felt like I'd made a good shot from each spot. The ball careened all over the place on my misses, but Booker kept chasing it, sprinting down the driveway to catch it before it went into the street, jumping over the hedge into our neighbor's yard, fighting through the jungle of azaleas that lined our front walkway.

Sam bounced his way back up the driveway, cheering each time I made a basket. But when I was two steps inside the three-point line, the ball absolutely refused to fall through the hoop. I took eighteen shots from that spot before I finally made one. Sam cheered, which sounded like "Yay-ay-ay," because his voice bounced right along with the pogo stick. And instead of taking one step back, I decided to take those last two steps together to stand all the way back behind my chalked three-point line.

I took a big pre-free-throw breath and blew it out slow, bounced the ball, caught it, stepped into my shot, jumped, and shot. The ball arced up away from me, a bird flying from my hand...and dropped through the net.

I whooped and Booker whooped and Sam whooped and jumped off his pogo stick. It flew up, away from him, and crashed back down, banging and clanging like a car wreck.

Mom threw open the side door and charged onto the porch, calling, "What happened? Are you all right? What happened?"

And somehow I managed to stop whooping long enough to shout, "I swished a three! I swished a three!"

Mom looked at me, her face still creased with fear, then at Sam, who was spinning in circles, then at Booker, who had grabbed the ball after it fell through the hoop and was jumping around, holding the ball over his head.

Mom's face softened. "Well," she said. "I'm glad you swished a three, whatever that might mean."

Sam fell over on the lawn, laughing and shouting, "The world is twirling!"

"Oh, honestly." Mom put her hands on her hips. "What did I do to deserve such wild children?" She smiled, shaking her head, and went back inside.

And Booker and I looked at each other, then bent over and made the sound that explodes out of you when you've been trying not to laugh: *"Ppppbbbbffffttttt!"*

Later, when Mom and Sam and I were eating supper, Mom said, "What was all that business about 'swishing a three'?"

"IT WAS AWESOME!" Sam yelled.

Mom looked at him.

"Oh yeah, inside voice." He took a bite of his mashed potatoes.

Mom turned back to me. "What was that all about?"

"Well, you know those chalk marks we made on the driveway?" I said.

Mom nodded.

"That's where the three-point line would be on a basketball court. If you can shoot from behind that line and make a basket, it counts for three points. All the baskets you make inside that line only count for two points."

Mom nodded again. "And?"

"And I need to learn to shoot from behind the three-point line."

"Why is that?"

"Because...um..." And then it all came spilling out. Everything that had been going on—well, not the Black Hole stuff, but everything else. Not playing point guard, and all the big, fast players on the other teams who made it impossible for me to make the shots I'd always been good at, and being afraid of getting in the way of players like Kate who were so much better than me, and Coach saying he'd have to bench me if I didn't start competing harder. And then I told Mom about John Wooden, the UCLA coach, and how he said you shouldn't let what you can't do stop you from doing things you *can* do, and that if I could learn to shoot from outside, the bigger, faster players couldn't stop me from playing basketball.

By the time I finished talking, Mom had long since put down her fork and stopped eating. And now she just sat there, leaning toward me a little bit, her arms folded along the edge of the table. "I'm proud of you, Nikki," she said.

"For?"

"For not giving up." She picked up her fork. "I've told you before that I don't understand your enjoyment of this kind of physical challenge but..." She reached over and patted my arm with her other hand. "Must be those sports genes."

We finished eating, and Sam and I got up to clear the table.

"Mom," I said, picking up her plate, "I know I'm not allowed to have friends over after school when you're not home, and I know I shouldn't have had Booker over today, but he really helped me with my shooting. Would it be okay if he comes over to rebound for me sometimes? It's a lot easier to work on shooting if I have a rebounder."

Mom tapped her fingers on the table. "I'll need to talk with his parents."

"I'll get their phone number."

"And you will stay in the driveway. You will not invite him into the house until I get home."

"I know."

"And the same rules apply," she said, looking square at me. "Taking care of Sam is your top priority. And as much as you may love basketball, schoolwork comes before sports."

"I know," I said again. Even though I also knew that now that I'd figured out what I needed to do, I'd have a hard time putting anything ahead of basketball.

20

Mutants

"What'd you do yesterday?" Adria asked when she sat down next to me on the school bus Monday morning.

On any other day, in all the years I'd known Adria—all the years we'd been best friends—I would have told her exactly what I'd done on Sunday. Told her all about chalking the three-point line on my driveway and Booker coming over and my swishing that three. But that's not what I said. Somehow, I wasn't ready to talk about it. Not even with Adria.

So I said, "Not much. Slept late. Ate pancakes."

"Oh, your mom's pancakes!" Adria slid down and rested her head on the seat back. "To die for."

"What about you?" I said. "What'd you do?"

She sat back up. "Homework, mostly. And I went to an extra strength-and-conditioning class with Kate, since we didn't have games. My dad wants me to train more, especially after we got run to death by that first team on Saturday."

"I think I'm still tired from that game," I said.

Adria laughed. "Me too."

And I *was* tired. Not just from that first game on Saturday, but also from all the shooting I did with Booker on Sunday. My left arm ached and my feet hurt, including a new blister on my heel. I had it covered in salve and a big, thick bandage, but it still stung. I hauled myself up and down the school stairs, feeling like roadkill again, hobbled into science, and climbed onto my lab stool, groaning.

Booker laughed. "You sore?"

"It's not funny," I said.

He laughed harder, then said, "Does that mean you're not shooting this afternoon?"

I shook my head. "I'm shooting. I've only got two weeks until the next tournament."

"Nikki and Booker!" Mr. Bukowski said.

We sat up. "Sorry."

Mr. Bukowski adjusted his glasses, and I think he tried to look stern, but it's hard to look stern when you also look like an Albert Einstein bobblehead, and besides that, he was smiling.

He nodded at us, then said, "The DNA molecule."

He held up two parallel strings of colored plastic pop beads that were connected together by more pop beads, in different colors, spaced out like the rungs of a ladder. Holding the top and the bottom, he twisted the ladder of beads in opposite directions, making it look exactly like the picture of the DNA double helix in our science books.

"DNA is the instruction set that resides in the nucleus of every cell in your body," Mr. Bukowski said. "It's what makes you, you."

He turned his little double helix back and forth, staring at it, and I wondered if he'd forgotten he had a class of kids watching him, because he looked like he was totally lost in the fabulousness of DNA. But then he said, "Today you're going to work with your lab partner to make a model of DNA."

He passed out instruction sheets and boxes of pop beads and explained how we were supposed to build our models, using the different colored beads to represent each of the different molecules that make up the big DNA molecule.

"Pay attention to the instructions," Mr. Bukowski said. "The four base molecules of DNA always pair up the same way, so make sure yours do, too. Okay, get going."

Booker and I grabbed our box of beads and started popping beads together.

"I feel like I'm in preschool," I said.

"Yeah, it's cool, though."

"You are such a science nerd."

Booker gave me a little shove on my shoulder, and even though my arm was tired and sore, his hand on my shoulder still felt kind of nice.

Mr. Bukowski walked around the room, looking at the pop-bead DNA molecules kids were making and pointing out mistakes and answering questions. He got over to our table just as Booker and I finished our ladder. I held it up and twisted it.

"Very good," Mr. Bukowski said. "All your molecules are paired up just right."

We looked at it for a minute, dangling there from my hand. Then I said, "Mr. Bukowski, each of these beads represents a single chemical, right? A single molecule?"

"That's right," he said.

"Well, so the same molecules make up everyone's DNA?"

"Yes."

"So then..."

"Yes?"

"So then, if we're all made of the same stuff, how can we all be so different?"

"Ahh, excellent question." Mr. Bukowski adjusted his glasses. "To answer that, let's think first about how we're the same." He looked back and forth from me to Booker. "What do you think?"

Booker shook his hair away from his face. "Well, we all have a head and a body. And a heart and lungs and all that."

"Right," Mr. Bukowski said. "And a brain and skin and arteries—all the organs and systems that make our bodies function. All those things are the same, right?"

Booker and I nodded.

"So what are the differences?" Mr. Bukowski asked.

"The size and shape of all the stuff," I said. "The color of your hair and skin. The shape of your face. The size of your body."

"Exactly right." Mr. Bukowski tapped his knuckles against our lab table. "It's only the details that make us different. More than ninety-nine percent of our genetic code is the same in every human. But there are three billion of these base pairs in our genome, so even if only a fraction of one percent of them differ, that's still thirty or forty million possible differences in the sequence of the bases."

"But it says in our textbook that DNA copies itself every time a cell divides." I looked back at our pop-bead model. "If it copies itself, how do the differences happen?"

"Another excellent question," Mr. Bukowski said. "This is getting into material you'll learn in high school, but there's something called spontaneous rearrangement, which means that the genes you inherit from each of your parents get mixed together. So for example, while you might look similar to each of your parents, you don't look exactly like either one. And then, of course, mutations occur. Sometimes there are mistakes when the DNA copies itself."

Booker laughed. "So we're all mutants?"

Mr. Bukowski laughed, too. "I don't think I'd put it quite that way, Booker. But, yes, that's the basic concept. As genes mutate, changes occur."

I twisted our DNA model back and forth. "That's what happened with my eyes, isn't it? The DNA copied itself the wrong way. So my eyes came out different colors."

Mr. Bukowski pushed his glasses up. "You know, Nikki, when we talk about mutations in genetics, we're not saying they're bad or wrong. In genetics, mutations simply cause variations. I don't want you to think there's something genetically wrong with your eyes. Heterochromia occurs in about one percent of people. And it's fairly common in some breeds of dogs and cats."

"It's the same kind of mutation that causes calico coloring in cats, right?" Booker said.

I stared at him.

He shrugged. "I looked it up."

Mr. Bukowski smiled. "Yes, I believe you're right, Booker.

In any case, it's the mutations that make us interesting, isn't it? It would be a pretty dull world if we were all exactly alike."

"Like clones," Booker said.

I set down our DNA model. "I guess I'd rather be a mutant than a clone."

That cracked us all up.

Booker and Sam got to our driveway at the same time that afternoon, Booker jumping off his bike and leaning it against a tree and Sam slamming up the street, hollering, "Nikki! Booker! Guess what!"

I'd already finished warming up, so we just had to listen to the third-grade news before we could get to work.

"We starting in the same place?" Booker said.

"I guess." I turned to Sam. "Do you think we can spend half an hour out here today instead of twenty minutes, then work extra hard to get our homework done when we go in?"

"Okay!" Sam yelled.

Booker and I both put our hands up to our ears.

"Oops, sorry," Sam whispered. "I'm gonna jump on my pogo stick."

"Put your helmet on!" I called after him.

I went to my favorite spot, left of the free throw lane, and Booker got ready to rebound, and then...and then it was like magic happened, like the ball really was a bird flying from my hand, arcing up away from me, slipping through the net. Over and over, as I stepped back and back.

"Awesome shooting," Booker said, firing the ball to me.

"Yeah, well, here comes the hard part." I stepped back to just inside the three-point line.

And it was definitely harder from there—I missed five shots before making one—but the shots still felt good, still felt smooth. And even when I stepped behind the line and shot ten times before I made one and took six more shots before I made another, I felt focused, locked in, almost like I was in the zone during a game. Like I could have kept going forever.

But I couldn't. Our half hour was up.

Booker grabbed the last rebound and tossed the ball to me. "Making progress."

"It felt good," I said.

"Looked good, too."

"Really?"

"Really. You've got a supernice shot, Nikki. All that one-armed shooting must be paying off."

My face was getting hot. "Thanks," I said.

"Okay, gotta go." Booker got on his bike, rode a lap around Sam and me, then headed for the street. "See you later, mutant," he called.

"You're the mutant," I yelled after him, and Sam bounced down the driveway, shouting, "Bye, Booker-er-er!"

And standing there, watching Booker pedal away, I thought, *Wow, that was fun.* I mean, being with Booker was fun, but my shooting...my shooting was *so* fun. Feeling the energy zing up from my feet all the way out through my fingertips, the ball sailing from my hand, the swish of the net. It was the most fun I'd had with a basketball in my hand since I'd started playing on the Action. And it made me hope that if I really *could* learn to shoot from outside, then maybe, *maybe*, playing on this team could be fun, too.

I was still thinking about that the next night when Mom and Sam and I got to the gym for Action practice, and still thinking about it when I stepped into line next to Kate for our warm-up.

We all headed up the court doing ankle flips, and when we turned to come back the other way, I said, "Kate, do you think basketball's fun?"

"Yeah, I love this team. Everybody's fun."

"No, I mean when you're playing. Do you think it's fun then?"

"If we're winning."

"How about the rest of the time? Practice and everything?"

"Well, I hate sprints," Kate said. "And Coach's ridiculous planks and sit-ups. I really hate them."

"Who doesn't?"

We got to the baseline, turned, and Frankenstein-walked the other way.

"I guess I never really think about whether or not basketball's fun," Kate said. "It's just, like, my job. It's what I do." She laughed. "That sounds dumb, doesn't it? That basketball's my job? But, yeah, I guess I do kind of think of it like that. It's always been so important to my dad. I guess it's always been important to me, too."

We turned again.

"But do you like *playing*?" I asked.

"Oh yeah, I love playing. I love competing in games. Unless I don't play well. Then it's no fun at all, because Dad spends the whole drive home telling me everything I did wrong. And now he's keeping a shot chart every game because he wants me to shoot farther away from the basket."

"Is that why you always throw up?"

"Yeah, I get nervous."

We got to the baseline again and headed back the other way, skipping backward.

"Does your mom ever come to games?" As soon as the words were out of my mouth, I couldn't believe I said them, because, you know, it wasn't like my paper dad ever came to games. Or anything else.

But Kate didn't seem to mind. "My mom lives in Florida with my brother right now. He goes to this big tennis academy down there. It's only for another year, though. Then he'll graduate from high school and either turn pro if he's good enough or play in college. When our Action season's over, I get to spend the rest of the summer with him and Mom."

I was about to say something about sports genes, but Coach blew his whistle, so it was time for sprints and line drills and all the rest, and even though I wanted to keep talking to Kate, it's pretty darned impossible to talk while you're gasping for breath.

We had to make twenty-five layups in a row with the heavy yellow balls that week, but somehow I wasn't thinking of them as horrible anymore, and maybe we'd already started getting stronger, because most of us made all our layups, and it only took us a few minutes to get to twenty-five in a row. We all clapped and slapped hands, and Maura did this goofy high-five-low-five-behind-the-back-five thing with Sam.

Then we worked on defensive closeouts, which meant springing forward and sprinting two or three steps, then screeching to a stop with our butts down and our hands up.

Which also meant that every time we hit that stop, our toes slammed up against the front of our shoes, and after about ten minutes of that, all I wanted to do was tear my shoes and socks off and lie down with my feet in a bucket of ice water.

Lying down was definitely not part of the program, though. As soon as we finished the closeouts, we went straight into learning a complicated new offensive pattern. It got us all bumping into each other, going the wrong way, or passing the ball where somebody wasn't, so I had to think so hard I forgot about my feet.

Maybe Coach had planned it that way.

At the end of practice, after we shot free throws and ran sprints for the misses, we all dropped down by our gym bags, pulled off our shoes, and rubbed our feet.

"Ohmygod, my toes hurt so bad," Jasmine said.

"Dude," Maura said. "I already had an ingrown nail. I think it just grew all the way through my toe."

"I'm asking my mom to get me thicker socks," Autumn said.

"I'm asking my mom to get me socks with those little grippers on the bottom like babies wear," Taj said.

And I don't know why, but sitting there, listening to everybody complain, made me think about what Mr. Bukowski had talked about the day before, except sort of in reverse. I mean, looking around at my teammates, we all looked so different from one another, ran at different speeds, jumped high or low. But defensive closeouts made everybody's feet hurt exactly the same way.

We were all sore-toed mutants.

We finished taking off our shoes and gathering up our stuff. And just about the exact second we pushed open the big gym doors to step outside, there was a gigantic crack of thunder and rain came gushing down out of the sky. We all shrieked and ran, and I don't know about everybody else, but by the time Mom and Sam and I got to our car, we were soaked.

Which meant we had a long, wet, clammy ride home.

It also meant that by the time we got home, every last speck of my three-point line was streaming down the driveway in big, multicolored, wet-chalk streaks.

Mom and Sam and I stood in the garage and watched it disappear, and Sam slipped his hand into mine.

"Don't worry, Nikki," he said. "I'll help you draw it again."

21

A Librarian Finds
Some Answers

Booker and Sam and I had just begun rechalking the three-point line the next afternoon when Mom pulled into the driveway.

"Why are you home so early?" I asked her.

"I took the afternoon off." She opened the trunk of the car and lifted out a can of paint and a paintbrush. "I had a small research project of my own to do, and I wanted to get this for you." She held the paint can toward me.

"Paint?"

"Asphalt paint. It's what they use to mark the lines on the road. It won't wash off."

"Really? We can paint a permanent three-point line on the driveway?"

Mom nodded.

I hugged her and thanked her about a hundred times. Then Booker and I decided that since we wouldn't have to do this again, we should go ahead and mark the whole arc. There was no way we could paint a long, smooth line like the ones on real basketball courts, though, so we decided to make a dotted line, with a big dot of paint every six inches or so.

Sam wanted to help, so he held the end of the tape measure on the big X under the basket, Booker measured out nineteen feet nine inches, and I painted the dots. After about five dots, Sam got bored and needed to run around, so Mom put her foot—in her hideous clog—on the end of the tape measure at the X, re-adjusting as Booker and I moved around the three-point arc.

"Would you like to hear about my research project?" she said.

Listening to Mom talk about research projects was usually about as exciting as, well, worms or oranges, but since I was pretty happy with Mom right then, and since Booker always wanted to know about everything, we both said, "Sure."

Mom pulled a little notepad out of the pocket of her pants. "I went over to the university athletics department this afternoon and met with the women's basketball coach."

I looked up from my paint dot. "Why?"

"To ask her about three-point shooting."

"You just walked into her office and asked her about shooting threes?"

"Actually, I called her first to see if she had a few minutes to talk. We've been friends—well, friendly acquaintances—for a long time." Mom flipped the notepad open. "The coach, whose name is Becky Wheeler, by the way, said that when you're learning to shoot from outside, the most important thing is to maintain your shooting form and rhythm, so that you shoot the same way, whether you're six feet from the basket or behind the three-point line. She said they video-tape their players during shooting drills so the players can see if they're altering their shots, because if they have to alter their shot, they're not ready to shoot threes."

I didn't know what to say. This was my mom, my clue-less, book-obsessed librarian mom, giving me information straight from a college basketball coach.

Booker knew what to say. "Your phone takes video, doesn't it, Nikki? I can videotape you while you shoot."

Mom turned a page in her notebook. "Becky said you shouldn't worry too much about whether or not the ball goes in at first; you should concentrate on shooting in rhythm. Also it's important to shoot straight. It's okay to miss long or short, but if you consistently miss left or right, you don't have sufficient control of your release." Mom looked at me. "I don't know what that means. Do you?"

I nodded. "That's something Adria's dad made us work on. Shooting straight and holding our follow-through straight."

"Nikki doesn't miss left or right much," Booker said.

"Well, good. You've already got that down." Mom turned another page in her notepad. "Becky also said you should email your schedule to her, and if your team plays in one of the recruiting tournaments she goes to, she'll come by to watch you play."

You know, sometimes having a mom who's a university research librarian is beyond annoying. But right then it was beyond cool.

I smiled up at her, and she smiled back at me. Then she told Sam to stop beating our neighbor's hedge with a stick and suggested he help us finish the rest of our three-point dots.

"Only if I can paint the dots," Sam said.

"Fine," I said. "But I'm going to help you."

"I want Booker to help me."

"Fine."

Mom went inside, and I took over at the X, and by the time Booker and Sam finished all the paint dots—which weren't quite as neat as my paint dots—it was time for Booker to go home. So then, since we had to let the paint dry, Sam and I went in to do our homework and eat dinner. But after dinner, Mom said that since it was still light outside, she'd help Sam finish his homework if I wanted to go back out to try out my new three-point line.

I did a quick warm-up, then started my take-a-step-back-after-a-make shooting routine. It went pretty well at first, and I didn't have to chase too many wild rebounds until I got two steps inside the three-point line.

Then it went terrible.

I shot and shot and shot—twenty-six shots—with the rebounds flying all over the place. The sky was on the dark side of twilight, and the net hanging from our old, rusty hoop looked like a black spiderweb against the last glow of the sky before my ball finally dropped through the basket.

Mom opened the side door and stepped out on the porch. "Time to call it a night, Nikki."

"I haven't made a three-pointer yet."

Mom looked from me to the basket, then back to me. "Did you make your last shot?"

I nodded.

"Then it's time to stop. It's too dark to see what you're doing anymore."

"I don't want to quit yet."

"You're not quitting," Mom said. "You're postponing the

rest of your shooting until tomorrow. And you still have home-work to finish, don't you?"

"Yeah." I put my ball away in the garage and climbed the little porch steps to stand next to Mom. "Thanks," I said.

"For?"

"For the driveway paint. And for talking to Coach Wheeler."

"You're welcome." Mom put her arm around my shoulders, and we watched the last glimmer of light fade from the sky and the first stars come out.

"Remember when I was little I used to make wishes on stars?"

Mom patted my shoulder. "You usually wished for a puppy, as I recall."

"Maybe I could make a wish that one of those stars will help me learn to shoot threes."

"Did the stars help you get a puppy?"

I laughed. "Good point."

"I guess you'll have to keep practicing," Mom said.

"I guess so."

I couldn't practice threes on Thursday, because Sam and I both had too much homework to finish before Action prac-tice, but when I got off the school bus Friday afternoon, I was ready to go to work. Unfortunately, since we didn't have a tournament that weekend, Coach had worked us extra hard in practice, including having us run a passing drill with the heavy yellow balls. So by the time I finished warming up on Friday and Sam thundered up the street and Booker rode up the driveway on his bike, my left arm was already tired.

"Ready for filming?" Booker said.

"I might need a new arm first."

"Complain, complain."

I laughed. "Easy for you to say."

I talked Sam into rebounding for me, gave my phone to Booker, and trotted over to my favorite spot. I shot from there until I swished one, then took two steps back after each make, figuring I'd try to save my arm a little bit. That turned out to be a good idea, because my arm was so tired by the time I got back to the three-point line I didn't know how I could shoot anymore. But I bit down on my bottom lip and thought about Mia and how she probably pushed herself this hard every day. So I bounced my ball, squared up, and shot. It took me seven tries to sink a three. It wasn't pretty—the ball bounced all around the rim and up against the backboard before it finally dropped through the net—but it was a three and it was good enough.

Booker hadn't filmed the whole time, but he got me shooting from each spot a few times. We all grouped around the phone to watch. It wasn't all that interesting at first—just me shooting from midrange. But when my video-self shot from the three-point line, my real-self saw a big problem.

"I'm jumping forward," I said. "Look." I pointed my finger at tiny video-me. With each three-point shot my whole body leaned forward and my feet landed three feet ahead of where I'd jumped from.

We ran the video again. "See," I said. "When I'm shooting close in, my body is pretty straight and my feet land only eight or ten inches from where I jumped up. But when I get back by the three-point line, I jump forward. I'm altering my shot." I clicked off the video. "If I have to alter my shot, I'm not ready to shoot threes. Isn't that what the coach at Mom's college said?"

"I bet you're just tired," Booker said. "You said your arm was sore."

"You're just being nice."

"No, I'm not. I'm, umm..." Booker paused, which let me know he *was* just being nice, but then he said, "I don't think you were jumping forward that much Monday night. And anyway, you can't change your plan based on one data point. It wouldn't be scientific."

I laughed. "You're good, Booker."

"Yeah, I'm serious, though."

An SUV drove by, stopped, backed up, and stopped again

right at the end of our driveway. The front passenger window rolled down, and Kate stuck her head out. "Hey, Nikki!" she called.

I trotted down the driveway with my ball tucked under my arm. "Hi, Kate," I said.

"Hi, Kate!" Sam bellowed.

"Hi, Sam!" she yelled back.

I ducked my head to look inside the car. "Hi, Mr. Nyquist."

He nodded at me, drumming his fingers on the steering wheel.

Then the back window rolled down. Adria sat in the back seat. "Hi," she said.

"Oh, hi," I said. "You guys going to a strength-and-conditioning class?"

"Yeah. An extra one." Kate opened her mouth and stuck her finger in, like she was gagging.

But Adria looked past me up the driveway. "I thought you weren't allowed to have kids over when your mom's not here," she said.

I looked back at Sam and Booker. They both waved at her.

"Oh, um," I said. "Um...Mom made an exception. Booker's helping me with a project."

"A project?" Adria said. "With your basketball? In the driveway?"

"Um, yeah." It sounded so lame, even to me.

"Hey!" Kate said. "Do you have a three-point line painted on your driveway?"

Mr. Nyquist snapped his head around and raised himself up in his seat, looking at the driveway, too. "Doesn't look very accurate."

I turned and looked back at my "court." The dotted-line arc did look lopsided from this far away. "It's accurate," I said. "We measured it really carefully."

"You painted it yourself?" Kate said.

"I had some help."

Mr. Nyquist pulled off his sunglasses. "You're working on three-pointers?"

Man, Mr. Nyquist was about the last person I wanted to talk to about this, but I couldn't really deny it, so I said, "Yeah."

"Who are you working with?"

"Well, uh..." I looked back at Booker and Sam again. "My little brother and my friend Booker."

"Oh, for crying out loud. You know what I mean. Which shooting coach are you working with?"

"Well, really just my little brother and Booker. And my mom helps, too."

Mr. Nyquist gave a sharp bark of laughter. "Good luck with that."

Kate's face reddened, and my face got hot, too. It was one

thing to call me a Black Hole on the Basketball Court—it was a whole other thing to laugh at my mom.

I glanced at Adria, but she had her arms folded and was looking away from me, so I bounced my ball a couple of times, then bent down and looked right at Mr. Nyquist. "Actually, Becky Wheeler is helping me, too. Do you know her? She's the women's basketball coach at Wilder University. My mom is a research librarian there. She might not know a lot about basketball, but she knows how to find out about anything, and she's good friends with Coach Wheeler." It wasn't exactly a lie.

"Wow," Kate said. "Cool."

But I wasn't really looking at her. I was looking at Mr. Nyquist, who wasn't laughing anymore. Now he was clenching his teeth. He slammed his sunglasses back on and threw the car into gear.

Kate waved out the window as her dad drove off. "Good luck with your shooting," she called. "See you Tuesday."

But Adria didn't say anything. She just rolled her window up.

Oh boy.

Booker walked his bike down the driveway. "What was wrong with Adria?"

"She knows I'm not allowed to have friends here after school." I rotated my ball around my waist. "I haven't told her about working on three-pointers. Or about working with you."

"You think she's mad?" Booker said.

"Yeah, she looked pretty mad. I'll call her later."

Booker rolled his bike back and forth. "I've gotta go. See you tomorrow?"

"Don't you have better things to do on the weekend?"

Booker shrugged. "How'm I going to know if you quit jumping forward if I don't come to watch? I'll be over after I cut the grass and stuff."

"Um…" I said.

"Um?"

"I could come over and help you," I said.

"You don't have to do that."

"You're helping me."

Booker smiled. "Okay," he said. "I'll text you in the morning. Wear jeans."

"What?"

"Wear jeans or sweats or something. Not shorts."

He swung onto his bike, waved, and headed off.

Sam and I went inside. He wanted to play a video game, but I told him I needed to start my weekend homework so I'd have more time on Saturday and Sunday to work on threes. I went up to my bedroom and dropped onto my bed, but before I pulled my books out of my backpack, I looked up at Mia.

"Can I do this?" I asked her. "Teach myself to be a three-point shooter?"

As usual, Mia didn't have a lot to say, but the determination on her face, the effort straining through every muscle, made me think that if she were actually here in my room, not just in a poster on my wall, if she were here talking to me, she'd say, *There's only one way to find out. Keep trying. Then try harder.*

The Three-Point Line

I tried calling Adria three times that night, but she didn't answer her phone.

I texted her, *Call me.* But she didn't do that, either.

I tried again—three times—Saturday morning. Same result.

So I gave up and headed over to Booker's.

When I got there, he was standing in his driveway with his parents. For a second I thought, *Wow, he doesn't look anything like his parents*, until I remembered, duh, they adopted him. But Mr. and Mrs. Wallace *really* didn't look like Booker. Booker had blondish hair and blue eyes. Both his parents had dark brown hair and brown eyes. But more than that, they were totally different shapes and sizes. I mean,

Booker was pretty tall and really skinny. His dad was shorter than Adria. And Booker's mom wasn't just short. She was tiny. Like maybe-not-quite-five-feet-tall tiny. And a little bit round. She wore wire-rimmed glasses and, honestly, if she were older and had white hair, you might think she was Mrs. Santa Claus. Which probably made her a perfect person to teach kindergarten.

She came over to shake my hand when I got off my bike. I had to tilt my head down to look at her, which felt funny— I was so used to craning my neck to look up at basketball moms.

"Isn't it nice of you to help Booker with his chores?" she said.

"He's been helping me a lot," I said.

"Even so." She smiled with her whole face, her eyes crinkling up into little crescents.

Yeah, the perfect kindergarten teacher.

"Ah, the basketball phenom," Mr. Wallace said, and Booker said, "Dad, don't embarrass her!"

"I'm hardly a phenom," I said, laughing.

"Oh, I've heard you're quite the shooter. But the question is"—he whipped a Weedwacker out from behind his back— "how are you with the business end of a Weedwacker?"

"I, uh…"

Booker shook his head. "Dad, come on, you're scaring her. Sorry, Nikki," he said. "I should have warned you my dad thinks he's hilarious." He took the Weedwacker from his dad and held it out to me. "I thought it'd be easiest if I mow and you weed-whack."

"Okay." I took it from him and turned it around, looking at it.

"Have you used one of these before?" Mr. Wallace asked.

"Well, actually, no. A boy who lives on our street mows our lawn. My mom says it's her one indulgence."

"Your mother sounds like a smart woman," he said. "But there's nothing to weed-whacking. You'll pick it up in a minute. Booker will show you. Meanwhile..." He picked up something that looked like a giant's scissors, clacked the blades together, and said, "Chop, chop."

I jumped back, and Mrs. Wallace said, "Honestly, Len, Nikki's going to think you're an ax murderer. Put those hedge clippers down."

I looked at Booker.

He was clearly trying not to laugh. "Come on, Dad. I thought you wanted me to make friends. You think Nikki's ever going to come over again?"

Mr. Wallace smiled. "I'm sorry, Nikki. I'm not really an ax murderer."

"That's okay," I said. "I didn't really think you were." Even though the thought maybe *had* crossed my mind for a second.

He put the clippers down and handed me a pair of plastic glasses. "Please, wear these while you're working."

"So I'll look goofy?" I said.

Mr. Wallace shouted one big "Ha!" of laughter. "No, not to look goofy. To protect your eyes in case the Weedwacker kicks up a rock or a stick. I pulled a piece of barbed wire out of the backyard last week. God knows how that got there. But you can see how overgrown everything is. Who knows what's lurking in the bushes." He made his voice sound like an old-movie vampire.

"Dad!" Booker said.

Mr. Wallace laughed again. "Sorry," he said. "Please wear the glasses, Nikki. You only get one set of eyes."

"Okay." I put them on.

"Sharp," Booker said.

I gave him a shove. "Don't you have to wear them?"

"Yeah." He pulled a pair out of his back pocket. "Okay, let me show you how to weed-whack."

Mr. Wallace was right—it didn't take long to learn how to use a Weedwacker. But, boy, was I glad Booker told me to wear jeans. I was covered in little weed shreds in about two minutes.

Booker mowed the grass and Mrs. Wallace went around with a wheelbarrow and collected sticks and piles of old leaves and the big clumps of weeds I whacked down. And Mr. Wallace chop-chopped away at the huge bushes that grew across the front of the house.

When Booker and I finished our jobs, he asked his mom what else we should do.

She set down the wheelbarrow. "You've done plenty. Go help Nikki with her basketball." She smiled up at us with her whole face and waved us away.

Booker went inside to change into basketball shorts, then we got our bikes out of the garage.

I turned back to say good-bye to Mr. Wallace. He was up on a ladder now, singing, clipping away at a tall bush near their front door.

"Booker," I said. "Does it look like, um, does it look like your dad's clipping that bush into the shape of a giraffe?"

Booker looked at his dad's creation for a minute, then shook his head and laughed. "Oh my god," he said.

We got on our bikes and headed for my house.

"What does your dad do?" I asked.

"You mean for work?"

"Yeah."

"He's a high school physics teacher."

"Really?"

"Yeah. Go figure."

When we got to my house, I ran in to change into shorts and hollered to Sam that Booker and I were back. Sam exploded out of the house before I'd even gotten my shoes tied.

Sam wanted to do the filming, and Booker said he didn't mind rebounding. So I did a quick warm-up, then shot and stepped back, shot and stepped back, over and over. Then we grouped around the phone to watch the video. And when little video-me shot from the three-point line, I didn't jump forward nearly as much as I had the day before.

"See?" Booker said. "You were tired yesterday."

"I'm still jumping forward, though."

So we went back and did it again, with me trying hard to think about shooting the same way, no matter where I was. I got a little better, but still not great, so we did it again and again until Sam got bored and ran down the street to play with Jeffrey and Omar.

Booker and I went inside to get something to drink. I asked Mom if she'd come out to rebound or shoot video, but she was reading—what a surprise—and said, "I'd like to finish this book. Can I help you later?"

"Is it the oranges book?" I asked.

"No, I finished that last weekend."

"Worms?"

Mom laughed. "No, I'm afraid I'm reading about tectonic plates."

"Wow. Fascinating," I said.

"Oh, it is. They're—"

"Mom! Could you tell me later?"

She smiled. "Yes, I can tell you all about it later."

Booker and I took our drinks and went back outside.

"It's times like this that I wish I had an actual dad who would come out and rebound or something, instead of just a paper dad," I said.

Booker looked at me funny. "Paper dad?"

"Oh, that's what I call the guy who was the, um, the, you know, donor. My mom has a report that tells about him. I read it a couple of weeks ago. So now I kind of think of him as my paper dad."

"What does the report say?" Booker asked. "Does it tell you who he is?"

I shook my head. "Donors are anonymous. There's no information about who they are. Just a description of what my dad looks like and where he went to college and his hobbies and stuff."

"So, what's he like?"

"Um…"

"Sorry. You don't have to answer that." Booker played

with the pull tab on the top of his soda can. "My mom keeps telling me I ask questions that are too personal."

"No, it's okay," I said. "It was actually interesting. The donor report, I mean. It made my dad sound like a cool guy. He lived in a bunch of different countries when he was a kid. And he was on the track team at the University of Virginia."

"You're kidding."

"No. He ran track in college."

"Wow," Booker said. "I guess you know where you got the sports gene."

"Well, I hope I got it. Hey, but listen to this—he could ride a unicycle and juggle."

"What?" Booker burst out laughing. "Whose dad can do that? Don't you want to meet him?"

I sat down on the porch steps. "I can't."

"How come?"

"Like I said, donors are anonymous."

Booker sat down next to me.

"Mom says I can try to find him when I get older, if I want to."

"Do you think you will?"

"I don't know. Maybe. But maybe not. It's not like he's ever been part of my life or anything. And, um, maybe he wouldn't want to know me, you know?"

Booker frowned. "I hadn't thought about that. That would suck."

"Yeah." I scuffed my feet on the step. "What about you? Do you think you'll get back in touch with your birth parents sometime?"

Booker reached down and picked up my basketball from the driveway. "I don't think so."

"No?"

He shook his head. "They were...they were horrible parents. I think they forgot I was there most of the time. When I was little, if I got hungry, I'd go over to the neighbors and they'd feed me."

We sat quiet for a minute.

"Also..." Booker bounced the ball on his knees. "You know how I did my science project on genetic links to addiction?"

"Yeah."

"Well, I could've inherited that, you know? I could've inherited a trait that makes it easy for me to get addicted to stuff." He stopped bouncing the ball. "I guess it sounds stupid, but that scares me. It makes me not want to have anything to do with my birth family."

"It doesn't sound stupid," I said.

We sat quiet again until it felt weird not saying anything.

"Hey!" I grabbed the ball and jumped up. "You want to play H-O-R-S-E?"

Booker looked at his watch. "I have to go soon. Don't you want to work on threes?"

"My mom said she'd help me later." I spun the ball on my finger. "Come on, I need a break from threes anyway."

"I haven't shot in a while." Booker stood up. "I'm probably pretty rusty."

"Good, then I'll win." I bounced the ball to him. "Just kidding. You go first."

Booker dribbled the ball right up to the basket, then took six steps back, turned to face away from the basket, closed his eyes, and tossed the ball backward over his head. It hit the backboard and dropped through the net.

"You are such a liar!" I yelled, and I would have slugged him, but he jumped away from me. "That's what you call rusty?"

Booker was practically doubled over, he was laughing so hard. "That's my one trick shot," he said. "Honest."

"Yeah, I'll bet." I picked up the ball, went over to the spot he shot from, and turned away from the hoop. "Cheater," I said. "Just wait until I go first." I closed my eyes, tossed the ball backward, and turned around in time to see it sail over the backboard.

I was laughing almost as hard as Booker when I grabbed the ball out of our neighbor's hedge, but I still managed to make a mean face and throw the ball at him. "Just wait," I said again.

"Oooh, I'm scared. You get an *H*."

Booker dribbled to the hoop and made a right-handed layup, so I did, too. Then he made a basket from around the free throw line, so I did, too. Then he did kind of a runner, dribbling straight toward the hoop and launching the ball up in a little arc. The ball banged the rim and bounced out.

"Ha!" I said. "My turn." I went over to my favorite spot, about ten feet back from the hoop, left of center, and put up a sweet little shot that dropped through the net without even touching the rim. "Oh yeah. Let's see you swish one."

"Swishes aren't in the rules."

"Maybe they are now."

We both cracked up again.

"Okay, you don't have to swish it," I said. "Let's see you make the shot."

Booker shot from my favorite spot, and even though the ball rattled on the rim before it fell through the net, it was a pretty shot—nice arc, nice spin.

I spun the ball in my hands. "Okay, let's see how you do on the left." I dribbled in for a left-handed layup, then tossed the ball to Booker.

"Yeah, left's not my best." He dribbled in for a layup. His form looked fine, but the ball didn't go in.

"*H!*" I called, pointing at him.

"Yeah, yeah, whatever."

I bounced the ball, trying to decide what to do next, what kind of shot I'd probably make that he maybe wouldn't. And that's when I saw Sam's pogo stick propped against the side of the garage. I ran over and grabbed it.

"What?" Booker said. "Are you nuts? You think you're going to shoot a basket while you're jumping on a pogo stick?"

"Sure. It's easy."

"You ever done it before?"

"Millions of times."

Booker made the *Pppppppbbbbffffffttttt* sound.

"Okay, I've never done it. But I bet I can. Here, hold the ball." I got on the pogo stick, bounced twice, and my foot slipped off. "I haven't pogoed in a while. Let me get going."

I got back on and bounced around in a circle. It really had been a while since I'd been on Sam's pogo stick, like maybe a year. But I got my balance and held out my hand. "Give me the ball."

Booker tossed me the ball, and I managed to swing my hand up and around, the way I would to shoot my warm-up shots. I bounced over to the hoop, holding the handle with my right hand, the ball balanced on my left hand, then I bounced, bounced, bounced, and, on the up bounce, extended my arm and flicked my wrist, and the ball arced up and dropped through the net.

"No way!" Booker shouted, and fell over on the lawn. "No way! No way!"

I bounced in a big circle, whooping and laughing.

"That was unreal." He sat up. "I can't believe you made that shot."

I jumped off the pogo stick, still laughing. "It was pretty unreal. Too bad I can't use a pogo stick in a game. I could shoot way up above everybody."

Booker looked at his watch. "Oh man, I gotta go. My folks decided we should all take golf lessons."

"That sounds fun," I said.

He got on his bike and rode a circle around me before heading down the driveway. "Not as fun as pogo basketball."

I went inside and made myself a turkey sandwich and thought about how, even though Booker didn't share any DNA with his parents, he'd still inherited their funny-and-nice genes.

I tried calling Adria again, but she still didn't answer, which was annoying. How could she be that mad at me? I mean, come on, she'd been spending a bunch of time with Kate. Did she expect me to just hang out by myself?

I set my phone on the counter and ate my sandwich—chewing a lot harder than I needed to—and decided I didn't have time to think about Adria right then. The only thing I had time for was figuring out how I could train myself to not jump forward when I was shooting threes.

By the time I finished eating, I had an idea. I ran back out to the garage and searched around for the little plastic cones we'd gotten when I was on my kindergarten soccer team. I finally found them, wedged behind an old hose on the shelves, covered with about a hundred times more spiderwebs than Mom's flowerpots.

Ick.

I picked up the cones with the very tips of my fingers, ran out of the garage, threw the cones on the lawn, and rolled them around with my foot to scrape the spiderwebs off on the grass.

Then I set them in a row a foot inside the three-point line—if I kicked over a cone when I shot, I'd know I was still jumping forward. Which is exactly what I did on my first three shots. I went back closer to the basket to get my form right again, then back to the three-point line, focusing harder on keeping that form, and only kicked over a cone once in five shots.

Then I kept going like that, moving the cones around to shoot from different spots along the three-point arc, shooting closer to the basket to get my form right again if I kicked over the cones, chasing down my rebounds, trotting back, squaring up, shooting again. I kept shooting from each spot until I hit a three, which sometimes only took six or seven tries and sometimes took twenty. When I got all the way around the arc, shooting from ten different spots, I started back the other way.

Mom came out with some lemonade and stayed to rebound for a while, but by that time I was getting really tired. I missed my shots and kicked over the cones ten times in a row.

"Let's take a break," Mom said. "You can help me get the laundry started."

"Some break," I said, but we both laughed.

I went in with Mom and helped her sort the laundry, then ate a banana and drank some juice and thought really hard about how good it would feel to lie down on the couch and watch TV until suppertime, but instead I filled a water bottle and headed back outside.

To give my left arm a little more rest, I shot some right-handed layups, then I marched back to the three-point line and started back around the arc. But this time, I didn't stay in each of my ten spots until I made a three, I took ten shots from each place and moved on, even if I didn't make a basket.

And guess what: There were only three places where I didn't make a three-pointer. In a couple of places, I made two, and when I shot from the very top of the arc, I made three, which maybe doesn't sound like all that many—three baskets out of ten tries—but it felt fantastic to me. And what was also fantastic was that I only kicked over the cones a couple of times.

Sam came blasting up the street at some point, and I talked him into rebounding for me again, then pretty soon after that I heard the side door open, and Mom said, "Nikki, I think you should call it a day."

"I'm okay," I said.

"You've been shooting all day long. Think about how sore you were after your first practice with this team. If you practice any more today, you won't be able to pick up a pencil tomorrow, let alone a basketball. Supper's almost ready. Come on in and wash up."

And I have to say, that supper, which was just grilled chicken and green beans and pasta salad, tasted about as good as any supper I ever ate.

My shower and my pajamas felt fantastic that night, too, and when I finally fell into bed, I think I was asleep before I even told Mia about my day.

Sunday morning, Mom and Sam headed off to Sam's soccer game. I was hoping Booker would come over, but he texted me to say his parents were going hiking along the Potomac and wanted him to go, too.

You want to come? he said.

Yeah, sounds fun, I texted back, but then I glanced out my bedroom window and saw my old, rusty hoop down in the driveway. I sighed and turned back to my phone. *Better stay home and keep shooting, though. Only a week before next tournament.*

Okay. Good luck.

Thanks.

I frowned at my phone. Was this stupid? Going hiking with Booker and his funny parents would be way more fun than standing out in the driveway by myself shooting threes over and over, chasing rebounds, getting a sore arm. I let my thumb hover over Booker's phone number, almost pushed it three times...but then I looked up at Mia, at her straining muscles, at her determination. And I heard Coach's voice—*Heading into the big tournaments now. Can't put you on the floor if you won't compete.*

I dropped my phone on my bed, pulled on my shoes, and ran outside.

In Case That Other Horrible, Awful Day Wasn't Horrible and Awful Enough

Monday morning I got on the school bus with a tired left arm. But, man, I was happy inside—happy that I worked so hard on my three-pointer over the weekend and maybe made enough progress that I'd be ready to shoot some in the tournament that was coming up the next weekend. I was pretty happy about having so much fun with Booker and his parents, too.

But all those happy feelings disappeared when Adria got on the bus.

Because, for the first time since the second day of kindergarten, Adria didn't walk down the aisle and drop into the seat next to me. For the first time since the second day of kindergarten, she climbed the bus steps, glanced around, and sat in an empty seat near the front of the bus.

Oh boy.

I sat through three more stops, staring at the back of Adria's head, then at the last stop before we got to school, I got up, plowed forward past the kids getting on, and sat down next to her.

She folded her arms and looked out the window.

"You want to talk about it?" I said.

She whipped her head around and glared at me. "Why didn't you just tell me you didn't want to hang out with me anymore?"

"What?"

"What do you mean, 'What?' You can't come over to my house after school because you have to take care of Sam? And, oh, I can't come over to your house because you can't have friends over when your mom's not there? But, gee, Booker can come over. Because Booker's helping you with a project. Really? Why'd you lie to me?"

"I didn't lie! I...I..." I pulled my hands through my hair.

"Yeah." Adria turned back to the window. "So he's your boyfriend now?"

"No!" I slumped down in the seat. "He's...he's helping me learn to shoot three-pointers."

"Oh, right. Because he's an expert at that?" She shook her head. "That's pathetic, Nikki. You didn't think my dad could help you?"

"No, it's not that. I...I wanted to ask your dad to help me, but I..."

The bus bumped into the school parking lot, and Adria picked up her backpack. "You what?"

"I didn't want to tell you about it in case I couldn't do it. I didn't want you to laugh at me."

"Nikki, that is so lame. Why would I laugh at you for that?"

"Because you did before! When I told you about Mr. Nyquist calling me a black hole."

"What? Nikki, get over yourself!" She grabbed the back of the seat in front of us, pulled herself up, and shoved past me. "I laughed because it was funny."

"It wasn't to me," I said.

Adria turned back and looked at me for a second...and then she was gone.

After that beginning, I didn't think the day could get much worse, but I was wrong about that.

In homeroom, our teacher passed out third-quarter report cards. She said, "Open them after you get home, please."

Yeah, right. Like anybody was going to do that.

I held mine under my desk and opened it as quietly as I could.

C in history, B in everything else except PE. I got an A in PE.

Which, you know, wouldn't seem like a total catastrophe, right? Except for the fact that on my first-quarter and second-quarter report cards, I got a B in history and an A in everything else.

Great.

At lunchtime, for the first time since the first day of kindergarten, Adria and I didn't sit together. She sat with Mary Katherine Pentangeli and her friends, and I sat with some of the girls from our science class. Adria and I didn't sit together on the bus ride home, either.

But as upset as I was about Adria and as much as I dreaded showing Mom my report card, as soon as I got home I headed straight out to our driveway with my basketball. I had work to do. I couldn't waste time worrying.

Booker couldn't come over because he had too much homework, so it was just Sam and me. He came blasting up the street like usual, but instead of shouting out the fabulous third-grade news, he waved a piece of paper over his head. "Nikki! Nikki! Guess what! I got all A's on my report card. First time ever!"

I grabbed him and swung him around. "Sam, I love you! I think you just saved my butt!"

"Really?"

"My report card isn't good. Let's show Mom yours first."

"Okay!" Sam yelled. "You want to ride bikes?"

"I need to keep working on my shooting this week. Can you jump on your pogo stick?"

I'd already done my warm-up shooting, so I set out my little orange cones inside the three-point line and got to work. And even with all the bad stuff that happened that day, my shooting went pretty well. I didn't kick over any cones and I made a couple of threes from each of my spots around the arc. I was feeling so good I said, "Hey, Sam, bounce around inside the three-point line, okay? I can pretend you're a tall player that I have to shoot over."

Sam bounced over and I kept shooting. And it worked. I had to try so hard to ignore Sam and concentrate on what I was doing that my shooting actually got better. Pretty soon Sam was whooping and yelling, taking one hand off the pogo stick to wave at me, but I stayed focused—stepping into my shot, letting the ball fly, collecting it after it fell through the net or chasing the rebounds, then back to the three-point line to do it again. Sam jumped and jumped and laughed and yelled, and then...and then I put up a shot that didn't fly like a bird—it streaked like a jet, smacked the front of the rim, and shot straight back, and before I could yell "Look out!" it slammed into the pogo stick at the exact second Sam bounced up. The pogo stick exploded away from him, and he stuck his hand out to break his fall and crashed onto the driveway.

"Sam!" I ran to him.

He rolled over, his face pinched tight, eyes squeezed shut. When he opened them and looked at me, tears ran down the sides of his face.

"Are you okay?" I kneeled down.

"My arm kind of hurts." He tried to sit up, winced, and lay back down. "Good thing I was wearing my helmet."

I almost laughed. "Show me where your arm hurts."

He pointed at his left wrist, and I bent down to look at it, looked at his right wrist, then back at the left. It had already started to swell.

I sat back on my heels. "I think I better call Mom."

I stayed home while Mom took Sam to the emergency room. I did homework and tried to get dinner started. And worried.

It was almost eight o'clock before I heard the garage door open, then Sam blasted into the kitchen with his arm in a sling and a brace on his wrist.

"Nikki, look!" he hollered. "I got a sling! Nobody in my class has had a sling before. And when the swelling goes down, I'll get a cast! I'm going to get a chartreuse one like Kritika's!"

I'm not sure I'd ever seen anyone so happy about a broken arm.

Mom didn't look as happy as Sam when she came in, though. She kicked off her clogs, hung up her jacket, and got a glass of water. "Oh, you made a salad," she said, looking at a bowl on the counter. "Thank you."

"It's not fancy," I said. "Just lettuce and carrots and tomatoes."

"Unfancy is fine."

"I set the table, too."

Mom smiled a tired-looking smile and sat down at the counter next to me. She rubbed at her forehead. "I can't remember what I was planning to make for dinner."

"There's a pizza in the freezer. I could make that."

"Yeah, pizza!" Sam called from the family room.

Mom nodded. "Pizza will be fine."

I got the pizza out of the freezer, read the directions, and turned on the oven. "Is it a bad break in Sam's arm, Mom?"

"No, thank heaven. A small crack in the ulna."

"Which is?"

"One of the bones in his forearm." She rubbed at her forehead some more. "Tell me again how this happened, Nikki."

So I told her, leaving out the part about all the laughing and whooping and how hard I had to concentrate to ignore Sam.

She shook her head. "It doesn't seem like you made a very good decision, does it? Asking your brother to jump around in front of you."

"No," I said. "It was stupid. I'm sorry, Mom. I'll be more careful."

She went to change her clothes, and I put the pizza in the oven and took it back out when it was done, cut it into slices, put everything on the table, and called Mom and Sam. I even put a piece of pizza and some salad on Sam's plate since he wouldn't be able to serve himself.

Mom sat down smiling. "I'm afraid fixing dinner doesn't quite make up for a broken arm, but I appreciate your effort, Nikki."

We must have all been hungry, because we ate without saying much, until Sam finished his piece of pizza, jumped up, and shouted, "Oh, Mom! I GOT STRAIGHT A's! Where's my backpack, Nikki? Where's my report card?"

I got up and got his report card, thinking, *Man, why couldn't he have forgotten about this for a day or two?* I handed his report card to Mom.

"Well, this is happy news," she said. "I'm proud of you, Sam. Good work. Did you get a report card today, Nikki?"

"Yeah." I fished it out of my backpack, handed it to her, dropped back into my chair, and closed my eyes. When I opened them, Mom was frowning at my report card.

She looked at me. "Nikki, when I agreed to your taking care of Sam after school, we made a deal, didn't we? Your top priority was to *take care* of your brother. And you would not let your schoolwork suffer. You agreed to that deal."

"I know." I scrunched up my shoulders.

"How do you think you're doing?"

"Not very well."

Mom set my report card on the table, picked it up, and set it down again. She pushed her plate to the side. "I'm afraid you've played your last game with the Northern Virginia Action."

"Mom, no!" I jumped up. "You can't do that! You can't take me off the Action!"

And Sam yelled, "No, Mommy! Don't do that!"

Mom sat back and spread her hands, palms up. "Do you think I'm happy about this? I can see how hard you've been working to succeed on this team, Nikki. Unfortunately, it looks like you've stopped working hard at school."

"I haven't, Mom. I just..." I sat back down. "It was only the first couple of weeks of the Action season, when I was trying to get used to the practices that were so much harder than county league, and I was tired all the time, and I had that big genetics project and a big test in history. And I also had to figure out how much time I needed to spend with Sam on his homework and...and look at Sam's report card, Mom. That's the first time he ever got all A's, right, Sam?"

Sam nodded about eighteen times. "Nikki's a way better homework helper than the helpers at after-school-care."

"See?" I said. "I'm doing a good job at that. And Sam and I have the time figured out now. We're getting all our homework done."

Mom drummed her fingers on the table. "I hear what you're saying, Nikki, but I'm afraid I'm not convinced. Your brother has a broken arm. Your grades are down. Put yourself in my place. What would you do?"

"I'd give me another chance!" I was almost crying now. "I know I didn't take care of Sam the way I should have today, but I won't ever make that mistake again."

"Nikki made me wear my helmet!" Sam said.

"See? At least I did that," I said. "I'll pull my grades up, Mom, I promise. I don't want to get C's. But please don't take me off the team. I'm working so hard. I'm trying to do something I've never done before. You have to give me a chance to show Coach Duval that I won't let what I can't do stop me from doing what I can. Please, Mom. Please!"

She didn't say anything for a whole minute. Maybe longer, because it felt like five years.

I grabbed my napkin and wiped at my eyes and chewed at my bottom lip.

Finally, Mom said, "All right. I'll give you another chance. You can play in the tournament this weekend. But Booker will *not* come over after school. You don't need any extra distractions. I want to see any graded work you get back this week, and I want to see your assignment book and the work you've done to complete your assignments. Every night. Then we'll reevaluate."

She stood and picked up our plates. "But I'm not making any promises, Nikki. You've got to earn back the privilege of playing on the Action."

24

Game Time

The rest of that week was probably the longest four days of my life.

I don't know how many times I texted Adria or tried to call her, but she kept right on ignoring me. And even though I'd been really mad at her—or at least really annoyed—during the past few weeks, we'd still been friends, you know? But now...now I didn't know, and I felt like half of me had broken off.

And to make things worse, we got in trouble for not talking to each other at practice Tuesday night. We each missed a couple of passes and made mistakes on defense, mistakes we'd never make if we'd been talking.

"Nikki, Adria!" Coach called, his voice sharper than

usual. "What're you two doing?" He blew his whistle and stopped practice. "Ladies, there are a lot of things about basketball that are difficult to learn. Communicating with each other on the court is not one of them."

And wasn't that just great?

Having Mom go over my homework every night wasn't a whole lot of fun, either. She made me fix every missed comma or clunky sentence in my English essay and quizzed me on the chapters I read in my history book. She even made me explain how I got my answers on my algebra homework. And all that time I worried and worried. Did she think I was working hard enough? Would she let me keep playing on the Action?

And on top of all that, I missed Booker. I mean, we still talked in science—when Mr. Bukowski wasn't—but that wasn't the same as hanging out together, talking and laughing and goofing around while I worked on my shooting, which was also harder without him rebounding or even just encouraging me to keep going when I missed a bunch of shots in a row.

I did keep going, though.

In all, from that first Sunday when Mia McCall took on LeBron James and I realized my father had given me his sports genes—that Sunday when I started learning to shoot three-pointers—then after school all through that week, then the next weekend, when I shot all day on both Saturday and Sunday, then after school all through the next week, I figured I'd spent thirty-eight hours working on my three-point shot, which, you know, compared with how much time Mia probably puts in, maybe wasn't all that much. But still, I felt like I worked pretty hard. Actually, I felt like I worked *really* hard.

On Friday night I asked Mom if Booker could come with us to the tournament that weekend, since he'd helped me with my shooting so much, and she said yes.

"Let me ask," Booker said when I called him. He called back a few minutes later and said, "I can't tomorrow. Chores, chores, chores. And golf lessons. But maybe Sunday."

"Okay."

"So listen," Booker said, "you have to shoot at least one three-pointer in every game, all right?"

It made me sweat just thinking about it. "All right," I finally said.

"Promise?"

"Yeah."

"Good. Put Sam on the phone."

"Why?"

"I'm going to tell him you promised."

At seven o'clock on Saturday morning, when Mom and Sam and I climbed into the car, heading for the Action's first "big"

tournament—the first tournament that would count toward whether or not we made it to nationals—I was already nervous. What if I airballed every shot? What if Kate or Adria or Taj were open down low and I didn't see them and airballed a three? What if Linnae or Maura or even JJ had a clear path to the hoop, and I didn't pass the ball and airballed a three?

Why had I ever thought I could do this?

Finally I fell asleep, thank god, and didn't wake up until Mom pulled into the parking lot of the huge recreation center in Maryland that was hosting the tournament.

Most of the other Action families were already in the gym lobby when we walked in, grouped around a big table. The girls sat on the floor, putting on their shoes and braiding each other's hair and stuff like that. In every other basketball game of my life, I would have sat down next to Adria and laughed and joked with her, but that day, I sat down between Linnae and Jasmine.

"Do you believe this?" Linnae said. She pulled two kneepads from her gym bag and shook them in front of Jasmine and me. "My mom saw Autumn take that bad fall in practice last week, so now she thinks I'm going to bruise my knees and die."

"Ohmygod," Jasmine said. "I hope my mom doesn't notice those. And keep your mouth guard in your mouth today, okay, Linnae? Don't pull it out and chew on it like

Steph Curry. You did that Thursday night, and my parents talked the whole way home about all the money they'd spent on me at the orthodontist."

"I'll try," Linnae said. "But that thing is so annoying." She pulled out her ankle supports and began the long process of wrapping them up and down and around her ankles, shaking her head and muttering to herself about her mom being "such a whack job."

Kate sat down in front of me. "I'm mad at you," she said.

I think I almost started to cry—did I need one more person mad at me? "What did I do?"

"You painted a three-point line on your driveway, so my dad bought a stencil of the three-point line to paint on our driveway. He says I'm getting"—she lowered the pitch of her voice to sound like her dad—"outworked by that left-handed guard."

That cracked me up. "Oh, yeah, like I'm ever going to be better than you."

"You never know," Kate said.

Coach stood up and clapped his hands to get our attention. "Game time, ladies."

We gathered up our stuff and followed Coach down a hallway and into a gym where four games were finishing up on four courts, which seemed pretty calm compared with the other tournaments we'd played in. It was still plenty loud, though, especially since we could also hear the roar from the five other four-court gyms that opened off the main hallway.

We warmed up along one end of the gym, and Kate threw up into a trash can. Then the game clock blared, so we ran onto the court to warm up our shooting. Then the game clock blared again.

I didn't start, but I hadn't expected to, especially since we were playing a team from New York full of big, tall girls. But five minutes into the first half, with the score tied, Coach called me to sub in for JJ, who had already picked up two fouls. He clamped his hand onto my shoulder and said, "You ready?" I nodded, and the ref whistled me in.

"Go, Nikki!" Sam's little-kid voice piped at me from the bleachers.

I hustled onto the court, got my butt down and my hands up, ready to play defense, but before I was even set, Kate blocked a shot and swatted the ball out to half-court. I jumped forward, grabbed the ball, and drove it all the way up the court for a layup.

Cheers erupted from our bench and bleachers.

And then it happened again. A blocked shot, a long outlet pass up the court that I caught and took in for a layup, left-handed this time, because a girl from the other team had sprinted down the court with me and was defending the right side of the basket.

I couldn't believe it—at last, I'd done something right.

We were up by six at halftime, but the New York team battled back, and with three minutes to go we were tied. And then there I was, wide open behind the three-point line. Maura whipped the ball in to Jasmine, the defense collapsed toward her, and she zipped the ball back out to me. I heard Sam squeal, "Shoot, Nikki!" and I squared my shoulders and stepped into my shot...and passed the ball back to Maura.

I couldn't do it.

Couldn't risk an air ball.

Couldn't take the shot.

Coach subbed me out and put JJ in. She managed to muscle her way to the hoop for a layup, got fouled, and made her free throw. Then Taj and Kate took over. They each hit a couple of big shots and blocked a couple from the other team. And we pulled out a win.

We all jumped around and yelled, then trooped out to the lobby to wait for our next game.

"All right, ladies," Coach said. "First one down. We win the next game, we'll be in the top bracket tomorrow. Which is where we need to be to win the tournament, right? And why do we want to win the tournament?"

"Because we want to go to nationals!" Maura yelled, and all the rest of us whooped and clapped.

I texted Booker, *Hit 2 layups!!*

He texted back, *Big deal. Shoot the 3.*

I stuck my tongue out at my phone. Easy for him to say. He didn't have to worry about shooting an air ball.

But still.

Why had I spent thirty-eight hours working on a three-point shot if I wasn't going to try one in a game?

I sat down on the floor to take off my shoes and change my socks, and Sam sat down next to me.

"You promised to shoot a three-pointer in every game, Nikki," he said.

"I know, Sam." I stuffed my sweaty socks into my gym bag. "I got scared."

He slipped his hand into mine. "Why would you get scared? Nobody's going to hit you or anything if you miss."

I couldn't help laughing. "I guess you're right about that."

He held out the snack bag Mom had packed. "You want an apple?"

We each took an apple and sat there crunching together while I tried to squeeze every thought of air balls out of my head. I made myself focus instead on one thing—Mia taking on LeBron. Over and over, Mia pulling up at the three-point line before LeBron got close enough to block her shot, her face determined, her muscles straining, over and over and over.

Then Coach said, "Get your shoes on, ladies. Game time." And we were back in the gym.

Our next game was against a team from Ohio called the Blasters. Their uniforms were yellow—the same yellow as the block of sulfur in the rock case in Mr. Bukowski's classroom—with a burst of orange in the middle of their jerseys that looked like a bomb exploding. I guess they made their uniforms look like that on purpose, because, as it turned out, the Blasters played basketball like a bomb exploding on the court. JJ looked like a sissy next to them.

They shoved, they hacked, threw their elbows around on every rebound. They smashed into us when we tried to make layups, threw Linnae into the gym wall behind the basket, sent Jasmine hobbling off the court when she got hit midjump and came down sideways on her ankle. Then one of them slammed into Autumn when she jumped to shoot, knocking her feet out from under her. She hit the court flat on her back with a *whomp* that got players and coaches and parents from all the other games in the gym turning to see what happened.

Coach Duval stormed onto the court, shouting at the refs, "This isn't football! Call a foul!" He helped Autumn up and half carried her to the bench, and Autumn's mom—sweet, petite Autumn's mom—stood up and screamed at the Blasters coach, "You are awful! What are you teaching your girls?"

He turned, looked up at her, and laughed. "I'm teaching them to play ball," he shouted back.

And the game kept going.

We were halfway through the first half and we had two girls hurt, which meant we only had eight girls to finish the game. Then Taj went up for a rebound, and a Blaster caught her with an elbow, square on the bridge of her nose. Taj doubled over, her hands covering her face and blood gushing down the front of her jersey.

Taj's dad said a bunch of words that would get me grounded, and her mom ran out of the gym and came back with a tournament official, who had a box of those instant ice packs you squeeze to make cold. He squeezed three packs and gave them to Jasmine and Autumn and Taj, who was now leaning back in her chair, holding a towel to her face. Then another tournament official came in, pulling on latex gloves, spraying a bottle of something at all the little splatters of Taj's nose blood on the floor, then wiping it up with about fifty paper towels.

So now we had three injured players and seven girls to finish the game.

And I was in.

We battled back and forth and the score stayed close. Then I grabbed for a rebound and took an elbow to my ribs that knocked me sideways. But I held on to the ball, passed it out to Maura, and charged up the court after her.

She called a play, and we set up our offense, and the ball went inside to Adria, then out to JJ, back in to Kate down near the basket, then out to me on the wing, just outside the three-point line. Sam's voice yelled, "Shoot!" and Mom's voice yelled, "Shoot!" and Coach Duval's voice yelled, "Shoot!" and I stepped and jumped and shot, and the ball arced up away from me…and fell through the net.

The ref threw her hands in the air like a football official signaling a touchdown, and our bench and bleachers cheered and yelled, and…and I had scored a three-pointer.

Oh. My. God.

Behind me, a deep voice boomed, "For crying out loud, Kate! Don't kick the ball out. Take your shot!"

But Sam's voice shrieked, "THREEEEEE!"

And Coach's voice, quiet but cutting through all the rest, said, "Yeah."

And honestly, I don't have any idea what happened after that, but I have to think I played defense, then sprinted back up the court to run our offense, then played some more defense and some more offense, then the game clock blared for halftime.

We all dropped into our chairs and guzzled water, and Coach said, "All right, now you know the way they play. Tougher than tough. But we're bigger than them, and we're faster than them, and we're *better* than them." He paused, looking slowly down the bench, looking each of us square in the eyes. "You ready to take it to 'em?"

We nodded hard and said, "Yeah, Coach!" and "Let's go!" and bounced up and down in our seats. Then we guzzled more water and showed each other our scrapes and bruises, and then the game clock blared, and Coach clapped his giant hands and said, "'Action' on three. One, two, three."

"ACTION!"

And we were back on the floor, with Kate stuffing the Blasters' shots, and Maura and Kim-Ly zinging the ball up the court for our outlet player, and Linnae or JJ or me grabbing their passes and jumping toward the hoop for layups, and Adria and Kate rocketing up behind us for a put-back if we missed. I tried two more three-pointers and made one, and I heard the Blasters coach yell at the girl guarding me, "Shut her down! Shut! Her! Down!"

By the middle of the second half, we were up by twelve, and the Blasters were mad as hornets.

Their coach and parents yelled and cussed, and the Blasters whacked at us harder and harder, and then, there I was behind the three-point line with no defender on me. Kim-Ly flipped the ball to me, and I stepped into my shot and let the ball sail from my hand...and a Blaster threw herself at me, hitting me in the face with her forearm and ramming her shoulder into my chest, smashing the air from my lungs. I flew backward, slamming into the line of empty metal chairs at the end of our bench. The chairs exploded up around me and crashed back down, clanging and screeching across the floor.

Everything stopped.

Every sound. Every movement. Every breath.

And then Adria was bending over me, shouting, "Nikki, Nikki, are you all right? Are you okay?" And her hands on my shoulders and her voice again, "Nikki!"

I blinked, grabbed her arm, and sat up.

Then Coach was kneeling beside me, holding up two fingers, asking me how many fingers I saw.

Somewhere behind him a whistle shrieked, and a ref yelled, "That's enough! Clear the floor! Clear the floor! This game is *over*!"

A furious roar erupted from the Blasters' side of the court, and tournament officials ran into the gym, and then Mom was there, bending over me, and Sam, too, crying, "Don't die, Nikki!" and throwing himself into me so hard I fell over sideways again.

And that's when I started laughing. "I'm not dying, Sam," I said between breaths. "Hey, did my shot go in?"

Coach chuckled and shook his head. "Not even close." He patted my knee. "That's okay. The refs stopped the game. We get the win." He stood up. "You just keep shooting, Lefty."

Adria held out her hand to pull me up, and even though it probably looked really dopey, I kept hanging on to her arm, even when Coach gathered all the girls and families together.

"I haven't seen a game that crazy in a long time," he said. "But crazy games mean crazy parents, so before any of them start cursing at our girls, let's get out of the gym. Grab your stuff. We're going to stay together and we'll walk as slow as the slowest one of us."

Jasmine couldn't walk at all by that point. Her ankle had swelled up to twice its normal size, so her dad and Taj's dad linked their arms together to make a sling and carried her. And all the rest of us followed, packed tight together—the parents saying stuff like, "Unbelievable!" and "I've never seen anything like that!" and "What could that coach be thinking?" and us girls saying stuff like, "That was awesome!" and "Did you see Kate's monster block on their center?" and Maura pounding me on the shoulder, which I suddenly realized really hurt, shouting, "Dude!" and throwing her hands in the air, and Coach and Kate's dad coming up behind us like walking trees. The only crazy Blasters parents we ran into were two women coming out of the bathroom who called us some ugly names as we walked by, and JJ gave them a mean, scary glare.

When we got out to the parking lot, Taj's family and Jasmine's family went straight to their cars to go to an emergency clinic, but the rest of us grouped around Coach.

"Let's hope we don't see another team like that for a while," he said.

"Or ever," Autumn's mom said.

Coach boosted his ball bag up on his shoulder. "But we got two wins, so that puts us in the upper bracket tomorrow. We'll be playing against good teams and it looks like we'll be down a couple players. So go home and get lots of rest." He looked around at us. "I'm proud of you girls. See you in the morning."

Everybody headed for their cars, but I hung back with Adria.

We didn't say anything for a minute, then Adria said, "You okay?"

I nodded. "I guess I'll have some pretty good bruises tomorrow." I twisted my arm around to look at a big purple spot that was already showing on my elbow. "I guess we all will."

"Yeah." She looked at her elbows, too.

We stood silent for another minute, then I said, "I'm sorry I didn't tell you about working on three-pointers, Adria. And about Booker helping me. I just... I'd been playing so bad and I was afraid—"

"I'm sorry I laughed about the black hole thing," Adria said. She kicked at the gravel in the parking lot. "Oh god, you're going to think I'm the meanest person in the world when I tell you this."

"Adria, I know you're not the meanest person in the world."

She looked at me, her eyes sad. "I was glad Mr. Nyquist called you that. I was glad you were having such a hard time."

"What? Why?"

"Because...because you know how my dad always said you were the most important player on the team?"

"Yeah."

"Well, that always made me so mad. Even though I knew he said it because you were the point guard and you had to lead the team, he was *my* dad. Why didn't he say I was the most important? So then, when Coach Duval didn't put you at point guard, even though I could see how upset you were and how much you were struggling, I was glad because... because you weren't the most important player anymore." She shook her head. "And then you started hanging out with Booker and..."

We stood staring at each other and then...and then I burst out laughing.

"Nikki! What are you laughing about?" Adria said.

"Us! You were mad at me. I was mad at you."

"What were you mad at me for?"

"For being tall! For getting new shoes and knowing so much more about basketball than I do and going to extra training and hanging out with Kate. And for not struggling to learn your new position."

"Are you kidding? Moving from center to forward? I don't have any idea what I'm doing half the time."

I picked up my gym bag. "I wish you'd told me that."

"I didn't want to admit it. Even to myself."

We started walking, following our parents, and dopey or not, I looped my arm back through Adria's. "I hated not being friends," I said.

"Me too." She hooked her arm tighter through mine. "Let's don't do that again."

"Duh," I said. "Double-triple-quadruple-duh."

Shooter

When we walked into the gym lobby the next morning, you would've thought our team name really was the Northern Virginia Roadkill.

Jasmine was on crutches, with a bad ankle sprain, so she'd be on the bench for a few weeks. And even though Taj's nose wasn't broken, she had two amazing purple-and-green shiners, and her doctor said she shouldn't play for a week or so, either. Autumn said she was ready to play, but she looked stiff and sore from hitting the floor on her back the day before. Even JJ was all bruised up.

Booker had come with us. I'd told him all about the Blasters game on the way to the tournament, but when we got there, he looked around at my teammates and said, "Geez, I thought you were exaggerating."

"You want to sit with us while we put on our shoes and stuff?" I said.

He shook his head and stuck his hands in his pockets. "I'll hang with your mom and Sam." Then he grinned at me. "Let's see some field goal kicking, okay?"

I smiled back. "Okay."

We had the first game that morning, so Coach led us straight to our court. But when we came through the doorway into the gym, we all stopped short, piling up against one another.

Because there was a team already warming up on our court.

The bright purple Philadelphia Chargers.

The team we played against in our first game of our first tournament. The team with the giant bigger than our giant and the sharpshooter point guard.

The team we played against when I played like a Black Hole.

"Well, well, well," Coach said. "I didn't realize we'd be playing the Chargers this morning. This is going to be interesting." He gathered us all together by our bench and told us to get our shoes on double-quick so we'd have extra time to warm up. And then he said, "Ladies, that purple team is in for a surprise. You're a different team than you were when you played them before. Let's have some fun."

I rubbed my hands up and down the sides of my shorts, bunching up the shiny fabric with my fingertips. Yeah, we were a different team. Two of our bigs were hurt and couldn't play, and most of the rest of us were banged up. And...and what if the Chargers were still so good that I played like a Black Hole against them? And Mom and Sam and Booker were here to see me play like a Black Hole. And...I squeezed my eyes shut.

"Nikki?" Adria grabbed my shoulder and shook it. "What are you doing? Get your shoes on. Look," she said when I opened my eyes. "There's nobody on a couple of the other courts yet. We can run over there and warm up our shooting."

I shoved my feet into my shoes and jumped up. I didn't need to tie them to stand in front of the basket and shoot with one hand.

We grabbed a ball from Coach's bag and jogged over to an empty court.

"You first." Adria handed me the ball.

I balanced it on my left hand, bent my knees, powered up, released the ball at the top of my stroke, and...*swish*, one. I kept going, three swishes in front of the hoop, three on each side, then Adria shot and I rebounded.

Kate came out to join us. "Hey, look." She pointed at

a small group of people standing along the baseline of our court or sitting in a row of folding chairs that had been set up there, some of them watching us, some of them bent over their phones, juggling notebooks and coffee cups. Then a white-haired man in a green shirt came in and sat down in one of the chairs.

"Is that the college scout who was at our first game?" I said.

Kate nodded. "And those other people? They're coaches."

"College coaches?" Adria said.

And I said, "For an eighth-grade game?"

"Yeah, go figure." Kate laughed. "I bet they're all like fourth assistants to the fourth assistant."

But then I saw something else—a woman in what I recognized as a Wilder University ball cap, and my mom waving at her, and her waving back at Mom. "That's Becky Wheeler," I said. "The head coach at Wilder University."

"Kate!" Mr. Nyquist's voice wasn't loud, but sharp and insistent. He walked toward us, pointing at the college coaches. "You see those coaches? They're here to watch you."

And you know, if you asked me a thousand times why I said what I said next, I'd answer a thousand times that I had absolutely no idea. Because what I said was, "Becky Wheeler is here to watch me. I emailed her our tournament schedule."

Mr. Nyquist looked down at me like he thought I was not

only the stupidest ant in the universe, but the ugliest one, too. For a second, I was afraid he might step on me.

Then he looked back at Kate. "There are several coaches here from *powerhouse* programs. I sent them film, and they're here to see *you*. So when the ball gets passed in to you under the hoop, I don't want to see you kicking it back out. You take your shots. *Every* shot."

Kate said, "Dad—"

"Every shot!"

And then I said something else I can't believe I said. I said, "If Kate takes every shot and never kicks the ball out, the whole defense will collapse in on her, and she won't be able to shoot at all. If she kicks it out, and I make a basket, or Linnae does or JJ, then the defense can't collapse, and Kate will be open the next time the ball comes in to her."

Then we all stood there for, like, ten hours while Mr. Nyquist and Kate and Adria stared at me. And then I said, "Basketball's a team game. That's what Coach says, right? The Action plays team ball."

And then, thank god, Coach Duval blew his whistle for us to run our regular warm-up, and Kate and Adria and I sprinted away from Mr. Nyquist before he could say anything else. And you know what? This time, while we warmed up, Kate didn't throw up into a trash can.

When there was a minute left of warm-up time, Coach

called us over. "All right, we've got all kinds of distractions here this morning. A team that beat us the first time around. A couple of injured teammates. Coaches watching. But we're here for one reason. We're here to play ball. So that's what we're going to focus on and that's the *only* thing we're going to focus on. You with me?"

Kate chewed on the side of her thumb, Maura bounced on the balls of her feet, and all the rest of us nodded.

"Starters," Coach said. "Adria, Kate, Linnae, Maura, Nikki. And, ladies, I want to see you attack that hoop. All right, 'Action' on three. One, two, three."

"ACTION!"

We ran onto the court and took our places for tip-off. The Chargers took their places, too, and the ref blew her whistle and tossed the ball up. Kate's hand found the ball first and tipped it to Maura.

We all took off to start our offense.

I set up on the wing, down on the left side of the hoop, outside the three-point line. Maura fired the ball in to Kate, and the Chargers' center stepped in behind her with her hands up. My defender collapsed in toward Kate, too, just like I told Mr. Nyquist she would. Kate held the ball a second, then she flicked the ball out to me. I caught it, and before I could think about Black Holes or Booker watching or coaches along the baseline or anything else, I squared my shoulders, stepped into my shot, jumped, and let the ball fly from my hand. It soared up in a long, high arc...and dropped through the net.

The ref threw her hands in the air, signaling a three-pointer, and our bench exploded. Even Jasmine jumped up on one foot. The parents cheered and Sam and Booker whooped, and Coach said, "Yeah. That's how it's done."

I ran down the court to play defense, hustling, closing out, then sprinted back the other way when Kate grabbed a rebound, my hand in the air, looking for the outlet pass, hustling and hustling, and...

Everything else fell away.

All the yelling and cheering, the whistles screeching, the college coaches watching, Booker and Sam and Mom and Black Holes, and the Chargers coach hollering "Shooter!" every time the ball came to me—it all fell away. And now it was just me and the ball and the hoop and my teammates, out on that shiny wood floor, playing like we were connected. *In the zone.* Together.

I know I shot more threes in that game and hit at least two and I know we won, but I couldn't tell you what the score was or anything else about it other than that it was the most fun I'd ever had playing basketball in my whole entire life.

When the game clock blared at the end of the game, we all whooped and jumped around, then lined up to slap hands and say "Good game" with the Chargers, then followed Coach out to the lobby. He talked to us for a few minutes, but I didn't hear much of what he said. I was still too excited about having so much fun. But when the team meeting was over, Coach clamped his hand on my shoulder and said, "Good shooting, Lefty. Looks like you figured out how to not let what you can't do stop you from doing what you can."

"I'm trying," I said.

He nodded. "Keep it up."

Then Mom and Sam and Booker were there, hugging me. All of them, even Booker, which, you know, was pretty embarrassing since I'm sure I was completely sweaty and gross.

"I have a message for you from Becky Wheeler," Mom said. "She can't tell you herself—something about NCAA rules that don't allow coaches to talk to young players. But she said she enjoyed watching you and that it was obvious you've been working hard. And she said you have a pretty shot." Mom put her arm around my shoulders and pulled me close. "Must be those sports genes you didn't get from me."

We had three hours before our next game, so we all hung out around a couple of big tables in the lobby. Adria and Kate and Booker and I all sat together—Sam, too, when he wasn't running around with Kim-Ly's little sisters or getting people to sign his chartreuse cast. We ate snacks and sandwiches and drank Gatorades and laughed at Maura ("Dude, you guys, check this out") spinning basketballs on her fingers.

My mom sat with Adria's parents, talking and laughing, and Jasmine's mom sat with Linnae's mom, talking about ankle braces and mouth guards. "Ohmygod, Mom," Jasmine said. "Don't make me wear those. Not the mouth guard, anyway. Maybe the ankle braces would be okay."

Taj made goofy faces while we took pictures of her black eyes, and JJ relaced her shoes with navy-blue and orange laces, saying she guessed they could be lucky, too. Then she said, "Hey, Nikki, for real, what's the deal with your eyes? What's wrong with them?"

"There's nothing wrong with Nikki's eyes!" Adria said, jumping up in JJ's face.

JJ stumbled back, looking at me. "Oh, okay, uh, sorry."

"It's a genetic thing," I said.

And Booker said, "Heterochromia iridis."

Everybody looked at him.

His face got red. "Our science teacher told us."

After that, Autumn decided Booker needed orange and blue nail polish on his thumbs, and Sam did, too. So we had to take pictures and laugh about that.

And then Mr. Nyquist sat down next to Kate and said, not in his usual booming voice, "You played a nice game." And I think that might have been the first time I saw Kate smile at her dad. And the first time he smiled back.

Then Coach was standing in front of us, clapping his

hands. "Ladies," he said, "you remember at tryouts I told you I've been coaching club teams for twenty years? I've coached a lot of good teams in those years, and a couple of *very* good teams, but I've never coached a team better than this one." He paused and looked around at us. "This team deserves to go to nationals."

We all whooped and cheered.

"So listen up," Coach said. "If we win this next game, we win the tournament. And that could give us an automatic bid to the national championships. But I'm not going to kid you—this is going to be a tough game. We're playing a team from Delaware called the Lightning and they're good. Real good. So let's dig down deep. Let's leave it all out there on the court. You ready?"

We all bounced around and said, "Yeah!" and "Let's go!" and "Action!"

And I shouted extra loud, because even though Mom hadn't said she'd let me keep playing—even though I might never play another game with the Action, let alone play with them at nationals—I was determined to do exactly what Coach said. I was determined to leave it all out there on the court.

And when the game started, it looked like all the other Action girls felt the same way. We came out on fire.

The first play of the game, Adria popped open under the basket, caught a pass from Kim-Ly, and put the ball in the hoop. Then Kim-Ly stole the Lightning's inbound pass and took the ball straight back to the basket.

We got back on defense and Kate blocked a shot and tipped the ball out to me, and I fired it up the court to Autumn. She took it in for a layup.

One minute into the game, and we were up by six.

The Lightning's coach called a time-out.

We were all feeling great, bouncing around, but when the refs whistled us back on the floor, a tougher Lightning team came out to meet us. They ran off fourteen straight points before we got ourselves back together, so instead of being up by six, now we were down by eight.

And that's how the game kept going—we'd go on a run, get a few points ahead, then they'd fight back with their own run and get back on top. Kate was a beast on the boards, getting a ton of rebounds, and Adria scored ten points in the first half, but my three-pointer wouldn't fall. I shot three or four in the first half, and didn't make any. I tried to make up for it on the other end, playing the toughest defense I'd ever played, my butt down and my hands up, springing forward to close out fast on every girl I guarded.

At halftime we were down by three and we were tired—playing two games in one day against really good teams was enough to make anybody tired, but playing two games in one day against really good teams when we only had eight players was getting close to exhausting.

We sat on the bench, guzzling water, and Coach talked to us about strategy and which Lightning players to guard closer and stuff like that. Then, right before the buzzer sounded to start the second half, Jasmine, leaning on her crutches, and Taj, squinting at us through her shiners, stood up in front of us and said, "Dig deeper, you guys! You can do this! Come on, 'Action' on three. One, two, three."

"ACTION!"

And we were back on the floor.

The game stayed close. Coach subbed us in and out a lot, trying to give us little rests, and Taj and Jasmine kept up a steady pep talk from the bench.

With five minutes to go in the game, I finally hit a three. And then I hit another, and we were up by two.

The Lightning fought back, hitting some really nice shots, and with thirty seconds to go, we were down by one.

Kate caught a pass under the basket, but her defender stepped in with her arms up, and Kate had nowhere to go. She pivoted away and passed the ball up to Adria, who drove toward the hoop, got stopped, and fired the ball out to me. My defender charged toward me. I shot-faked, getting the girl to jump up, trying to block the shot she thought was coming, and with the clock ticking fast toward zero, I shot-faked again. Kate's defender ran at me, I zinged the ball back to Kate, and she turned, barely jumped, and put the ball in the hoop.

The game clock blared.

We won!

I jumped and whooped and ran toward Adria and Kate, and we all jumped and whooped together.

Then our whole team was out on the floor jumping and hugging—all of us, even Jasmine on her crutches—whistling and yelling and chanting, "Action! Action!" The tournament officials came in with the trophy, and we all had to take turns holding it, even Booker and Sam and Kim-Ly's little sisters, posing for pictures, laughing and shouting and hugging some more.

And then Coach pulled us together, quieted us down, and said, "Ladies, you did good." He smiled around at each of us. "See you Tuesday."

And even though I didn't know if I'd be at Tuesday's practice, didn't know if Mom would let me stay on the team, I jumped around and shouted, "Action!" as loud as anybody.

Maybe louder.

On the way home, Booker and Sam and I and even Mom talked nonstop for about the first twenty minutes, then I fell asleep, and I think maybe Booker and Sam did, too, because a couple of times when I woke up a little bit, the only thing I heard was the car stereo playing that Beethoven symphony Mom likes—the one with the big choir of people singing out Beethoven's version of joy.

When we got to Booker's house, his parents were outside working in the yard again. We all got out of the car and Mom shook hands with Mr. and Mrs. Wallace, and Mrs. Wallace looked at Booker's hands and said, "My goodness, don't your thumbs look fancy," so Sam had to show her his thumbs, too.

"Looks like a good time was had by all," Mr. Wallace said. "And how was our phenom today?"

"Phenomenal!" Booker said.

My face got hot.

Sam ran onto the front lawn, then stopped, staring at the bushes. "Hey, Booker!" he shouted. "You have plants that look like animals!"

Booker and I looked, too.

"Oh gosh," I said. "A camel has joined the giraffe."

Booker shook his head. "What next?" He reached for my hand, and...and I reached back, lacing my fingers through his.

Mom called Sam and got in the car and Sam raced over, and Booker squeezed my hand before he let go and I squeezed back, and by the time I got in the car, my face was burning hot.

When we got home, I headed straight for Mia McCall, leaning my hands against the poster, bending my head forward until my forehead touched hers. "Thank you, Mia," I said. "Thank you for showing me how to love basketball again."

And then I just about fell into the shower.

By the time I was done, I could smell dinner cooking, and I realized I was starving.

When I got downstairs, Mom was sitting at the kitchen counter, reading.

"Tectonic plates?" I said.

She shook her head. "Jellyfish."

"Sounds slimy." I sat down next to her. "Have you decided?"

"Decided?"

"If I can keep playing with the Action?"

Mom closed her book. "Nikki, do you know what I saw this weekend?"

I shook my head.

"I saw the girl with joy in her face again." She put her hand on my cheek. "How could I possibly take that joy away from you? Especially when you've been working so hard. So, yes, you can keep playing on the Action."

I jumped up and grabbed Sam and danced around the kitchen.

"But," Mom said.

I turned back to her.

"You will bring your grades up."

"I will, Mom."

"And I'd rather not see any more broken bones." She held a small box out to me. "I have something for you."

"What is it?" Sam said.

Mom shrugged. "Open it, Nikki."

I untied the ribbon, opened the box, and looked down at three little beanbags and a book called *How to Juggle*.

Mom put her arm around my shoulders. "You obviously have the sports gene," she said. "I thought you might have the juggling gene, too."

My eyes burned. I picked up the beanbags, covered in soft, rainbow-colored fabric, and rolled them in my hands.

"What is it?" Sam said again.

"Beanbags." I tossed one to him. "So I can learn to juggle."

"Why?" Sam said.

"Because…" I looked at him. "Sam, have you ever wondered about your father?"

"Yeah."

"And you know he was a, um, sperm donor, right?"

"Yeah."

"Do you know what that means?"

"Not really."

"Okay, good. Mom can explain that later. Come on." I took his arm and headed for Mom's office.

"Nikki," Mom said. "Sam's too young for this. It won't mean—"

I turned around, taking her arm, too. "You waited too long to tell me, remember?"

"Yes, but..."

"He should know, Mom," I said. "He should know something about his father."

Mom took a deep breath, the kind of breath you're supposed to take to calm yourself before shooting a free throw, then blew it out, long and slow. "All right," she said at last. "You're right, Nikki. But I'm coming with you."

So we went into Mom's office and she sat in the big chair by the window and pulled Sam into her lap. I opened the file drawer where she kept our paper dads and pulled out the two folders. Then I sat on the arm of the chair and held the folders out in front of Sam.

"These files tell about our fathers." I flipped the *Nikki, Donor* file open and leafed through the pages, pointing at things. "See? My paper dad has brown hair and brown eyes, and he was on the track team at the University of Virginia, and he can ride a unicycle and juggle."

Sam grabbed the *Sam, Donor* file and pulled it open. "Can my father juggle?"

Mom put her hands around Sam's, holding the sides of the folder, and I pulled the green paper clip from the top of the forms. "Let's find out," I said. "Here's what your father looks like. He has brown hair and brown eyes, like mine. He's six foot four inches tall and weighs two hundred and ten pounds." I started to turn the page. "Wait, what?" I grabbed the form and looked closer. "Six foot four! Mom! My paper dad is five foot eleven, and Sam's is six foot four?"

"Oh dear," Mom said, "I'd forgotten about that."

I picked up the rest of the pages and shuffled through them. "What does he do? Med school, grew up in a small town, played high school football, baseball, *and* basketball?" I dropped the pages into the folder, grabbed Sam's hand, and pulled him out of Mom's lap. "Come on. We're going outside."

"Why?" Sam said. "What are we doing?"

And Mom said, "Nikki, it's almost dinnertime."

"Doesn't matter." I'd already pulled Sam halfway across Mom's office, but I stopped and looked down at him, holding his shoulders in my hands. "Sam," I said, "you got the sports gene and you got the tall gene. Good thing it's your left arm that's broken. You'll only need your right one to develop good shooting form."

I clapped my hands, loud and slow, the way Coach Duval always did. "You ready to learn how to shoot a basketball?"

Acknowledgments

I'm extremely grateful to the faculty, staff, and students of the Master of Fine Arts in Writing for Children and Young Adults program at Hamline University. I could not have completed this novel without your instruction, help, and support. I'm particularly grateful to my faculty advisers: Claire Rudolf Murphy, who taught me how hard a writer needs to work; Marsha Wilson Chall, who showed me how fun writing for children and young people can be; Mary Logue, who made me push my characters to be uncomfortable; and Gary D. Schmidt, who gave me encouragement at a time when I needed it most. Thank you all.

I'm also grateful to Kate DiCamillo and to the family of Frances and Kermit Rudolf for the scholarships that helped me complete my MFA at Hamline.

An enormous Thank-You to my wonderful agent, Ginger Knowlton, and to her wonderful assistants, Megan Tripp and Natalie Edwards. Thank you for loving this book and for finding it such a great home at Little, Brown Books for Young Readers.

And speaking of which, I cannot imagine a more perceptive, insightful editor than Lisa Yoskowitz. You made me work so much harder than I wanted to on revisions and, in the process, made this a much better book. Thank you.

And thank you to Michelle Campbell, Jackie Engel, Shawn Foster, Marcie Lawrence, Christine Ma, Annie McDonnell, Christie Michel, Hannah Milton, Emilie Polster, Jessica Shoffel, Victoria Stapleton, Karen Torres, Megan Tingley, and the entire team at Little, Brown for bringing Nikki's story to life.

To the Hamlettes—Dori Graham, Jamieson Haverkampf, Tina Hoggatt, Andrea Knight Jakeman, Lily LaMotte, Jan LaRoche, Regina McMenamin Lloyd, Aimee Lucido, Christy Reid, Blair Thornburgh, Lily Tschudi-Campbell, and Stephanie Pavluk Wilson—I could never have done this without you. Write on, sisters!

Thank you to Coach Chessie Jackson at The College of New Jersey for answering my questions about the arcane rules of the NCAA.

Thank you to Jamie Coniglio and her fellow research librarians at George Mason University for answering my questions about their world.

A big shout-out and thank-you to the Western Fairfax Mustangs, the Potomac Valley Vogues, and the Oakton High School girls' basketball teams. What a joy it's been to watch you girls play. And to Coaches Tommy Benton, Fred Priester, Krista Jay, Kathleen Rose, Gus Taylor, Jeff Robinson, and Willie Diggs, thank you for your dedication to young athletes, for teaching them the skills they need to succeed, and for inspiring them to work hard, dig deep within themselves, reach high, and love the game.

And finally, thank you to my family for always believing I could do this. I love you.

Barbara Carroll Roberts

is a graduate of Hamline University's Writing for Children and Young Adults MFA program. She played competitive sports in high school and always wished there had been books in her library about athletic girls. That desire—and the realization that there still aren't many books about girls who truly love sports—inspired her to write this book. She lives outside Washington, DC, with her family and their many pets. This is her first novel. You can visit her at barbaracarrollroberts.com.